22 March

For Nancy –
a gal in the grand
Europe tradition –
but with a style
all her own –
with warmest regards.

[signature]

OTHER BOOKS BY NIVEN BUSCH

The Gentleman From California
The San Franciscans
California Street
The Actor
The Hate Merchant
The Furies
Day of the Conquerors
They Dream of Home
Duel in the Sun
The Carrington Incident
Twenty-one Americans

The Takeover

A NOVEL BY

Niven Busch

Simon and Schuster : New York

Published by Simon and Schuster
Rockefeller Center, 630 Fifth Avenue
New York, New York 10020

SBN 671-21368-7
Library of Congress Catalog Card Number: 72-90388
Designed by Irving Perkins
Manufactured in the United States of America

The author wishes to thank Peter Davison for the right to reprint a portion of his poem "Into The Future," which was originally published in the *Atlantic Monthly*.

2 3 4 5 6 7 8 9 10 11 12 13 14 15

For Suzanne

In city times like these
One never retraces steps. Forward
Is the only direction. Beyond this corner
The wind gusts cold. . . .
What will come at me from my blind side?

—PETER DAVISON

CHAPTER ONE

BEFORE leaving town, Jed Basco had seen his new office only in the rough, the plaster newly troweled and raw-smelling. Now everything was finished. Basco & Western had moved from Rockefeller Center to their new building on the East River. The great pale carpets had been laid and the refectory table Jed used as a desk had been set in its proper place at the end of the room with the skies of Manhattan and the mysterious smoky life of its roofs visible in the background. On the walls were photographs, theatrically enlarged, of the famous dams he had built—the Yellow Mountain Cut, the Grand Teton, the Horseshoe, and the St. Cloud Canyon. Sometimes, in a restless mood, he would stroll from picture to picture, puffing his pipe, looking at the great structures so artfully photographed with a dab of cloud in the sky and lodgepole or ponderosa pine growing in the background. He would take pleasure from such studies, remembering what segment of his life had gone into each immense bow of concrete—thinking of the problems and the battles and the great feeling when he'd worked them out, as he had this last business at American Canyon.

It was a fine office, an impressive and livable office, but it lacked one item.

"Where's my gun cabinet?" he demanded.

He put the question, rather more gruffly than he intended, to the dark, handsome girl he had found in the outer office. She was using the desk of his regular secretary, Elsie Lasof, and had introduced herself as Adeline somethingorother. He hadn't paid much attention, since Elsie always got a substitute from the steno pool even if she was just stepping out for coffee.

"I'm sorry, Mr. Basco," Adeline said, "I didn't know about any gun cabinet. Was there supposed to be one?"

Jed gave Adeline the quick undershot look which meant her answer had not pleased him.

"Yes, there was."

The girl hesitated. She wanted to be helpful.

"I'll check, Mr. Basco," she said. "It might not have come over in the move. Shall I check with Mr. Surabaya in transportation?"

"By all means," Jed said. "Where is Elsie?"

Adeline looked surprised. "She's on vacation, Mr. Basco. I thought you knew."

"I didn't hear anything about a vacation for Elsie."

He was now genuinely irritated. First no gun cabinet. Then no Elsie. All you had to do was leave for a few days and everything got bollixed up.

"She left you a note, Mr. Basco. I have it right here."

Adeline rummaged in the desk with one hand, dialing with the other. She handed Jed an envelope with his name typed on it.

"I have Mr. Surabaya for you."

Jed went to his own desk to take the call. He had not previously met or spoken with Mr. Surabaya, but in a corporation employing, worldwide, some twenty thousand people, you were not expected to be everyone's kissing cousin.

"Do you happen to know where my gun cabinet is?" Jed said.

Mr. Surabaya answered with careful politeness. He had a slight foreign accent, Middle Eastern or Asiatic. "I have an invoice for it right here on my desk, Mr. Basco. I'm certainly sorry, sir, if some error has occurred."

"I appreciate that," Jed said. "Now let's find out where the cabinet is, and then get it where it belongs. If you say you have an invoice for it, then somebody must have signed that invoice. Why don't we start with that?"

"The gun cabinet was delivered to your home, Mr. Basco. Somebody there signed for it, the man servant, I believe, Mr. MacNeice. If you wish it brought here I'll see to it at once."

"I do wish it brought here," Jed said evenly.

"Very good, sir. It will be delivered before noon."

"Thank you," said Jed. "Now the only point that puzzles me is this: That gun cabinet has been in my office at Rockefeller Center for two years, going on three. Why would you think I wouldn't want it after we moved?"

"Well, there was some question about the personal

belongings. Some of the executives thought their things wouldn't fit with the new decor. Miss Conquest, the assistant office manager, was assigned to handle that aspect of the move. Do you wish her to call you?"

"No, I don't," Jed said. "All I want to do is get the gun cabinet back here."

"That I can take care of," said Mr. Surabaya. "It will be done immediately. And once more, sir, my apologies."

Jed hung up. There had been an annoying undercurrent in Mr. Surabaya's rather too elaborate explanation. Even his anxiety to pass responsibility along to someone else seemed to suggest—some undue propriety? The gun cabinet had initially belonged to Jed's father. It had been built by a Scotch cabinetmaker, Stewart MacKenzie, in Edinburgh, 1921, and it had held four guns. Jed kept two shotguns, a Winchester Model 21 and a Browning 16 over-and-under, and two rifles—an 8mm Drilling, custom built for him in Belgium, and his old Savage .306, equipped with a new, sophisticated telescopic sight. You didn't need such weapons in a city office—but it had always given Jed a good feeling to have the cabinet there, a sense that he wasn't tied to the refectory table desk or the blueprints in the filing cabinet or the big dams or even Basco & Western. He was Jed Basco, a fifty-two-year-old corporate executive but one who still thought of himself as an engineer, an anachronistic old prick, perhaps, by some standards—but not by his own. He still had a far piece to go, and he meant to go all the way.

He realized that he was still holding Elsie's letter. Taking it out of the envelope, he read:

Dear Boss:

I'm off—two weeks in the West Indies, all expenses paid by Basco & Western. Surprised? I am. Annoyed? I hope you're not. I tried to reach you in Dallas, but they said you'd just left for the dam. Christie Clarke, Admiral Stranahan's secretary, thought you might be there awhile.

I can almost hear you saying, since when does Admiral Stranahan's secretary give orders to my secretary? You're right, of course, but you hadn't called in for six days and the opportunity seemed too good to turn down. But if you are angry or need me (and I like to be needed) just whistle. The address is Grand Hotel, Kingston, Jamaica.

Pardon my haste. But do you realize this is the first vac (as the British would say and no doubt are saying right now in Kingston, Jamaica) that I've had since the Big Acquisition? And that, boss, was two years ago. Oh, not that I'm complaining. Honest I'm not.

With best regards,
Elsie

Jed laid the letter on his desk, placed it face down as if its true meaning was not contained in Elsie's crisp typing but must be drawn from some other source: the corporate climate around him.

The letter in essence conveyed the same message as the mislaying of the gun cabinet: there was trouble in the air.

Office administration at the command level of a major corporation permits few accidents. Too much is at stake—egos ruffled at that altitude can send shocks shuddering down, with unhappy results, through every operational tier below.

Nobody, as Jed well knew, disposes of the president's belongings except the president. Nobody gives a member of the president's staff a vacation except the president. Yet here were two such boggles in a single morning—an incredible record, unless one did not choose to regard the incidents as boggles but elected instead to identify them as the classic maneuvers initiated against an executive under fire: reduction of office status (personal property removal) and secretary got out of the way (she might detect danger and report it to her boss).

Jed drummed on the letter with his short, square-tipped fingers. He had arrived at a value judgment he was later to regret but which seemed reasonable at the time. He had decided that—rather than containing any larger implications—today's annoyances were acts of spite. And when spite was the issue he knew where to look for it.

There are men with whom you can fight and still remain friends. Steve Vishniak was not one of them. Oppose him once and you made a lifelong enemy. Knowing this, you kept your guard up, as Jed had usually kept his up with Steve. Until now. Until, busy with other concerns, at a bad point in company affairs, he had become vulnerable.

On review, he was not sure that Steve had ever been a friend, not even in the beginning when Steve was romancing Basco Precision for possible merger or acquisition. The result of that courtship had been the purchase of Basco by Vishniak's General Western. Jed had not really wanted to sell; he had not even wanted to be rich particularly, but richness—Steve Vishniak's kind of richness—was coming into style, and for getting rich the deal had been perfect. The principal issue had been control. Jed had hung tight on that and Steve had met him halfway. More than halfway it had seemed then. Steve had given him the presidency of the parent company, plus two additional places on the board for men of his choice—seats in which Jed had promptly installed his attorney, Felix Linus Rupke, a man of notable political connections, member of a prestigious Washington law firm, and Loris Dominici, an old friend who was also a large stockholder in many companies associated with the building trade.

Three places on a seven-man board. A new president could hardly ask for more. The concession was proof, if any additional proof had been needed, of how badly Steve Vishniak had wanted Basco Precision. He had paid more for it than anyone else would have paid, a price which conferred instant, fantastic personal wealth on Jed Basco while at the same time moving General Western from financial difficulty to firm and happy ground.

Vishniak loved acquisitions. A bull-necked man with steel-gray eyes and a face shaped like a shovel, he had once mailed out to shareholders a singular 33⅓ rpm record stating his views on "The Implosion Theory of Corporate Growth." The basis of the theory was that the more companies one mashed together, the more money juiced out. Vishniak bought corporations the way his father—a Detroit junk dealer—had bought automobile carcasses: a restaurant franchise chain, a car-rental agency, a facility for making battery-powered tractors for use in coal mines, a laundry equipment factory, and firms manufacturing, respectively, fire engines, granite aggregates, hose nozzles, bedsprings, ladies' slacks and automatic sprinklers. As acquisitions speeded up, accurate data on divisional operations had to be accepted pretty much on faith; cash flow was not always what had been anticipated, and the purchase of a new business with large, liquid capitalization seemed indicated.

Basco Precision fitted this need admirably. A construction company, operating mostly on government contracts, it showed earnings of 11 percent on annual turnover of a billion and a half dollars. What was more to the point, its liquid revolving fund of some four hundred million dollars could be siphoned, with a little bookkeeping effort, into dividends flowing upstream to the parent company; even giving Jed Basco five shares of General Western for one of Basco Precision, this happy arrangement, over a five-year period, would reduce the purchase cost of Basco to zero.

The new nomenclature, Basco & Western, had been designed to lend the acquisition the façade of a merger—perfectly all right, if that was Jed's wish.

The board of Basco & Western divided down the middle like one of those before-and-after advertisements for hair dye in which, on opposite sides of a center part, one patch of the head is revealed in some glistening youthful shade, the other gray.

Vishniak, Thorpe and Pulaski were all under forty—and all well on their way to being billionaires.

Jed and Rupke were both well past forty, Dominici sixty-one.

It was a contest of age against youth, and each of the younger men was unusually aggressive and fast-moving.

Thorpe had been a Harvard Business School Whiz Kid, hired away from IBM at twenty-nine to head General Western's real-estate division at a six-figure salary.

Pulaski, inheritor of a massive third-generation oil fortune, had been a playboy until he found that securities could provide as much action as girls. He had bought his way onto Western's board in a move which, without Vishniak's wariness, could have been a takeover.

Admiral Stranahan had seemed to hold the deciding vote—and he was nearing seventy. A recently added board member (sales to the military was the coming thing), he had sat, until his retirement, as Chairman of the Joint Chiefs. Rupke had felt that, after proper wooing, the admiral, because of his age if nothing else, could be swung into Jed's faction, thus giving him control.

It hadn't worked that way. Vishniak had kept the board firmly in hand, and the board together controlled more stock than Jed, although Jed as an individual held more shares than any other member of the board. This was an advantage, but a more important edge which Jed conceded to Steve was that Steve headquartered at the Manhattan office where the power game was played, while Jed spent over half his time out in the field. Jed, so rich now and so busy, had concentrated on his work and refused to worry. He had allowed points in the way a nationally seeded tennis player might spot a club champion thirty a game and still beat him. More important, there were quite a few men, in and out of Wall Street, who could give Vishniak thirty points and beat him for power or money, but no engineer in the world could build a better dam than Jed. Jed knew this and Vishniak knew it. What was more, Vishniak needed him. Thorpe and Stranahan and Pulaski needed him. Or so he had figured. . . . And still figured! So if it pleased Steve to refute that need with annoying little put-downs when Jed's back was turned the appropriate reaction might be to pay him no heed.

By mid-morning the irritations attending his settlement

in the new office seemed less significant, and his good humor was further restored when, shortly before lunch, two men in white coveralls with B & W stenciled on their backs brought in his gun cabinet. One of them ventured a compliment on the rifles, and Jed opened the cabinet to show him the Drilling. Engaged with this, he ignored the flashing of his telephone until Adeline came in and told him Herman Pulaski was calling from Texas.

Rather coincidentally—if one related the call to the weapon Jed was holding at the moment—Herman wanted him to fly to his ranch for a deer hunt.

"The bucks are up and moving," Herman said, "and the sun is bright on the Brazos."

"You're a poet, Herman," Jed said. "That should be set to music."

"Then why not dance to the tune?"

"I just got back, remember?" Jed said. "Somebody has to mind the store, even if it's only the boss."

Herman laughed in the quick, yapping way he had, as if Jed had said something very funny.

"Stop being boss for a while," he said. "It might do you good. Steve and Coleman are here now, and the admiral's flying in tomorrow."

"Tomorrow is impossible."

"Then come Saturday. I'll have a car at the Dallas airport for you."

Herman was being curiously insistent. The last remark, for instance, sounded almost like an order. But perhaps he only meant to be genial and hostlike, Texas-style.

"Not much chance, Herman," Jed said. "But thanks for the invitation. Ship me a haunch of venison if you get one that isn't shot to pieces."

He fully intended to stand by his refusal, but after a productive afternoon and a good night's sleep he thought better of it. Saturday, hmmm. A hunt in the warm Texas weather, on the sweet windy range, could be pleasant, restorative. And with this came another notion, less agreeable but perhaps no less constructive. If he observed the four members of the board in the close atmosphere of a hunting party—if he checked them out (and Steve especially) he might sense what (if any) antagonisms were working against him beyond Steve's propensity for schoolboyish harassments.

He got off a telegram to Herman Pulaski and sent word to Bart Quinlan, his private pilot, to have the Learjet ready for takeoff sometime Friday evening; he himself might go a little short of sleep, but by napping during the five-hour trip he would arrive reasonably refreshed and in plenty of time for an early-morning hunt.

Yes, the Learjet would do. For a real bed, if he'd wanted one, he could have preempted B & W's luxurious Gulfstream II—a regular flying motel—but the Lear was his own, and he preferred it even for trips as long as this. Handy and almost as fast as a carrier-borne fighter, the Lear's resilience made it well worth the price, close to a million dollars, that he'd laid out for it. He'd had Quinlan set it down in some places no jet aircraft was meant to go—and the last had been the worst, a sagebrush strip near a Nevada cowtown, the gateway and loading depot for the American Canyon Dam.

Jed, aloft now, pulled a light blanket around him and composed himself for sleep. As he drifted off his thoughts turned back to the crisis at the dam project and his satisfaction with the way he'd worked it out.

American Canyon was the biggest job Basco & Western had ever undertaken. It had been cursed from the outset by late-arriving materials, floods, landslides, epidemics, isolation, reckless bidding and sheer, inexplicable human cussedness.

The most recent trouble had been a strike by the high-scalers. Their union, a CIO affiliate, alleged that Basco & Western hadn't been meeting legal safety requirements. The union operated a life and accident insurance program, and the program had been paying too many claims at American Canyon. Basco & Western's compensation carrier had opposed the union's position, suggesting that if a high-scaler died after a fall which had broken a number of his bones and perhaps crushed or ruptured certain essential internal organs, it was still possible to ascribe his demise to the pneumonia he had developed while waiting in some inaccessible spot for a rescue vehicle to reach him. Anyone could see that if he had succumbed in this fashion to natural causes, the awards to his dependents would be minimal.

Jed had agreed to meet the union adjusters and the insurance people on the job. His problem was to avert both a strike and a premium escalation, either of which at this point could put the dam down the tube.

A copter picked Jed up when he got off the jet. It drummed its tilting flight along the Sierra foothills with the sun pushing through reddish streaks of cloud against the starboard windows. Jed was out of his seat before the skids had touched in front of the operations shack at Construction City; he climbed down and the helipilot handed him a bulging Gucci briefcase.

Roy Hendrix, the construction boss, stood on the tamped earth of the company square with Fritz Latour, the chief engineer, behind him. Both men wore thick parkas against the morning cold. Hendrix was tall and skinny with a small, wrinkled monkeyface perched precariously on a long, thin neck.

"Man, am I ever glad to see *you,*" Hendrix said as he gripped Jed's hand.

American Canyon was the fourth job on which they'd worked together. It had been more grief than all the others combined.

Latour, who had a clerkly look despite his outdoor clothes and weathered skin, took a stogie out of his mouth by way of greeting, nodded shyly to Jed and put the stogie back again.

The negotiators were waiting, six in number—three from insurance and three from the union. They were indoor people, wearing city clothes. Behind them was a gray, mud-splattered Dodge Powerwagon, fitted with seats like a bus, with a hardhat driver at the wheel. The car had been assigned to take the party into The Cut, that vast tear in the earth's surface left by the diversion of the American River.

A road snaked down the sandstone cliffs, risky but negotiable by four-wheel-powered vehicles.

Pink blotches of light brightened the sky. Around the three sides of the square which faced The Cut stretched a city of tin-roofed, plywood houses. The workers lived in this city. It had been built for them. They had been there for six months and would be there for whatever time was required to finish the dam.

Out on the high mesa, half a mile away, lay another town. It was called End of the Line. This was a rest and recreation area. It consisted mostly of tents which housed cribs, bars, keno games, slot machines and sex movies. Once a week a staff physician from Construction City inspected the prostitutes who worked in the two officially recognized brothels. Most of the girls submitted for their own protection. Freelance hookers took their own chances, and the men who visited them took the same.

The only architectural element which the two loosely conjoined communities shared in common was The Cut—a sleazy gulf of blackness at night, by day a giant stony pit, where excavators chewed up rocks with goose beaks shaped like the snouts of dinosaurs.

For Construction City and End of the Line, The Cut fulfilled the functions which for more sophisticated cities might be supplied by a cathedral or a glittering Prado, with this difference—the existence of the cities depended upon the activities that went on here. From the complicated and hazardous tributes which The Cut exacted from the inhabitants of the twin cities flowed the power, hostile and demanding, that gave life to the population; once it withdrew this power (as it surely would), a great lake and forebay would replace it. The people would drift off and the houses in which they had lived would crumble into ruins and blow away.

The construction of the tunnels diverting the river and making The Cut had been the first steps taken by Basco & Western in the preparation of the dam site. It was one of the processes which the unions had denounced as faulty. There had been cave-ins. Corpses had been dug out of sandstone crypts. These had been demolition men, but the casualty rate among high-scalers also had been formidable. The high-scalers, who had their own union, drilled holes into the face of the granite cliffs to make the notch which would anchor the dam. They dangled on ropes operated on winches by comrades above. Skillful, wary and impertinent, they were the best-paid workers on the dam. They used hand signals to communicate to the winchmen their need to be raised or lowered. When no raising or lowering was necessary but merely horizontal movement along the cliff face, the high-scalers provided their own propulsion. They would brace their feet against the rock and kick out so that their bodies, on the end of the ropes, looped through the air. They would make these mad jumps and get to some other nub of granite and drill a hole in it. They did this many times a day. Later another detail would come by and put dynamite charges in the holes.

Naturally, what with the jackhammer work, the signaling, the springing-off and the mad grasshopper jumps along the face of the cliff, several hundred feet from the ground, there were accidents. Some unusual abrasive in the stone cliffs would fray the ropes and they would break, by God, even though they were manufactured of the best quality nylon woven around a metal core. Finding a better type of rope was the logical correction for the high accident rate; B & W's Research and Development Division had come up with a type they thought would serve. Jed had samples in his briefcase.

He marched over to the Dodge Powerwagon. Hendrix followed on his right, Latour on his left. Hendrix made the introductions, and Jed shook hands all around.

"Gentlemen," he said, "I'm sending this vehicle down to The Cut. It can pick us up later. No use our making use of it now. Takes too long."

He started walking then, Hendrix still on one side, Latour on the other. The adjusters and the union people, blue with cold, did not look happy. They could see Jed was heading for the Skip, and the Skip was bad. They had been warned about it.

"Don't get in that thing with the Man."

"The Skip, now, that's a one-way trip to hell. They don't like Basco on this job."

"Oh, he rides it. Every time he comes here. All the old-style bosses do. Him in particular. But if you figure to live out your time, leave him alone in there."

The Skip was a square box made of planks. It had four sides and a floor but no roof. The planks were bolted together, reinforced with angle irons at the corners. The sides were about waist high for an average man though Jed, due to his stocky build, took the rise near his armpits. He pushed back the bolt that secured the gate—really no more than a hinged section of timber. He stepped in, Latour and Hendrix following. The rest had no choice except to follow.

It was all very well for somebody to tell you, don't get in the Skip, but it was something else to refuse if the boss got in. You couldn't suddenly remember that you had to phone your wife or go to the john, though the latter might be true. Was almost sure to be true. If you were a union negotiator or an insurance adjuster you got in, little as you might like it.

The Skip dangled at ease. It nestled in a small notch like a boat slip, sliced out for it on the edge of The Cut. From its corners four steel cables connected it to a steel ring which in turn was supported by a grooved wheel. The wheel acted as a trolley. It worked on a cable strung across The Cut. By applying traction to the trolley through another cable the operator, from his shack on the opposite side, could move the Skip to the center of The Cut. This he did forthwith, obeying a hand signal from Jed. When the signal was repeated the operator, yanking back on one of his levers, stopped the Skip's horizontal motion at the cross-cable, then started lowering toward the canyon floor. The lousy crate was falling, hurtling downward at a terrifying pace. Was the stinking birdcage out of control, the cable cut, the operator laughing at what was to follow? And far below, when it was impossible to resist the compulsion to look down, there was stone, sharp rock, torn-up ground and inescapable, splintering, horrible death.

But the fall had stopped! The operator had yanked back on his lever. By some miracle the Skip came to rest on a spot leveled off for it on the canyon floor. It settled there as delicately as a wineglass which a waiter, trained in the best establishments, might put down on a white tablecloth.

Jed opened the gate. The men stepped out, and he led the way to the jeeps waiting at the landing place to take the party into diversion tunnels 4 and 5—the ones about which the complaints had been raised.

Jed had placed considerable hope in the Skip. You couldn't be sure of the results. But this much he knew from experience: the best and maybe the only way to handle a crew of fussy adjusters and arrogant union leaders was to scare the shit out of them. That was why he had sent one of Basco & Western's brightest young public-relations men to Construction City with instructions to circulate the rumor about dropping the boss into The Cut. This young fellow, Bill Grady, had done his job well, and the negotiators were now less likely to keep harping about the lack of safety precautions. They were a hell of a lot more inclined to pay attention when he, Jed Basco, president of Basco & Western, explained how and why, from now on, the accident rate would be cut back. They would be more impressed when he laid out pieces of the new nylon rope on the tailgate of a truck and passed out the Xeroxed memoranda from Research and Development about the rope's virtues. Later, out of deference to their possibly still spastic sphincter muscles, he would lift them topside in the Powerwagon instead of the Skip.

That night he flew them into San Francisco for a party, and two days later the unions decided not to strike. The outcome, Jed felt, was a real coup—one that would restore confidence in Basco & Western's Construction Division and distract attention from the bad third-quarter report (largely caused by losses by less stable subsidiaries).

He had worked hard. He had earned this weekend in the sun, by God. And as the Learjet, having achieved cruising altitude, set its course southwest, Jed fell asleep with the serenity of a man who could face the future with confidence.

Pulaski's big spread backed up to the Brazos. Standing on the ridge where the jeep had set him down, Jed could see patches of water far below, dull as tin behind little screens of willow and scrub cottonwood. He wanted now to cleanse his mind and blood of city thoughts and to put himself in place here in the wilderness; to identify with the stirrings of another day, the dryness of the wild rye-grass and the filaree under his feet and the dampness of the night still held in the scoop of the draw. The creatures who lived by night were ending their hunt, and those that lived by day were awaking to the joy of daybreak in this lonely place, though the day for some of them might be their last. Especially it might be the last for any bucks getting up now from their nest in the sage laced with trails made by cattle and the padded tunnels of jackrabbits on the sides of the draw.

Pulaski had been the first out of the jeep. He had taken the worst station, partly because he was the youngest and the best shot and also because he was the host. He would walk slowly up the bottom of the draw, hopeful to move game ahead of him to hunters positioned farther along, though not of course without a chance for a shot himself. The rest of the party was strung along the crest that rimmed the draw: Stranahan and Thorpe midway, Jed at the end. The guide at the wheel of the jeep then made a sweeping half circle to put Vishniak on the opposite side; if a buck were sprung from the sage to the south, Steve would get the action. He had the best place of all.

It was almost light enough to shoot now. Jed had moved from a squatting position to sit more comfortably, his back against a liveoak and the Drilling in his lap.

He felt part of the ridge now. He belonged to it and it to him. He was alert for the hunt and yet full of peace at being close to the earth once more. It had never occurred to him, but this sense of earth, of its integrity, and the importance of it, had given him the drive to change it, to make an impression of his will on it, diverting rivers, creating structures to hold back natural forces, to turn their flow into power where no power had been before. He felt in some unexpressed way that such power came from him, from the thrust within him to live and be, and his identification with and recognition of natural laws and forces.

It was time to move. He got up slowly, grimacing to find a slight stiffness in his legs after their few minutes of motionlessness. He kneaded the muscles in his thighs and flexed them to remove the ache. Then he slid open the bolt of the rifle and slipped three rounds into the magazine.

He walked softly along the ridge. There was deer-sign here, some of it fresh. In a clump of hackberries the trail divided, a narrow spur tapering slightly downward, leading toward the draw. Jed took this direction. Almost at once he heard the movement of a heavy animal below him: the slide of earth as a hoof pushed the slope indicated weight and size. Jed stood still, sucking in his breath. Something big was down there feeding and it wasn't one of Herman Pulaski's steers—Herman had moved his cattle off this portion of the ranch a week before the hunt.

Jed crawled to the edge of the drop. Sixty feet below him upwind stood the biggest buck he had ever seen. It was looking away from Jed, senses alerted by the presence of the men farther down the draw. The big animal knew how to take cover and had it now. He was totally protected except from Jed directly above him.

The buck stamped one of his delicately muscled legs, and again there was a trickle of earth and shale. He was concerned about the hunters but not too worried as yet. He had observed hunters in this draw before. Now, with kingly head high in the buckeyes, he was taking stock of this bunch, calculating how to deal with them, not aware that if Jed willed it so, there was no escape route, only death.

Jed considered removing the scope secured to the Drilling by two clips. It could be taken off in a second, without a sound or the need for a tool. With a scope sighted in for two hundred yards you could easily miss an animal at point-blank range. The iron sights would be better. One shot would do it. Jed wouldn't even have to dress out the big bastard or pack his carcass up to the rim. Herman's ranch hands would attend to all of that. He could pull the trigger once and be much congratulated in camp that night, and the buck's huge rack, properly mounted, would look splendid in his new office, right above the gun cabinet.

Jed knew all this, but he could not pull the trigger. He could no more have killed this buck than he could have killed his son. He moved the safety to its locked position, laid down the rifle and looked around for a pebble. He flipped it so it would fall in the buckeye shrub, but he had to toss another before the buck trotted off, keeping the bushes between himself and whatever idiot was throwing stones at him. He headed down the draw, but Jed was sure that, having detected hunters there, the big deer would cross, then double out the other side.

Just then he heard the whap, then the reverberation and two more whaps. The uproar, he learned later, came about when Vishniak gutshot, then finally brought down a little forked-horn, legal but only barely so—the only game anyone in the party took.

The big buck would live a while longer to bed down in the sweet sage and mate with his love at the proper season before somebody with a firearm made a trophy out of him.

In the weeks to come, looking back on the day, Jed wished he had been given just half the chance he had given that buck.

They let him have it a few hours later by the campfire. All four were against him, and four was all it took—a quorum of Basco & Western's board, whether they sat tall at a teakwood table or squatted on a hunk of earth. They must have been planning this for weeks, and now that the time had come they reveled in every second of it—Thorpe's face tight as a walnut; Stranahan's pale and ice-cream plump, the basic military-industrial puss; Pulaski all business, the role of genial host forgotten, mocking and mean now as an Arab selling a sick camel.

Vishniak was in charge of the execution; he did a good job of it, his dry Polish voice squeaking along like the rasp of a rope in a dry pulley. Jed didn't want to look at him or at any of them; he kept busy, working a finger around, drawing some kind of design in the soft, silty ground—he didn't know what (though the shape he had traced was to return to him weeks afterward with a queer shock of horror). He listened quietly, the creases on his ruddy face deeper than normal in the weave of the gentle flames and his eyes in their set-back hollows careful, attentive and hooded. He waited until everything appeared reasonably clear, then threw in some curt, contemptuous questions that elicited whatever, out of tact or desperation, Vishniak had left out.

They were still afraid of him. He had realized that at once. They had blocked him off in every direction—they'd probably discussed a dozen different settings for the final confrontation before deciding on the hunting trip. They were secure, they had the majority they needed, but they were still afraid. This had amused him, and it was a weapon in a fashion. He'd have to see what use he could make of it. Apparently Vishniak had expected some appeal for a stay, but Jed avoided giving him that satisfaction; he carefully dribbled the dregs of his coffee onto the finger patterns on the ground and walked out of the circle of light to his bedroll. He had his shaving kit and ammunition and a little other gear there along with a pint bottle of bourbon, half full. He had taken one slug straight out of the bottle and another in a tin cup with some water and turned in.

He learned long ago that you did not face up to disaster in your sleep. Your mind went on with the ordinary churn of dream-shapes and dream-movements, putting some kind of protective film around the badness, softening it to where you could deal with it. Tired from the long day, he dropped off quickly while the campfire slowly faded from red to gray and the stars wheeled grandly over his sleeping shape. Vishniak's buck stiffened in its shroud of mosquito netting, and the hobbled pack horses grazed in the sagebrush.

Stranahan, Vishniak, Pulaski and Thorpe sat up late, talking among themselves.

The next morning Jed made the hour's ride from the camp to the ranch. He showered and changed, then packed and rode in state in one of Herman's three Rolls-Royces to the Dallas airport. He'd had a drink before he left the ranch, and he poured himself another from the teakwood bar that glided out from the Rolls's back-seat panel; he wondered whether news of the action at the campfire boardroom meeting had yet reached the marketplace. Probably not, though splinters of it might already be flying around, passed from hand to hand in Wall and Montgomery and Spring and LaSalle streets like pieces of the True Cross; the devil and all to do now and not much time to do it in, July half gone by already and the annual stockholders' meeting scheduled for October.

The Lear was ready for him; Jed had been about to board when, stopping for a cup of coffee in the small lounge of the maintenance hangar, he picked up the morning's Dallas *Herald.* A headline on the front page suddenly supplied the piece of the puzzle that till then had been missing. Still holding the newspaper in his hand, he crossed to an open pay phone and dropped in a coin. He gave the operator his credit-card number and the number in Washington, D.C., which he was calling. "This is a person-to-person call," he said. "Jed C. Basco here to Mr. Felix Rupke."

CHAPTER TWO

THE telephone operators at Cabot, Constable, Page and Rupke had seldom been busier than on the morning when Marie Klein, the younger of the two on duty, fielded Jed's call from Dallas. The switchboard—always active—had heated up like a two-dollar pistol the previous afternoon. Most of the calls had been for Felix personally, though in some instances—those in which the client-counselor relationship had lacked the warmth which Felix injected into so many of his contacts (it was really marvelous how he managed this closeness, how actually he found time for it!)—the message had simply been left with his secretary.

You could pin down the exact moment when the calls began. The Dow-Jones ticker had carried the news a few minutes before the market closed. Cabot, Constable, Page and Rupke, like several of the larger Washington law firms, had a ticker in the office. The equipment was located in a small study known as the Partners' Room, adjacent to the library.

George Page was watching the tape when the flash came over. Related to a former Under Secretary of State (during the Woodrow Wilson administration), George Page had White House connections himself—not as good as Felix Rupke's, perhaps, but not bad. Two days earlier, George had visited the Anti-Trust Division of the Attorney General's office in behalf of a client and he had heard the coming announcement rumored—actually more than rumored: mentioned, one might say, as a certainty! As soon as he was back on Lafayette Square he had switched on his intercom and said to Felix Rupke, "Congratulations, old man, he's going to do it."

Felix Rupke was keeping a cool front, but he was too sophisticated by training and too canny by nature to pretend he didn't know what George was talking about.

There was a pause, during which Felix's breathing could be heard over the intercom, and then he said, "What makes you think so?"

"I don't think so," said George Page. "I know it for a fact. He'll announce it tomorrow—day after, at the latest. So I say to you again—congratulations."

"Bullshit," said Felix Rupke, "but thanks anyway."

And he cut off the intercom.

This was not a put-down. George would not have tolerated a put-down for an instant. He might not have done anything about it at the moment but, in the long run, through the abrasive interplay of business partnership, he would have taken revenge. Still, Felix would not have risked quite such casual brusqueness if he had not, by the very thing that was about to happen (this fantastic appointment!), moved beyond the firm's hierarchy. The flip of Felix's finger on the intercom switch indicated his own recognition of his new rating; it also confirmed exactly what George had just told him: that the appointment was coming through. Thus, put-down or not, the cutoff was a score for Felix Rupke, and it set George Page on his mettle to prove his prophesy correct.

Having calculated that the President's secretary would release the story for the wires the next afternoon, George strolled into the Partners' Room a little before 3:00 P.M. He tore off the bit of tape and took it into Aaron Cabot's office. Aaron got hold of Constable and then summoned Felix. Never a demonstrative man, Aaron rose and gravely extended his hand, as did Dan Constable. After this ceremony, the three waltzed around the big office with their arms around Felix while George Page stood by, his bone-colored head tilted sagely to one side. He was not quite participating as yet, but he was not abstaining either, and when Dan started singing "He's a Jolly Good Fellow," George finally joined in. Soon Aaron was pressing buttons, all the buttons within reach—and in a maneuver absolutely unprecedented at Cabot, Constable, Page and Rupke, except for the annual Christmas party, all the firm's employees began crowding into the big office with its heavy brocade draperies and antique furniture. Waiters from the Mayflower, summoned by Dan's secretary, moved through the press serving cold turkey sandwiches, liquor and champagne.

At seven o'clock, Aaron Cabot knocked on his glass.

"Looking back through history," he began, glaring formidably around, his relentless urbanity in itself enough to diminish the now somewhat drunken clamor of the crowded room.

". . . looking back through history, ahem . . ."

"That's two looks so far," said Dan Constable as his partner, comfortably at a loss for words, paused once more. "How many is it going to take?"

"Quiet, please," said Cabot, unruffled. "Looking back through history, one can perceive past occasions when members of this firm have been considered for high public honor. My father—I have this straight from no less an authority than my mother—was urged by President Harding to accept the post of Attorney General, an appointment which could well have been his ruin, and ours, had he not had the good sense to decline it."

"Hear, hear," said Dan Constable. He held a glass of champagne near his right ear, swirling it so he could listen to the bubbles popping.

"There was also an eminent person, related to one of our partners, who served with distinction in the State Department."

Aaron bounced a complimentary glance in the direction of George Page—the reference, of course, was to an Under Secretary, and George acknowledged it with a brisk wave of his hand as if, after all, everyone had had relatives in the State Department, and why not?

"But never before has a partner gone straight from a desk in this office to a seat on the highest court in our republic. Ladies and gentlemen"—and here Aaron Cabot, whose oratorical gusts had cleared a space around him, flung out a forefinger and aimed it with a bravura flourish at Felix—"I give you Felix Linus Rupke, new Justice Designate to the Supreme Court. Let us drink to his good health."

There was quite a stir as everyone present, even a girl who had been lying on one of the divans, apparently passed out, rose and drank to Felix.

In acknowledging the toast, Felix Rupke said in part, "The only trouble with this appointment is that—if the Senate in its generosity is pleased to confirm it, which is still by no means certain—it's for life. I'm concerned about that. I'd intended to spend that time, or what's left of it, right here with y'all."

The "y'all" was pure gimcrack. Felix had sprung, as all knew, from humble origins, but when he allowed himself some turn of phrase or mannerism culled from that remote background he did so only in order to appear disarming or endearing. To those who knew him well—and none knew him better than the people gathered around him now—the effort was largely wasted. There was little about Felix Rupke that was disarming and less that was endearing, and he had long ago eliminated from his person every trace and twang of the homespun. Far more easily perceived was the Rhodes scholarship that had followed the B.A. from a small Texas college, the European travel, the doctorate from Georgetown Law School and the long-time association with the Eastern Establishment elite. Not that his upbringing in a small county seat hadn't had value—it had. A common rural background had provided an important link with the man who had done more to forward Felix's career than all his clients or his money or his carefully acquired polish.

The town was still there. It had not changed much. Felix had gone back twice—once for his father's funeral, once for his mother's. He had become a citizen of quite a different world and in this world, at last, he had achieved the highest station to which he could aspire.

Felix stood firmly planted on the lifts which supplied added height to his small frame.

You would not, unless you observed him closely, have noticed the platform heels. You would have had to look even sharper to detect that the lift on the right heel was more than an inch higher than the left—a correction for a birth defect of the right hip. Felix had limped awkwardly, miserably as a boy, but in adulthood he had found some way of swinging or hitching the handicapped side so that the limp was less noticeable. The shortened leg provided a sort of health barometer. When Felix was at his best he hardly limped at all, but when he was tired or under pressure the hip ached and he used a cane.

Power and the consciousness of power, just as it masked off the limp, also served to make Felix appear larger than in fact he was, and his face and head, both disproportionately big for the body and neck, added to the impression of size and formidableness. The face was fleshy, the nose firm and dominating, the eyes well placed under thick black brows—small but magnetic, restless ink-black eyes which as a rule he kept slightly veiled or turned at an angle that would mask their impact. He had developed this eye trick not out of caution, for he was not a cautious man, but because he had learned that if he turned himself full on he frightened people. (It was no good to frighten people unless you had to!) His cheeks were sallow, his skin pasty, his lips thick, bracketed with heavy, fleshy grooves. Either the pleasure that he took in discourse or the wish to appear amiable, or both, made him, when chatting, curl the heavy oratorical mouth downward or pucker it in the middle in a way that lent to this portion of his face an alien old-maidish look. His hair was graying, growing thin on top; he wet it down daily with tonic and then brushed it across the bald spots. He had excellent taste in clothes. His dark gray hopsack had been tailored to his measure by an Oxford Street tailor whom he had first patronized when in England for his Rhodes. At that time he could afford one suit a year and he had bought the best. Always, in court, and often in the office, he sported a white buttonhole carnation—making the flower a sort of trademark. He wore none now. One of the secretaries, brasher than the rest, had pinned, instead, in his lapel the tickertape announcing his appointment; the bit of paper lent him a temporary raffish air like the confetti on a bridegroom's collar as he signs the hotel register.

". . . a call for you on Mr. Cabot's line, Mr. Rupke."

"Very well, I'll take it."

Throughout the rest of the party, and later, after everyone except himself and the switchboard girls had left, and then again early the next morning, long before the other partners (generally Aaron Cabot) had reached their desks, the calls had continued. Felix Rupke took all he could.

He had observed before, in other situations, that good tidings, like bad, can bring attention from unexpected sources.

His stepfather called him, collect, from Matagorgas,

Texas. Felix hadn't heard from the son of a bitch in years. This old redneck coot, Sol Bender, had fallen heir to the store. It was the same store Felix's grandfather had founded after he made a grubstake driving a mule team hitched to a peddler's wagon through central Texas ranchlands, selling pots, pans, bolts of cloth, medicine, tools, Bibles, corsets and in fact just about anything except food (that spoiled and most folks raised what they needed anyway) to the women, who would come out on the back porches pushing back their damp hair and drying their hands on their aprons, come out often not to buy—Lord no!—but to pass the time of day. The store, a hole in the wall in Civil War days, had expanded into an Emporium —Rupke & Sons (the "sons" not Felix or his three brothers but his grandfather and his granduncle), which covered half a city block and stocked more sophisticated merchandise than the wagon had, though pretty much the same line.

Sol Bender needed to call collect about the way H. L. Hunt would, but that was his style just as it was his style to take some dry-gulched rancher or franchise-skinned tradesman into the back room and lend him what he'd come to ask for, without security, and generally get it back.

Sol had inherited the whole kit and caboodle. He was the only man in Matagorgas who had been president of Rotary four times and the only man in the county who had been chairman of the State Republican Executive Committee. The county had never elected a Republican, but there might come a time, you never knew. Sol had put Felix through college but had stopped sending money when Felix got the Rhodes and then the scholarship to Georgetown. Felix could picture Sol, the collect call safely accepted, sitting at Felix's real dad's rolltop desk wearing the dark heavy pants he affected even in the hottest weather. Felix could see him lounging there with his galluses dangling down and his sixty-dollar alligator loafers propped in an open drawer.

"Well, son, we made it."

"Got to first base anyway, Sol."

"First base? Hell, son, you went all the way around. You're on the scoreboard now."

To Felix Rupke's way of thinking, he had been on the scoreboard for a long time, but there was no sense going into that with Sol.

"Yes, Sol."

"This is your nickel, but I guess you kin afford it. So I aim to speak my mind."

"Go ahead."

"You won't get riled now?"

"When have I ever been riled at you, Sol?"

"Plenty of times. When I married yore ma, fer one. Son, yore eyes was like a couple of nailheads. Yore tears was fallin' harder'n turds from a tall ox. You loved yore real dad, and I don't blame you, but we're friends now, Felix, ain't we, son?"

"We sure are, Sol. I'm glad you called."

"Mr. Justice?"

"Yes, Sol."

"Don't try to shush me, on account I aim to speak my piece."

"Go right ahead."

"We was strangers then. We ain't now."

"No, we're not."

"Okay, then. I want to tell you this: I had faith in you, Felix. Not when you got them scholarships. *Before* you got 'em. Otherwise I never would've put out what I did for your education that I got you."

A hell of a lot you put out, Felix thought. And it was only because Ma made you. But he just said, "A good education surely counts."

"That's the meat of it. Well, here's what I want to say. I had faith, but I got to say this now. I never figured you'd go this far. I'm proud of you. An' I hope when you git back and see the home town, like you always say you will, you'll come down to Rotary an' give us a talk."

"I just might do that someday, Sol. Right now I've got a call on my other line, so . . ."

"Don't shush me, son. I got to make an apology an' I hope it don't come too late. I just never thought you'd reach the Supreme Court. I wish one thing, jest one. I wish yore ma was alive to see this day." Sol was almost weeping now. "I miss yore ma every day of my life, son. I wisht she was alive. You made it, son. God bless you."

"Thanks, Sol. It was good of you to call," Felix said. But the line had already gone dead.

In the next hour other, less emotionally wearing calls came through: from the head of a national grocery chain (both the chain and the executive clients of the firm); from a member of the Senate Ways and Means Committee; from an Assistant Secretary of the Interior and then, on an extension of the same line, from the Secretary himself; from the mayor of an important Midwestern city, for whom Felix had negotiated an honorary degree, who was now secretly pleased that there would be no way in which he could be called on to repay his debt; from two governors, one a former fraternity brother, the other an important party darkhorse. There was also an urgent dialogue with a drunk whose name Felix could not identify but who claimed to have known him at Oxford and who assured Felix he would make the finest Justice since John Marshall, then asked for a thousand dollars to tide him over some desperate but undefined emergency; Felix, who invariably turned down such requests, agreed to wire him a hundred. He roared with laughter when the drunk gave his address as the Hotel Plaza, New York, but he wired the hundred anyway.

"There's a man who goes first class."

His secretary, Ann Tanner, a dignified middle-aged woman, shook her head bleakly. A day of feasting this might be, her manner said, but did that mean that one flushed money down the toilet?

"When you draw the hundred, draw yourself nine," he said, "and that will bring it out a thousand even. All right?"

"You'd better think that over, Mr. Rupke."

"I have thought it over. I consider it a very small expression of my long-felt esteem."

"Beautiful," said Miss Tanner. "That will wind up the payments on my car, and I need the car. So thank you very much."

"You're most welcome."

"Did it ever occur to you, Mr. Rupke, that you are buying a car also?"

"I've got a car, Ann," said Felix testily. He knew what she was leading up to.

"You do indeed, Mr. Rupke," Ann said. "You have a Jaguar XJ6 sedan. The most expensive Jag that's exported. You still owe seventy-two hundred and some odd dollars on it. I can give you the exact figures if you'll allow me to consult the file."

"Whatever it is, it will be paid."

During this interchange, Ann Tanner had been writing out the checks for the fellow in the Plaza and for herself; she laid them on Felix's desk for signature.

"Will I be going with you when you go to the Supreme Court?"

"I don't know, Ann," Felix said slowly. "I'll have to check into it. I imagine it can be worked out."

"Whatever you feel is best."

"That's fine."

One of the telephones was flashing. Felix reached for it, but Ann got there first; she answered, then set the switch on hold.

"I'm sorry I mentioned the Jaguar."

"In this office you are free to mention any topic you find appropriate."

"Then I would like to add one postscript. You own a car and last year you earned—this is correct, I think—two hundred thousand, six hundred seventy-four dollars and sixty-five cents, before taxes. I know that figure by heart because I've had the file out so many times to give to banks when they wanted a copy of your return for their loan departments."

"Just because a few investments happened to go wrong doesn't mean—"

But Ann went on relentlessly. "A few, Mr. Justice? Quite a few. Oh, I know you switched to blue chips, but not quite in time."

"I would hardly say I'm threatened with the poorhouse."

"Nevertheless, you still owe seventy-two hundred on your car. As a Supreme Court Justice you'll be making sixty thousand a year instead of the figure I mentioned. How will you manage? Have you thought about it at all?"

"Everything will work out."

Ann Tanner sighed. With this man it usually did. As she engaged the switch so he could take the waiting call, she tore up her check for nine hundred dollars and dropped the pieces into the ashtray.

It was past eleven before Felix's special telephone rang—the one with the red tab on it. Only one person dialed in on this number; it was the call Felix had been waiting for.

The voice said, "Has the Old Blister called you yet?"

"No, Mr. President. Not as yet."

The Old Blister was the President's private nickname for the Justice whose recently announced retirement had allowed for Felix's appointment.

"I rather anticipated that he would call."

"He will, you can take it to the bank. And I'll tell you what he's going to say. He's going to imply that I can't get you confirmed. Well, you tell him to eat it." The voice deepened conspiratorially. "We have counseled together and the boys will stand up and be counted."

"I'm not worried, Mr. President."

"You just tell me what he says, now. Call me back after you hear from him."

"Yes, sir. Thank you, Mr. President."

"Goodbye, Felix."

The two had been on a first-name basis for more than twenty years, but Felix had dropped this form of address after election day. Though the President himself retained the old familiarity, he never corrected Felix's new code. Each understood the rhetoric of high office, and each respected it.

The retiring Justice telephoned at 12:24. It occurred to Felix that the Judge might have chosen this hour for tactical reasons. The partners at Cabot, Constable, Page and Rupke lunched early, generally together, in the executive dining room. The Justice had sometimes joined them there when he had been in private practice. By placing his call at an hour when he assumed Felix to be away from his desk, the Justice might have hoped to make Rupke call him back. Felix might not have returned the call, but if he did some slight advantage accrued to the Justice since it placed Felix in the position of petitioner rather than petitioned, at least during those few moments while he asked the reason for the Justice's call.

Not that Felix didn't already know. If anyone was obliged to congratulate him on his appointment, it was Justice Harlan Spatafor. Felix was curious to see exactly what wisp of hemlock the Justice would wrap in the bouquet. Nor was he, at 12:24, unreachable since he had not gone to the dining room but had Ann bring a sandwich and a glass of buttermilk to his desk. Jed Basco would be due in from Dallas around one, or earlier, and Felix wanted to be on hand when Jed arrived. So when the light flashed on the Number Three and Ann told him who was calling, Felix, still sipping buttermilk, said, "Hello, Harlan. How are you?"

"Ailing," said Justice Spatafor. "I'm old and I'm ailing. That's been given quite some circulation. So I'm retiring. I thought you might have heard about that, too."

"I've heard it mentioned," said Felix. "I'm sincerely sorry. Your retirement is a loss to the law profession and to the United States."

"I agree with you," said Justice Spatafor. "Not that *he* would. Beyond that, I'll only say this much—*he'll* have a tough time filling my shoes."

"He's already filled them. Maybe you don't read the newspapers."

"I read them, Felix. I surely do. I could be as happy about it as I guess you are. Would be, if the boys on the Hill get around to seeing it *his* way."

"Oh, I imagine he's taken a fix on that," Felix said. "Don't you?"

"I do," said Justice Spatafor, "and that's what bothers me. Felix, I've known you for some time now, and I want to speak frankly. I hate to see you exposed the way this is going to. I'm speaking as a friend now. There's just no way in the world that he can ever sell it. I'd prefer to see you plead ineligibility. Health—or anything. Out of self-interest, if nothing else, you ought to spare yourself the hell that's going to break loose."

"You're most considerate, Harlan. I set the highest value on your solicitude."

There was a sigh, ending in a cough, at the Justice's end of the line. Perhaps he really was a sick man. His breathing sounded raspy.

"As I say, I can't expect you to accept my suggestion, but I wish you'd give it some thought."

"You can count on that. And I appreciate your generosity. Goodbye, Harlan."

"Goodbye, Felix."

Felix picked up the phone with the red tab on it.

"Well?" said the voice.

"He said just what you figured."

"Did you tell him to shove it?"

"I did, Mr. President."

"Good, talk to you later."

Felix buzzed Ann.

"I'm going to the sauna. Mr. Basco might like to join me. He's had a long plane ride. You can ask him. Otherwise, ring me when he gets here and I'll come back up. Whatever he wants."

"Yes, Mr. Justice," said Ann Tanner.

CHAPTER THREE

FELIX Rupke did not reach the sauna as soon as he'd expected. One of the junior partners, meeting him on the way to the elevator, begged his presence at a conference concerning Shields Petroleum, a corporation which had recently obtained a permit to import an amount, not to exceed 25,000 barrels daily, of South American oil to the United States. Since the Congress had recently barred the importation of any oil from South America, the permit had come up for question on the floor. The possibility that it would be revoked was of moment to Shields Petroleum Corporation since it meant the company would be losing $25,000 per day profit. Shields was not a client of Cabot, Constable, Page and Rupke, but the South American government was and the latter had a tax interest in the action.

It was such profitable and fascinating nuisances which forced the partners to stay in Washington when everyone else was escaping the summer heat. By the time Felix Rupke reached the pool-massage-sauna complex in the basement, Jed Basco was already seated in the steam, a glass of ice water in his hand, his chunky body bathed in sweat.

Jed moved over slightly and Felix settled himself on the sanded birchwood bench. An attendant entered, a bony Finn, nude except for a loincloth. He handed Felix a plastic glass of ice water similar to Jed's, then went out. Felix waited until the door was closed before he spoke.

"I never heard of anything like this. You'd better fill me in."

"I already told you on the telephone—they fired me."

"In *Texas?*"

"We'd been hunting. I didn't know at first it was open season—on me."

"Simply incredible!"

Felix's voice contained commiseration, but his face, growing ruddy in the heat, reflected no pain.

Corporate emergencies were his stock in trade. When fortune smiled on his clients he shared their joy, but when disaster fell he was less than totally dismayed. Either way, Felix profited. That was the advantage of the trade he practiced and the reason for his even temperament.

"I hear there's some red ink coming up for the third quarter," Felix said. "They could have needed a scapegoat for that."

Jed picked up the hose and sluiced cold water over his feet.

"What they needed was your resignation from the board of Basco and Western. When I saw the headlines about your appointment—you *have* resigned, haven't you?"

Felix Rupke was busy rubbing salt into his bony chest, covered with little curls of black hair that resembled ill-matched buttons.

"I have, yes. Effective as of yesterday."

"Then someone—probably Steve—got advance notice."

For the first time in Jed's experience Felix Rupke seemed embarrassed.

"My appointment," he said stiffly, "was top secret. At least until *he* chose to announce it. I've stripped myself to the nub. Sold every stock I own. Resigned from all my directorates, even membership in my own law firm. Have to be squeaky clean when the Senate Judiciary Committee checks me out."

"There's such a thing as being too clean," Jed said rather grimly.

Felix did not overlook his tone.

"If there was any leak, it wasn't at my end."

"Maybe they were playing a hunch then. Let's allow that possibility. With you still on the board there was always the chance that you and I and Dominici could pull Stranahan our way. With your resignation that chance ended and so did their hesitation, if they'd ever had any. Dominici, incidentally, wasn't invited to the campout. I didn't have a shoulder to cry on."

"It might have happened even if I had stayed on the board," Felix said.

There was a crash, then a ferocious hissing as the Finn

dumped water over the hot rocks. When the noise subsided Jed said, "All right. I'll accept that."

"I think we've always leveled with each other."

Jed said, "So let's level now. Here's something you *can* leak—right to Vishniak, Stranahan, Pulaski and Thorpe. I'm going to get my company back, and if their balls come with it, that's all right with me."

In the thickening steam, Felix Rupke shoved his face close to Jed's. He spoke almost plaintively.

"You sold your company, Jed."

Jed said, "I know I did. Biggest mistake I ever made. Or you ever recommended."

"If we had to do it over, I'd make the same recommendation. That purchase moved you from maybe a hundred million net worth to three hundred? Three hundred and fifty?"

"I've never been quite sure. All I know is that I'm now a millionaire bindlestiff."

"I would hardly apply those terms to you."

"I would. Where can I go? What's in the cards for me?"

"I'd say—anything you want. The ex-president of Basco and Western won't stand long on the auction block. That is, if you insist on working, at a time when you—"

"Have everything to live for? All that money? Well, yes, I suppose I could buy a yacht and a scuba-diving outfit and convince myself that loafing is as good as living. What do you want me to do, lay up in some Vegas hotel with a water bed full of diamond-eating whores?"

"My friend," Felix said, patting Jed's hard-muscled shoulder with a tentative placating hand, "you're upset.

Not that I blame you, but you can't make decisions in your present state of mind."

"Then you make them. Let's hear some of them."

"Give me a day or two. I'm convinced there is no lack of opportunity for—"

"Failed corporate executives? Horseshit! I'm distress merchandise. I don't fool myself about that for ten seconds. Sure, I've seen data proving Basco and Western is the United States' fifty-seventh biggest conglomerate, or some statistical crap like that. The fifty-eighth biggest conglomerate won't be in a rush to bid me in. Neither will the fifty-sixth. What does that leave? Some nifty little single-enterprise package capitalized for a hundred million dollars?"

"I never suggested a smaller company, though I certainly would not rule out—"

"Well, I would. And I'll tell you something. In that type of show I wouldn't last five minutes. Assuming that I'd sign on for a lower-echelon spot, which I wouldn't, the men under me would be trying to boob me, to prove their own worth, and the ones above would be afraid I'd climb over their backs. Between the two, they'd cut me into bite-size chunks, and the sooner they did it the happier they'd be."

Another Finn, chubby and bald, opened the door and was beckoning them out, but Felix waved him away.

"You are Jedson C. Basco," he stated with conviction. "A big name. You don't want retirement. That is understandable. So with that name and your knowledge—" he gestured oratorically—"a new enterprise is born."

"From scratch. And I take my hard-earned fistful of

dollars and start bidding on state hydroelectric or county highway bridges and retention dams. No thanks. I'll handle this on my own ground. I think I can win. God damn it, I know I can."

Felix groaned. He started for the door.

"Heat like this, you can only take so much of it."

They were lying on adjacent tables, the rubdowns almost finished before Felix spoke again.

"Vishniak and his bunch will still outvote you."

"That can change."

"If it doesn't," Felix said, "we are shipwrecked. That is my fear. I know shipwrecks. They are not pleasant, even if one lives through them."

Jed grunted, his face half buried in a towel rolled to simulate a pillow.

"The ship has already sunk, Felix. We're on a raft."

Felix sat up. "I like your simile. Take it from there. When five men battle for a jug of water on a raft, the one who survives is the one who gets the water. But the odds are still four to one."

"I've bucked odds before."

The Finn was trying to make Felix lie down.

"On your face now, please, Mr. Rupke."

Felix flopped forward.

"I don't like it," he said. "I don't like it at all."

Jed, all through, was sitting on the edge of his table putting on his socks.

"Your liking it is not important. All I want from you is advice."

"Advice, yes. Once I could have been of assistance. Not so much now."

"Oh, I'm aware of that," Jed said heartily. "The Supreme Court owns you. Or will. I don't expect much in the way of help."

"I wish I could give more," Felix said.

"You can give some, Felix," Jed said. "There's still one piece of you that's working for Jed Basco, eh, Felix? There's still," he said softly, "one little portion that *I* own, and let's not forget it."

But Felix Rupke, quiet on his table, did not answer. It was not even clear that he had heard.

Oh, you hardhat bastard, he thought after Jed had left. You stubborn, betrayed corporate son of a bitch. Why did you have to walk in just when everything was falling into place? Why did you have to come staggering to me with your bag of woe? The idea of his forced complicity in Jed's defeat or any defeat, coming at the moment of his own success, disturbed and irritated him; he scowled and fretted and finally got up to roam around the office, his small fists clenched and his mouth pulled into its characteristic droop.

The liquidation of a high corporate executive—an entirely ordinary and inevitable incident in a competitive industrial culture—could fall into one of several patterns. Sometimes by the time the end came the victim was almost relieved to escape from challenges to which he no longer was equal. As a face-saver, a reward for his numb acceptance of the blindfold and bullets, he would be given the title of honorary president or honorary member of the board. His colleagues would tender him a testimonial dinner and he would take his money and go home.

These were the easy cases. There were others, almost

as common, who spasmed in wild agony, kicking and spattering gore, caring little whom it fouled. They could not understand that their careers, after a steady upward curve of forty years or more, had been ended in five minutes. They would turn haggard, resign from clubs, avoid friends, accuse their wives of infidelity and sometimes end by blowing out their brains.

Jed was the rare type—a man who assessed his situation correctly and at the same time refused to submit to it. He had elected, at utter risk, the only option open to him—a hand-to-hand duel to the death.

Felix lit a cigar. He speculated, though without much interest, on Jed's plans for revenge. It was the sort of thing that only a bull-assed hardhat dam builder would try.

The two had gone up to the office and talked. Relaxed and glowing from the sauna, they had evaluated Jed's options.

Felix had been over the course before. He knew every ditch, every slippery corner. He had figured the odds and outlined the procedures. This kind of contest cost a lot of money. You went for broke—there was no middle course. You got out a letter to tell stockholders how current management erred and explained why you would serve them better. You nominated a new slate of directors and you staffed yourself with specialists who were not afraid to take risks if they could make a dollar—and then you had to watch them day and night to be sure the profit they turned was at the other side's expense and not, in the long run, at yours. You sought out experts in the practice of proxy solicitation to persuade the shareholders to support your program and a lawyer to keep your activities aligned with the requirements of the Securities and Exchange Commission. Above all, you needed a broker to accumulate stock for your account—one with the gall of a bullfighter and the cynicism of a pawnbroker, manipulating the market with a butterfly touch so as not to drive the price out of sight. All this you required and more than a little bit of luck.

Felix laid it out in painstaking detail. He refused to name names or make recommendations other than general ones. He wanted as little connection with the affair as possible. A voting contest for control of a big company—God, it was like a burglary: one wrong move and alarms went off. To bring his own connection with the affair to an end, if nothing else, Felix had been willing to devote some two hours of a busy afternoon, doling out cautious advice for which he could not even bill this burdensome client. He had then shaken hands with Jed and wished him luck and walked him out to the partners' elevator. The matter was settled. And yet . . .

Felix stared through a window at the portentous curve of the Capitol dome.

Something Jed had said hung in the air like the stink of the cheap, strong pipe tobacco that he smoked. Felix knew what it was though at the time, lulled by the Finn's big hands, he had pretended not to hear.

". . . there's still a little portion of you that I own . . ."

Felix knew well enough to what that remark referred. He had, through the years, done various favors, and not inconsiderable ones, for Jed—a matter of a phone call to a friend in the Department of the Interior, probing the price level of a construction bid. Or perhaps the conveyance of information that a certain type of project might be undertaken, that a plan was on the drawing board and that a meeting with a member of a Congressional committee might be desirable. Details of the meeting would be left to others, and sometimes Felix would not even bother to ask what had happened, but the word had been dropped. And often, as the result of such small gestures, inspired less by the lawyer-client relationship than the belly-warmth which had formerly existed between himself and Jed (a temperature noticeably lacking today, even in the blast of the sauna), Jed had made a lot of money.

And one thing you could say for Jed—he was not ungrateful. He had often talked about reciprocation. On several occasions Felix had been forced to explain in no uncertain terms the difference between the services for which he would take a fee and those for which he would not. The practice of law had its ethic. Nevertheless, there was an intermediate ground—an area in which certain special types of recompense could be arranged. After Basco Precision, on a tip from Felix, had bid in the forty-million-dollar Mormon Cutoff job, Felix himself, lunching one day with Jed in the L Street Club, pointed out such an area.

"Ever think of a foundation?"

"As a tax shelter? Yes, I have—I certainly have, Felix," Jed replied, slicing a delicate veal parmigiana. "Frankly, I'm not too sophisticated about taxes. Sometimes I don't know who robs me the worst, the IRS or my own tax accountants. But a foundation—I'm not sure I'm there yet."

"You might be," Felix said. "In fact, we have a man in the office who does nothing but foundations. Maybe you could have a talk with him sometime. Or there are outside people. Some of them just as good, even better. It would have to be your own choice."

Jed picked up the intent of the last three sentences.

"Possibly an outside person would be better," he said.

Shortly after this lunch, the Basco Research and Educational Foundation, a Delaware corporation, filed papers of registration with the State Department of Social Services, Bureau of Proprietary and Charitable Organizations, Charities Registration Section. Along with the executive personnel of the foundation, the name of Felix Linus Rupke was listed as general counsel. His salary was designated as $15,000 per annum, payable for life.

For some time now, the $15,000 check had come in on the second of each January, a welcome and dependable, if minor, addition to Felix's income. The duties he performed for this honorarium were not burdensome—some years, in fact, they were nonexistent. Chief among them was the supervision of contracts transferring grants and scholarships from the foundation to selected recipients such as universities, medical facilities and honor students; since Jed had placed only $85,000 in the foundation treasury and added little since, not many such transfers had been made. There was no way of knowing, on the other hand, when funding would be increased and more gifts awarded. Should such a circumstance come about, Felix was ready to meet the resultant surge in legal activity. He would work, by God, if there was work to do!

He had accepted his appointment in good faith and expressed his appreciation for it in a letter to Jed Basco, a copy of which was in his file. His covenant was with the foundation, not with Jed. Jed had no claim on him—not even a hypothetical one. With that last handshake at the office door this afternoon, he and Jed had parted company, possibly forever.

Felix nudged an intercom switch and asked for a cup of coffee. He was surprised to find how clear his thoughts were on the subject. By the time Ann brought his beverage, he knew what he was going to do. He was going to keep the foundation job. It was clean. There was no conflict of interest involved. How could there be? It would be a cold day in hell before the activities of a charitable foundation came up for adjudication by the Supreme Court. He would have been willing to tell the Man, himself, about this connection, confident of his approval, though of course you did not discuss matters of this kind with the Man; if there was one thing that bugged him it was having to deal with chickenshit details.

Felix moved the empty coffee cup to one side. For some reason he stretched out a finger and touched the telephone with the red tab. It was precisely by dealing with chickenshit problems that he had won his new post. Now at last he had it. From now on he would continue to serve but no longer out of sight. Now he would sit in one of the great chairs behind the high bench in the marble palace only a few blocks from the Capitol and the Senate Office Building—but infinitely superior to them in dignity.

Felix's rise had begun one afternoon in 1948 when a dusty, bone-thin politician in a crumpled suit and a ten-gallon hat boarded Harry Truman's campaign train in Fort Worth and demanded an interview. He was running for Congress and he wanted the President to endorse his candidacy. Presidential aides were not impressed, but Felix Rupke had been and he prevailed on his boss, the Secretary of Commerce, to present the candidate to Mr. Truman. The President endorsed him, the candidate won and went on and up and up. Through the next two decades the skinny whistle-stop hopeful had miraculously fleshed out into the Man, with Felix—a wispy, knowledgeable counselor—limping along, right at his side, continuing to handle the problems no one else would touch.

When a presidential aide was blackmailed for adultery, Felix had kept the story out of the newspapers; when a department head, caught grafting, took too many sleeping pills, Felix drove to Bethesda Hospital behind the ambulance and saw to it that registration, treatment and, later, burial were managed with appropriate discretion. Although not a student of military tactics, he evaluated the amount of firepower which the Kremlin and the Chinese would put up with in Vietnam; at White House parties he kept drunks orderly and steered bores away from unprotected areas; he edited speeches, filled in at diplomatic dinners and suggested to TV comedians how they could modify humorous or satiric references to the President and still be funny. He was on call day and night, perpetually alert to exercise his talents for silence, discretion and camaraderie. For these services he had received not a penny, sometimes not even a nod or a friendly word. He never complained. He waited. Someday he would get his reward. He knew just what he wanted. Knowing this afforded him the courage to reject, with an affability that disguised his contempt, the important-seeming but inferior posts with which the Man had occasionally tried to discharge his obligation.

Ann had come in again. She had another sheaf of telegrams, these mostly from corporations:

CHICAGO TILE AND ROOFING EXTENDS . . . MISOBISHI STEEL CONGRATULATES . . . MIDLAND DISTILLERIES WISHES . . . FLOOD AND WALTERS . . . SIERRA AGGREGATES . . . GENERAL CARBIDE . . . THE BOSTON COMPANY OF THE PACIFIC . . . HALLMARK TRUST AND SAVINGS . . . FELICITATES . . . SALUTES . . .

Felix brushed through the stack, replaced them in the file folder. On the outside of the folder he scribbled a single word, "Acknowledge," then resumed once more his restless pacing in the big, opulently furnished room. His telephones were flashing but he did not answer them. He roamed up and down the thick, pale carpet, sometimes pausing to touch objects on his desk or the smaller tables scattered here and there—ivory elephants, Foo dogs from Gump's, crystal Tiffany unicorns, bronze bookends reduced by Knoedler's from Miura bulls by Picasso. His wife had surrounded him with these cultural tidbits. His wife, who had her own interior-decorating business, was endowed with good taste. Now these things had become precious to him, symbols of growing status.

On a table by itself was a gold-framed picture of a young officer, Lieutenant William Bender Rupke, killed by a guerrilla ambush as his regiment, the 171st Infantry, advanced on Huichon, Korea. No status related in Felix's eyes to the photograph—merely the memory of a searching loss, a sorrow never quite eliminated even now, from any day through which he lived. As much as his limp or his lowly start, the death of the boy had somehow forced him to move, to aspire, to keep busy, lacking as he did the companionship, the home-directed interests which Bill might have provided had he lived.

Felix's glance moved to the books, banking a whole side of the room. Three shelves were filled with Moroccan-bound volumes about the Court. There was little that Felix Rupke did not know about its history. As long as he concentrated on its pageantry, real or imagined—the famous Justices, the great murmurous room, the high bench, himself in judicial robes—he was able to still the doubts raised by Old Blister's envious spite, as long as he looked at the books and pulled on his cigar and touched as amulets the hard, smooth, glistening little artifacts on his tables, he felt increasingly confident.

Qualified? Of course he was. Competent? Beyond the slightest doubt. Yet—a quotation from some long-past year, remembered from one of the tomes on the big shelves, passed across his view as if printed on electric tape: *"The country seems to require that its Justices should possess high character, sound principles, great capacity and wide celebrity. . . ."*

Well, on the last count he might lack something. You couldn't be a celebrity when your stock in trade was running secret errands and submitting classified advice. But the members of the bar—that was a different matter; they knew him all right. He would never forget that Monday when, standing beside the Congressman from Texas who was serving as his sponsor, he had been moved for admission to the Supreme Bar. It had been a rewarding moment. Perhaps the pleadings he had later brought to the

Court had not been epoch-making; still, on the whole, he had acquitted himself well.

A quarter past six! He should be leaving the office. His wife had invited a few friends over for a celebration dinner; but still he lingered. Jed's face rose before him, saying, "I'm going to get my company back, and if their balls come with it, that's all right too." No use reasoning with a man who talked like that. All that he, Felix, could do for the moment was babysit, as it were, take Jed's calls, if he rang asking for more pointers, calm him as much as possible and, in brief, keep him under control—at least until the Senate returned his own appointment.

The phone box was flashing again. Felix knew who it was. He snatched the instrument out of its cradle, yelled into it, "I'm leaving right now" and slammed it down. Then he picked up his briefcase, took his hat from its closet peg and started through the door with his swinging, hitching stride which, in this hour of fulfillment, had become almost a swagger.

CHAPTER FOUR

JED had first given parties in this house at a time when people were still using cocktail shakers. Today they put the ice directly into the glass. What had happened to those cocktail shakers? Dorothy probably had several of them put away in the cupboard where she cached also the oversize flower vases, the broken electric mixers, the platters too ugly or too big to use, and the Saints Satin Wax furniture polish. If he knew Dorothy, and he did, the contents of that closet would not have changed.

The only changes in the house would be the disuse of certain rooms and the bunching or thinning of furniture in certain others to compensate for the fact that he no longer lived there and that his son Bob and his daughter Kitty, the latter now married, had also moved out. Dorothy was alone now. It was a big house for one person, but Dorothy liked the house—loved it, in fact. When anybody complimented her on its appearance, she would glow with pleasure at such compliments, as if receiving some intimate form of flattery.

"Oh, do you really like it?" she would say, her forehead creasing in reappraisal of what they had liked. "I'm so glad, because I do too. I just *love* it."

He had usually been ready first when they had been giving a party. He would inspect the liquor tray—set out in the library, the most comfortable room if it were winter, or the west patio beside the pool if it were summer. He would make sure that the glasses were cooling in a bed of shaved ice, that the bottles were arranged the way he wanted them and that the cocktail shaker, of course, was in its proper place. He would have on his dinner jacket, white in the summer, black in the winter; also the soft pleated shirt with the big cufflinks, and he would enjoy a quiet martini before the first guests arrived.

Jed turned into the familiar driveway and parked the car, choosing a location well to one side of the front door. A new Ford LTD wagon stood under the porte-cochere. He walked over to the door and rang the bell. This was something he had never done before. He had helped design this house and supervised its building and then lived in it for fifteen—no, seventeen—years, but he had never rung the front doorbell. He was still thinking about that odd fact when the door opened and Rosa, the housekeeper, stood before him. She was four feet six and as ugly as the devil's half-witted daughter, but she was also the best cook in Burlingame. She had never liked him. Now, instead of stepping to one side, as an invitation to enter, she stood squarely in the middle of the doorway.

"Mr. Basco!" she said without cordiality.

"Hello, Rosa," Jed said. "How have you been?"

"Just the same," said Rosa. "Mrs. Basco is down at the stable, Mr. Basco. She'll be back pretty soon. You could wait maybe."

"I'll walk down," Jed said.

Rosa said nothing. She still did not move out of the doorway. With her dumpy body and her toothpick legs she was protecting the rights of the mistress of the house. To reach the path that led to the stables one had either to circle the house or walk through it. Jed placed two fingers on Rosa's shoulder and gently moved her aside.

"Thank you, Rosa," he said, walking down the hall.

Rosa looked after him with hate. She lifted her slabby chin and spat carefully into the exact spot where he had been standing. Then she closed the door.

Jed strolled down the path to the stable. On the edge of the flagstone patio a lawn sprinkler brushed bright drops against his legs and spattered the trunk of a liveoak with a brisk sound that reminded him of a shooting gallery. He had stood in such a gallery a few days earlier, in the basement of a Frank Lloyd Wright house overlooking the Hudson River, watching a tall, punctilious man score five successive hits on a moving target. It was early afternoon of a fall Saturday—properly a time for play, but because of the pressures of Jed's problem the pistol-shooter had invited him to confer at his home. His name was Gordon Rice, and he made his living—apparently a good one—running contests for corporate control. He had been recommended to Jed by a friend in a very large corporation who had successfully made use of Mr. Rice's services in the past. Mr.

Rice was listed in the Manhattan directory as a proxy solicitor.

The pistol-shooter handed his weapon to the gallery attendant to be cleaned. He turned and smiled at Jed. He was in his early fifties, Jed judged: a tall black with a thick crest of curly, almost white hair which he did not dress in any special way. There was an ascetic quality about him, as if his interests concerned the soul rather than the purse. He apologized again (he had already done so when they met) for keeping Jed waiting while he shot.

"You are sure you would not like to take some targets yourself, Mr. Basco?"

"No, thank you," Jed said. "I wouldn't know what to do with a handgun. I've just never had the occasion to use one."

"But you hunt, sir," said Gordon Rice. "I distinctly remember that you enjoy hunting."

"Not as much as I used to," Jed had said, thinking of the buck in the canyon and at the same time wondering, if Rice had this information, how much checking Rice had done on him. With the growing vogue for surveillances, maybe everyone at a certain level checked out everyone else. The file rooms of major companies bulged, like those of governments, with cabinets of secret information locked with complicated mechanisms imported from West Germany. So this was what it came to, the microfilmed information: the last analysis. Rice knew he was a hunter, or had been, and he had known before meeting him that Rice was a Negro. The last fact had influenced his decision. A Negro in his field would have to be the best.

"I don't like to kill things any more," Jed said as they went upstairs.

"You can decide that because you have killed," said Rice. "But I live a sedentary life. What is there for me to eliminate?"

"Finance capitalists," Jed said. "Haven't you done some of that?"

Gordon Rice smiled again his gentle, soul-shriving smile.

"Oh, no, I would not put it in those terms. Maybe I have provided some of them with the means or the incentive to eliminate themselves."

"That's different from hunting, all right."

"Yes," said Rice, "I would say so." He took Jed's order, then went to a bar in the corner of the big room, decorated in the best surrealist modern, and made the drinks.

"Does one exercise anger in hunting? I have wondered about that. In my business I am not conscious of exercising anger, but I have been conscious of some anger. I suppose that is because I am black. I get rid of it by popping and plinking with a pistol. Now you, Mr. Basco, you are angry as the devil—and examining this data, I would say you have justification."

His gesture took in a card table in front of the divan. The top of the table and an area of the floor next to it were piled with material Jed had sent him by messenger—the B & W stockholders' list, the minutes of board meetings, the merger agreement and other related documents.

"Justification—we won't cop a decision with justification. What I want to know is, can we win at all? What are my chances?"

He looked at Rice over his glass, his expression one of total determination. "I have a lawyer friend—ex-lawyer now," he added, "who thinks I'm a damn fool. He would like me to retire from business and raise blooded cattle. Or collect stamps."

"And you do not want to raise blooded cattle or collect stamps?"

"No, Mr. Rice," said Jed, "I must work."

"I understand," said Rice. "My opinion is that given your priorities, you should fight."

"Right to the end of the line," Jed said.

"Good. Then we will start. The basic mistake, of course, was selling your company. You acquired great wealth, but you imperiled your lifeline—this necessity for work."

"I should have had my ass kicked. In fact, I *am* having it kicked."

Rice, who had been drinking iced soda, put his glass aside.

"You wanted it two ways—always a risk. However, don't blame yourself. Your analysis of your position, as you described it to me on the telephone, is perfect. You have nowhere to go. You have to make the fight right where you are."

"I'm glad that you agree."

"Of course I agree. At the top the air is very thin and the corridors are pressurized. If a door slams, you are done for. Your door has not quite closed. With the proper leverage, we can force it open. This is the pry bar." He laid his hand on the stockholder list. "My staff has been working on it."

He handed Jed a print-out of B & W's some nine hundred thousand stockholders broken down by age, income, religion, locality, racial origin and extent of their holdings.

"Mr. Vishniak's office requested this study a few months

ago. The research firm preparing it also does work for us. I arranged to have it available. What we can obtain from this, without further depth interviews—for which there is obviously not enough time—is size of holdings, geographical location, the breakdown between direct personal holdings, direct institutional holdings and holdings in the names of banks or brokers. Also, to a minor extent, ethnic backgrounds based on patronyms. We may require some crash survey techniques to arrive at figures on age, income grouping of holders and religious affiliations. We can pin down precisely how much of the stock is held by what percent of the people surveyed—it usually figures that from three to four percent of the stockholders own from seventy-five to eighty percent of the stock. These are the key people—we'll direct our campaign at them. We'll file the necessary papers with the Securities and Exchange Commission, stating your intention to solicit proxies. All this is routine, but it will have to be done at high speed. There are only sixty days left before the annual meeting. Somehow in that time you'll have to get enough votes to throw out Vishniak's board and put in your own. All right. There are two ways to obtain the votes—by appealing to the stockholders and by buying shares for yourself. I mean buying massively. You have an advantage here—this print-out is proof that you own more shares personally than any other individual shareholder. You also have two handicaps: you've given away a lot of your voting shares, which are Class A common. A good deal of what you have left is a special kind—the Class B common, which by its charter General Western was authorized to issue without voting rights. The Class B, as you know, is also restricted by a notice affixed to it—it is unregistered, or 'letter,' stock and it can't legally be sold or traded for two years. You acquired this when you sold your company to General Western?"

"Yes."

"I assume you wanted ordinary certificates, but somehow in the course of negotiations you were offered the letter, or unregistered, stock; the controls placed on it placated board members who would have objected to the dilution of their dividends caused by a large block of common being issued to you as a condition of the sale."

"Something like that."

"You know, of course, that the restriction on disposing of unregistered stock is a tight legal commitment, with rather drastic penalties if it is broken. You are not supposed to sell the stock until the date specified in the letter affixed to the shares."

Rice got up and threw another log on the fire. As a crest of furious sparks lunged up the chimney he said quietly, "Now as to the people to whom you've given your voting stock: Here I'm making another assumption—that the aim of the gifts was a tax shelter in creating several separate estates for members of your family—four parcels of twenty thousand shares valued at approximately a million dollars apiece at the current market price."

"One of the recipients was not a member of my family."

Rice looked at a memorandum.

"But Mrs. Dorothy Basco—she is your ex-wife?" Jed nodded. "Mr. Robert Basco—"

"My son. He's twenty."

"Mrs. William Wadsworth Bramstead."

"My daughter, recently married."

"And the other person is—"

"No relative."

Rice replaced the memorandum on the stack of documents.

"You will excuse one more question. Will these people vote their stock for you?"

"Some will."

"And the others?"

"I'll have to find out."

"There is no time to lose."

"I know."

Rice did not seem displeased with the answer.

"I'm grateful for your frankness. Many men would have said to keep face, 'My family? This dear friend? Of course they will vote for me.' But things don't always work out that way."

"You mentioned the non-registered stock—the letter stock. Isn't there some way we could use it? There's a hell of a lot and—"

A man servant came in and turned on the light. In this sudden illumination Rice's face seemed hollow and drawn.

"I have been thinking along those lines, Mr. Basco. Let me reflect a little longer. I'll let you know. . . ."

What Rice thought or failed to think of regarding the non-registered stock remained his business. Jed's was to talk to the holders of the stock he had given away. He'd start with Dorothy because she would be the toughest. If she went along, the rest could be easy.

She was exercising a young gelding quarter horse, stocky and very well made, with beautifully muscled hindquarters and a wedgy Arab head. She had him in the training enclosure, a half-acre oblong with a heavy redwood fence around it. The jumps had been taken out and a trainer Jed had not seen before was slowly walking Dorothy's show hunter, Dolley Madison, to cool her. Sweat darkened the thin canvas cooling sheet covering the big mare's back, flanks and shoulders. Dorothy worked a horse hard. She still looked very trim and she was in beautiful control of the quarter horse as she loped him slowly through the figure eight his hoofs had dug out of the soft, springy turf. The sorrel had not been saddle-broke long. That much was evident as Jed, very cautiously, stepped near enough to watch the action. The gelding's eyes rolled white and the ears went back, but he never broke his smooth, gathered stride.

Dorothy saw Jed at the same moment her mount did. She moved her head in greeting without changing the rhythm or position of her body as she pressed the gelding with her thighs and calves, delicately shifting her weight to make him change leads. She was wonderful with horses —so much better, Jed reflected, than she was with people. She liked control. It was only when she lost it—when events took hold of her and began tipping her this way and the other—that she became unpredictable and frantic.

She took her mount through one more cantering loop, then stopped him, speaking to him with a harsh female tenderness, as if addressing a lover— "Back, darling, back, back, *back*. That's my angel. Oh . . . lovely, that's so nice. *Back* now. All right. . . ." Her strong thighs released their pressure; her weight slid forward, she touched the sorrel with her heels and he sprang ahead, glad that the lesson was over, dropping his head in the hackamore as if shyly acknowledging the praise.

Dorothy swung her leg over the horn of the stock saddle and slid down, facing Jed across the fence.

"Isn't he adorable?"

"Nice animal. Where'd you get him?"

Dorothy pointed to the RO brand on the horse's right flank.

"Green Cattle Company in Merced. They still breed the best. . . . Now listen, Anton," she said as the trainer, having led the jumper to a box stall, came to get her mount, "don't put a sheet on him this time. I don't care what they do with thoroughbreds in Switzerland. Just let him roll in the dirt, the way he likes to, and then sluice him off before you walk him. . . . This is my ex-husband, Mr. Basco, Anton Moulin. . . . Anton trained the Swiss team that won the Olympics."

Anton Moulin raised a finger to his forehead in the European style.

"With hunters, yes . . . but with quarter horses, no. With them I am stupid, Mrs. Basco says."

"We all have to learn, Anton. That's what some of us forget when we become too famous. . . . I have some damned ecology meeting today," she said as she and Jed turned toward the house. "I forgot all about it when you phoned. Twelve o'clock. I'm the chairman. Margery is picking me up, but we'll still have time to talk."

She had not hidden the cocktail shaker in the mop closet after all. It was still available for use, a tall tube of Shreve sterling someone had given them for a wedding present. The donor had not put his name on record. The engraving simply read Jed and Dorothy and the date April 6, 1948. At that time Jed and Mike McGettigan, Dorothy's father, had been partners in the construction firm of McGettigan & Basco; they had just bid in their first dam, the Willow Hill, and a model of its projected outline, sculptured in ice, had adorned the table on Mike's lawn near the pool where the wedding gifts were proudly displayed. Mike had hired a Pinkerton man to watch them. Father Brian O'Connor of the Church of the Good Shepherd, San Mateo, performed the ceremony at four o'clock in the afternoon under a liveoak tree. Mike and Mrs. McGettigan had asked seventy guests by engraved invitation, but Mike had kept on inviting every friend he met so that some hundred and twenty (Betty McGettigan always said one hundred and sixty) were on hand by the time the orchestra hired from the St. Claire Hotel, San Jose, played the Wedding March and the bridesmaids paraded out of the house followed by Dorothy, her left arm lightly tucked under her father's right elbow.

Hems were down that year. The Dior look was coming, but Mrs. McGettigan had been uncertain of its official endorsement, so the bridesmaids' hemlines were a compromise. There was dancing after six, and Jed and Dorothy took a few turns before leaving for a short honeymoon at Pebble Beach.

Dorothy had been a good-looking bride. Not a beauty. Jed had not wanted a beauty. He had wanted a woman, and Dorothy had been that. She had been an attractive bride and she had been a good wife, up to a point. He too had wanted to be a good husband; though not a Catholic, he had agreed to the Catholic ceremony partly to accommodate the McGettigans but also from the superstitious feeling that a Catholic ceremony ensured a lasting marriage. Catholics demanded fidelity from the first coupling until the death of the husband or of the wife.

With a beautiful woman the long course might have seemed more tolerable but the problems would have multiplied. Jed had been to bed with only one woman who was truly beautiful and the experience had shaken him, less perhaps because of her looks than because of her style. She had made no commitments and required no avowals in return, but in some subtle way she had demanded a capacity for total giving which he could not meet. He had given her up to marry Dorothy through the medieval witchcraft provided by Father O'Connor, but he had never been sure, above all that day on the lawn under the liveoak tree, that he had made the right decision. The question had been, of course, academic even then and a thousand times more so now, but it recurred to him as he accepted a martini from the silver pitcher, and he remembered the dryness of his mouth as he had stood beside Dorothy under the tree with the big ice dam glinting on the table and the Pinkerton man sweating in his thick blue suit.

At forty-four Dorothy was still a damn good-looking woman. She had not broadened in the rump the way most horsy women did, as if the saddle pushed them out, and her thighs in the tight jodhpurs had a pleasing, muscular arch. In bed, those thighs had arched for his pleasure, moist and strong as the necks and flanks of the young horses she was always riding, and you passed from the domain of the thighs into a violent flow and urgency as Dorothy came again and again with a deep interior shuddering. There was no way to get tired of that, and during the early years of their divorce, when he had come to see her on some business matter, they had sometimes gone to bed, as a salute to happier times, and on these occasions the business later, whatever it was, had gone well. That it was not to be that way today seemed a pity, but such was the fact. Dorothy made this clear as she returned from taking a telephone call.

"That was Marge Halsey. She just wanted to be sure I'd be ready. She's a dear, but she always worries about punctuality. I wouldn't have let her pick me up today except that she might have thought it was peculiar if I didn't accept. Which wouldn't be good because . . . Can you keep a secret?"

"Probably not."

"I know you can—you never see any of these people any more. The *my* crowd that used to be our crowd . . . so I'll tell you. Besides which, Jed Basco, though you are and have been many things, you have never been a talker."

Dorothy refilled her glass. She made a questioning motion with the shaker, but Jed shook his head.

"I'm glad you're not drinking," she said. "You were always impossible when you drank. The secret is, I don't feel too comfortable with Margery any more, and she senses it. She's just a little suspicious, you understand? Which I cannot allow. So whatever she suggests I go along with it on account of I'm having just a tiny little temporary thing with Ed, her husband. I suppose I had to tell someone, otherwise where's the fun? And it might as well be you, but if you dare so much as breathe a word . . ."

"Ed Halsey, the golf pro?"

"Oh, good God, Jed, you're ten—no, seven—years behind the times. The pro was Halsey, but it wasn't Ed. Bo Halsey. Or Bud, that was it, Bud Halsey. He's been gone for ages. *Ed* Halsey is married to Marge now. She was Margery Holcum when we knew her before. Mrs. George Ellsworth Holcum. George died, and she married Ed, from Bakersfield. He's homely as a crutch and rich as hell. He does parlor tricks. Can you imagine? Parlor tricks. And he has a Continental with a horn that blows reveille. He had it custom-made."

"You're lucky women, you and Marge."

"I don't blame you for being sarcastic. It's utterly ridiculous. Reveille. He blew it at me just about one month—to be exact, one month and three days ago. Saturday was our anniversary. That's what he called it. He's a scream. I was coming off the freeway and I had a new car too, that LTD wagon. You probably saw it outside."

"I'd say you made a better choice with the LTD than with Halsey."

"Oh, he's not all that bad. But you see, this is the funny part, he only looked at the car, not me. Nobody around here recognizes you by your face when you're driving. They just look at the car. He thought he was scoring a coup. You should have seen his face when I pulled over and he found he'd picked up his wife's best friend. We wound up in a motel, I'll never know why. Of course it can't last."

Jed said rather heavily, "It sounds like the hottest romance since Taylor and Burton."

"Elizabeth Taylor and Richard Burton are an old married couple now, like you and I used to be. This won't last because one day I won't be able to stand the sound of that horn."

"Find out where he had it made. I might want one."

"You don't need one, dear. You have a better way of getting women. You buy them."

"Not as a rule."

"Don't lie. I happen to know. And at your age it's easiest. I approve. But don't sidetrack me again. I know what you're here about. You see, Ed's brother-in-law, Marge's brother—what does that make him to me? Don't answer—is Ken Shields, and Ken rides the early commuter train with someone in Dean Witter who is a close friend of Herman Pulaski. Does that ring a bell?"

"Herman is on the board."

"Then it is true?"

"What's true?"

"That the third-quarter report is really a disaster?"

Jed reached for the shaker.

"Could be down a little. Will be, I'd say. But nothing to worry about."

He wondered how much more Basco & Western news had reached her via the commuter trains.

"Is that what you came to tell me, that there's nothing to worry about?"

She was feeling for his intent with perceptions acquired during their marriage and not discarded since the divorce. You didn't fool around with Dorothy at this stage of the game.

"No, I didn't. I was in San Francisco and I have some business to take up with you. It's a rather urgent matter. It will involve Bob and Kitty too."

"Oh, I'm glad that you're concerned about Bob and Kitty. That's very fatherly and nice. Especially after all those months when—"

"I'm not concerned whether you think so or not. And I've been in touch."

"With Kitty. Because she happens to live thirty miles from New York. Not with Bob. Have you any idea what he's been up to?"

"He sounded great last time I talked to him."

"I'd be curious to know when that was. Because a week —no, ten days—ago some *men* were looking for him. And they were from the FBI. Would you have any idea why they consider him a public enemy?"

"I'm sure they don't. It was probably a routine check-out. He might have applied for a job requiring security clearance."

"He might have, but he didn't. Bob would never in this world apply for that kind of job, and you know it. Furthermore there was nothing routine about this. They knew *all* about him—what courses he took at Harvard, the one year he bothered to take *any* courses—when he went to Vietnam, when he left the Army. He's in some kind of trouble and if you know what it is I insist that you tell me."

"I'm afraid I don't know."

Jed was aware that since receiving his discharge Bob Basco had been working the Underground, assisting deserters and other military defectors to leave the United States. Bob—laconically referring to this activity in their telephone conversations—had added, "I wouldn't say anything to Mother"—a suggestion Jed was not eager to ignore.

"Well, if you're not lying, as I suspect you are, I'd certainly find out. Because Bob adores you and I have a feeling that he needs you. Maybe *desperately*. . . ."

Not as much as I need him, Jed thought, but he said only, "I've told you that I'm going to contact him."

"Oh, those corporation phrases. 'Contact him!' What does that mean, pray tell? He's your, our, *son!* He's reckless, always has been, and now . . . I don't see how you can turn your back on him, no matter how much trouble you're having with your conglomerate."

"I told you, we're not having any trouble."

"Which I know better than to believe. I'd really forgotten what a liar you are. But when I think of it . . ."

"Take it easy, Dorothy."

"I get so angry I . . . just . . . might . . . *throw . . . something . . . at . . . you!*"

The heavy silver tube whacked against the bookcase. Ice, gin and water spattered on Jed's suit. The top of the shaker rolled across the carpet like a child's toy.

Dorothy said with weariness, "Rosa will take care of all that. She had plenty of practice in the old days. . . . Oh my God, I have to go and dress."

"I brought some stuff for you to sign."

CHAPTER FIVE

DOROTHY made no reply. She walked out of the room, across the hall and up the stairs, Jed following, his eyes on the trim buttocks moving at the exact level of his eyes.

He sat in a small gold boudoir chair, one that he did not remember. A delicate chair, not constructed for a man's weight, but Dorothy had the only other seating place, and a move to the bed might be misconstrued, Jed felt. He stayed in the chair and lit a pipe while Dorothy, on the settee, removed her jodhpurs, then stood up, took off her bra and panties and walked nude into the bathroom.

"I do wish you wouldn't smoke in here," she said, speaking through the partially opened door. "You know how I hate it. It stinks up the whole house. . . . What is it you want me to sign?"

"A proxy. So that I can vote your stock at the shareholders' meeting."

"Vote it for yourself, you mean. Everybody knows that the directors fired you."

Jed approached the bathroom door and stood so as to project his voice through the chink Dorothy had left.

"Dorothy, I ran the company the only way the directors would let me. Now I intend to get it back and run it the way I've always wanted. If you're willing to let a bunch of strangers, greedy ones at that, decide how much income you're going to have, then don't go along. It's up to you."

He could see his image, as he spoke, reflected in the mirror on the bathroom door. His field of vision added angles from the mirrors lining the dressing room walls and somehow this instant multiself, a host of loyal replicas backing him up, restored his confidence. His voice had the combination of decision and disinterest which had always brought Dorothy to heel in the old days.

"You can come in," Dorothy said, "provided you don't get any ideas. You've said your piece, and now I'm going to say mine."

She was foundering in a Coral Sea of bubbles, lightly awash but with the crew at battle stations.

"Well?"

"I won't sign your proxy. I might have, except for one thing. I still don't like to be publicly humiliated by your association with that bitchy old lady you used to keep. And please put out your pipe. This room is too small."

Jed tamped out his pipe in the toilet and flushed away the burning chunks of tobacco.

"What bitchy old lady?"

"What bitchy old lady? he says. Is there more than one? If you don't know which, I'd suggest you read last Thursday's *Journal*—the one with the story about your trying to get B and W back. Very interesting. Highly colorful and definitely slanted in your favor, I would say. Tough old construction tycoon battling for life against slick modern combine. The reporter did a great job. He must have seen the Register of Stockholders because he listed some of the main ones—Vishniak's bunch, of course, and some old Rockefeller or Mellon cousins, they're always in there. You read the story too, so don't shit me."

"Rockefellers and Mellons? I suppose you're referring to Xavier Dupont. We've never had Rockefellers or Mellons, old or young—not that we wouldn't have been pleased to. And no one to my knowledge has ever been humiliated by being listed with—"

"Wait. I was mentioned too. And Bob and Kitty. Well, we *are* big stockholders. You made us that, and I was grateful even if you did it for tax reasons. But vote for you, no. I hope they pull your ass right through the wringer. It would give me great pleasure to go to the meeting and watch it happen—to you and Georgiana Gibbs jointly."

"Georgiana Gibbs. Oh my God."

"Exactly. Something to vomit over. Because I never knew until I saw the story that you had given her exactly the same number of shares that you gave us, your own family. You're not still seeing her, are you—that *grandmother?*"

"Georgiana Gibbs has no grandchildren that I know of. But you could be a grandmother yourself almost any time."

"You mean," said Dorothy, with something like terror, "Kitty is pregnant?"

"Not that I know of. But let's face it—she's been married now for over a year. And I understand she's trying."

"Well," said Dorothy, visibly relaxing, "I'd be very happy to be a grandmother, which no one incidentally believes possible. Why, when I tell people I have a married daughter they practically faint. So then I have to tell them my age, which is forty-four, if you'll recall."

"I hope you keep a supply of smelling salts on hand."

"How old is she—seventy?"

"Georgiana Gibbs is sixty-four."

"Got *that* little statistic down pat, haven't you?"

"I am familiar with Georgiana's age, yes. For your information I did give her some Basco Precision, and when Western acquired Basco her holdings—"

"Sure, she got three for one. We only got the B and W. She'd *always* had the Basco Precision. You've just talked yourself into another bind. You took care of her first and us second, your own family."

Jed, thinking only of his business dilemma, nevertheless found himself inadvertently staring at the thick reddish swab of Dorothy's pubic hair. Noting the direction of his glance, she dredged up a washcloth and primly covered her lower abdomen with it.

"If you want to stare at someone's pussy, go and stare at Georgiana Gibbs's. You don't mean to say you're still *seeing* her, do you?"

"I haven't seen her, in that way, since—"

He cast back trying to remember.

"Saturday night," prompted Dorothy, "at a geriatric sit-in, maybe?"

"Since before I gave her the stock. That would be—"

"I don't believe you. For some reason you always had a

penchant for whores. But I didn't know you were still interested in them when they were sixty-four years old. Or that you were willing to pay a million dollars. You must be the fourteen-carat sucker of all time."

From outside came the blast of the most unusual automobile horn Jed had ever heard. Dorothy's expression of composed fury dissolved into one of panic. She heaved herself out of the tub, inundating the floor, then crossed the bedroom, each footprint a dark puddle on the white rug. From a window overlooking the drive she peered down with frantic intensity, then gave a relaxed wave.

"Yoo hoo, Marge. I'm just out of the bath. Could you wait a minute, honey? I'll be right down."

Half dry, the wet towel she had been clutching to her breast now serving as a bath mat, she struggled into a girdle, back-hitched a bra, then put on in rapid succession hose, shoes and a flowered-silk print, ran a comb through her hair and dabbed on mascara, makeup and lipstick, all the time talking rapidly to Jed.

"I thought for a minute it had to be . . . and imagine, if he'd come up here on some kookie impulse, not knowing that she . . . but I guess she just borrowed his car."

"Dorothy," Jed said, "I'm going to leave this proxy here. I wish you'd reconsider. You understand that—"

"I understand everything, absolutely, and the fact that I understand is exactly why I won't—"

"Damaging your financial future and the kids' is a poor revenge for something that happened almost twenty years ago and that both of us have had plenty of time—"

"—help you in any way, shape or form. So go in there on your own, dear, and—"

"—to forget about."

"—give them hell. You can do it. I am not forgetting anything. And I am not signing. I'm sorry I'm in such a rush. Rosa will give you some lunch if you want it. There's some ceviche in the icebox. That's the Mexican thing she makes out of raw fish and salsa. We had it last night. I hope you have better luck with Bob and Kitty. Goodbye now."

Jed walked slowly downstairs. He could hear through the open windows the sound of big tires on the gravel and then, as the car turned onto Bridge Road, the horn again, can'tgetmeup, can'tgetmeup, can'tgetmeup in the mooorning.

"She's refused to sign the proxy," Jed told Rice on long distance. "I gave it my best pitch. There was no way."

"I think I expressed my fears about the family," Rice said.

"You did . . . you did indeed."

"In contests for corporate control, one has these problems. I hope you have better luck with your son and daughter."

"With my daughter, no problem. We've always been close. With Bob, well, I just don't know. It could be all right. He's a fine boy."

"And Mrs. Gibbs?" Rice said tentatively.

Jed stiffened. "I haven't seen Mrs. Gibbs for a number of years."

"But, in view of the size of the settlement—one would say she might feel . . ."

Rice's gentle voice, with its complicated meld of accents, trailed off.

"An obligation? Possibly. How's it going at your end?"

"We've filed with the SEC. We also have a statement out to the key stockholders, setting forth your position and asking for support. Ten thousand mailed so far. By the end of the week it will be four times that. You'll receive copies of everything."

"What about the letter stock? Have you found a way to handle that?"

There was a slight hesitation before Rice answered. "I approached several firms, two of them quite forcefully. Naturally, I couldn't lay it on the line. This is not the ordinary type of stock transaction, not at all. I sketched the situation in general terms, mentioning no names. There was resistance."

"But if we let it go at ten points under the market . . . you suggested that yourself."

Jed had a feeling of panic that surprised him. Without the use of his block of unregistered stock he would never have the capital to buy the B & W shares he needed.

"I brought it up," Rice said quietly, "and I believe I have the answer. There's a Boston firm, Donovan and Klein. They are—you might call them specialists in unusual deals. Donovan is handling it personally. They have branches in twenty cities. For clutch sale situations, there's no one better. While they are marketing the letter stock they will be buying for your regular account. News of the bad third quarter is actually helping. There's a flood of shares up for sale. I would be of very good cheer, Mr. Basco, in spite of your ex-wife's attitude."

"I am of good cheer," Jed said, "but I'll want daily reports. I'm not playing games, Rice. This is for my neck."

"I'm not playing games either, Mr. Basco," said Rice quietly. "I will be in touch. Peace and friendship."

"Peace and friendship," Jed said dourly.

CHAPTER SIX

THE vehicle was not an MP patrol or a black and white prowl car (a watcher in a jalopy parked across the street maintained an alert for such intruders and set off an alarm). The visitor must be all right. A cute chick who had been making sauce in a gallon pot for the Quaker ladies' spaghetti ran out in the yard and threw her arms around him as he climbed stiffly out from behind the wheel of the souped-up Chevy.

"I'm Susie Callan. You're Bob Basco, right?"

Bob rubbed her little sloping fanny sweetly and smiled wearily before shaking hands with the others who crowded up to him. By that time almost everybody was outside the meeting house, trying to get near him to touch him or win a smile or greeting as he moved into the house. He looked as tall as a ship's mast in his leather clothes, a beaded browband on his long red hair and his blue eyes bright above his dark beard.

Jed had not gone outside with the others. He had been starting to eat, and he stood holding his plate in the area they called the refectory, which was merely an extension of the huge, scrubbed, gleaming kitchen.

Bob spied him over a dozen clustered heads and strode over.

"So you made it," Jed said.

"Oh, I still read the ads," Bob said. "Habit I contracted in my childhood. What's that you're eating?"

"A repast these ladies were kind enough to offer an intruder. Good, too."

"I'll take odds on that," Bob said. "Is there enough left for me?"

Jed had made contact with his son through a classified advertisement in the *Berkeley Barb*. He had learned from an inquiry among Bob's friends, discharged soldiers who had served with him in Vietnam, that the FBI indeed had a warrant out for his arrest. In spite of the warrant, Bob made himself visible to his friends in the Underground like some pot-smoking resurrected saint.

A shot-up soldier in Letterman Hospital had recommended the ad.

"There's a number you can call," he wrote on a plastic tablet thoughtfully provided by hospital authorities to patients who could not speak because of wounds to the mouth and jaw. "It will reach Bob, but I can't give it to you."

He erased what he had written, lifting the plastic page so that the words on it disappeared.

Jed leaned over the wheelchair to bring his lips close to the soldier's ear.

"Please," he said.

The mutilated man shook his head.

He wrote on the pad, "That number is only for those who want out. You use the *Barb.* We have a drop going in the classifieds. Our ad is coded, but he'll read one that is not coded. Word it so he'll know it's not a trap."

Jed spent two hours working on the ad, though when printed it was only two lines long:

Bob B: You are tougher to hook than George the trout.
Call me. J.B.

He had inserted the number of his New York answering service.

Bob would remember George. This was the name they had given a big fish Bob had taken on a goofer fly when he was seven years old. The big brown was the first the boy had ever taken on a fly and the biggest anyone had caught that trip. Afterward Jed had put the little boy on his shoulders and carried him in triumph through the camps of several other fishing parties on that stretch of the Madison, and the catch had been properly admired.

Bob would remember George all right. If he saw the ad, he would get in touch.

He did, although he did not place the initial call himself. A strange voice on the telephone had directed Jed to the Quaker meeting house on Lemon Grove Avenue in Pasadena. He had been waiting two days, eating the good food provided by the Underground and sleeping in the meeting room on two pews turned face to face to form a bunk, a method also adopted by the fugitives quartered there.

The sanctuaried persons were three in number: two GI deserters and a conscientious objector. Leader of the group and by far the most impressive personality was a master sergeant, twenty-six years old, who had done nine months in Vietnam with the First Airborne Cavalry. A lanky, bony man, with a relaxed, good-humored air, he had adopted none of the accouterments of protest. He was clean-shaven, and his hair looked as if it had just been cut by a company barber. He had the Infantry Medal and the Purple Heart. Stationed at Fort Ord, waiting for his discharge to be processed, he had started an Underground newspaper, *The Lie.* The paper purported to state the true facts about Vietnam. The master sergeant had gone over the hill when tipped off, by a friend in the post Judge Advocate General's Office, that his identity had become known and that he was about to be arrested on the charge of "inciting to disobedience."

The master sergeant's friend, constant companion and admirer was an ex-Marine boot named Monash. He was a tiny individual, barely meeting the armed services minimum requirements of one hundred pounds and sixty inches. He had no political convictions but had joined the corps when a civilian judge indicated that if he did so a charge against him of grand theft, automobile, would be dismissed.

The third fugitive had no military background. This was just as well since he was like some sort of little animal turned out of his den or burrow too soon, his baby fat still on him and his eyes unused to the light. He was a dreamer and a letter writer, pale, chubby, loving and confused. Nevertheless, he had burned his draft card on the steps of Sproule Hall, University of California, Berkeley. A shy, blond girl friend living in Pasadena, not far from the meeting house, came to see him every day, bringing flowers, fruit and records. After giving out the gifts—which the two shared with everybody—she and the CO would sit together, often reading to each other out of the book *This Is My Beloved.* At night they would go to a pew-bench bed apart from the others and make love. His name was Andrew Gully.

Waiting for Bob, Jed had become acquainted with all three fugitives, but neither they nor the members of the Underground who assisted in operating the sanctuary knew quite what to make of him. They addressed him as "sir" or "Mr. Jacks," the name the Underground suggested he use. Everyone in the meeting was solicitous in seeing that his bed was comfortable, that he had enough food and even stuff to read. After talking to him for a while, though, most would excuse themselves—they had this or that to do. The Underground had put him there, but there might be some mistake: he was not the sort of individual you would expect to find in a counter-establishment sanctuary. That is, until Bob Basco arrived.

Jed could get into the office every day and use the telephone, making credit-card calls for several hours on end. In this way he kept up with the proxy fight, but the wait had been hard on him. The one part of life in the sanctuary that he had actually enjoyed was the late-night rap sessions. The master sergeant dominated the talk, but oddly enough he seldom talked about the war. It was as if, by deserting, he had ended his connection with all military activity—even protest against its continuance. What concerned him now was his future, and he happily detailed the sort of life he planned for himself after the Underground smuggled him into Mexico. He had been there numerous times for business or pleasure, and on one such trip he stumbled on a source of possible riches which had occupied his thoughts ever since. Mercury! That was what he intended to do. Start a mine from which mercury could be extracted—a mine like that had been there since Spanish times. "A quicksilver mine," the master sergeant called it, but the more picturesque term could not obscure the fact that it was an important ingredient in the manufacture of nuclear weaponry, selling now at a price per flask of $125 as compared to $40 before the bomb.

The mine was up in the Cordillera, east of Mazatlán, Sinaloa. The master sergeant had found it while hunting jaguar. He had drawn a map of the locale and, later, researched its history. During one period bandits had used it as a hideout; to exterminate them, the Rurales had dynamited the main shaft. But this could be repaired.

"Man, we go in there, we'll all make a fortune. Sure we'll have to pay off to the ricos. Some general owns the land, so we give him a bite—the *mordida,* they call it. But there's millions in it, more bread than you can imagine. The only problem is getting the quicksilver out. For that we've got to build a road and then . . ."

He would talk on and on, ruddy-faced, powerful and bony, with his easy Yankee voice that brooked no argument. Monash, who in his variegated past had actually done some mining, nodded, wriggling his tense small body in confirmation. Mercury, hell yes! It was better than gold. Money in the bank. Just took certain arrangements and then . . .

Jed remembered when he had heard that kind of talk before. Back in the Depression when there had been only dreams and empty bellies. In those days the young men had talked like this, forecasting the great projects in which they would participate after the hard times were over. Jed recalled a ride up mountains not so different from those that the master sergeant was describing, a ride on a bumpy road, sitting on the floorboards of a high old truck, sitting packed tight, young men going to a job, the stench of bodies, the shine of eyes above the bearded faces, the engine huffing and puffing and he himself, thin, sleepless, chilly and excited. That had been his first job, his first chance. That was what you remembered, the days when you could not be turned back, when nothing could stop you, when you were immortal, and you could do anything!

Out of that past he heard a young voice saying, "I know a piece of river bottom you don't have to pump no water to. Just stick a pipe in the river and you siphon it right into the furrows. Greatest place for growing apricots I ever seen. After I get me a little bit of money saved I'm goin' there and . . ."

Young men, riding up a mountain, going to a job.

Each evening at eight the meeting observed the Silence. The pews were arranged to form three sides of a square. Every person in the house, whether Quaker or not, took part. A log fire burned in the brick hearth fronting the open part of the square; apart from this ancient referral to older, less gentle faiths, there were no totemistic objects in the room. Now and then a Friend stood up and testified briefly on some subject of spiritual relevance.

The night before Bob's arrival the fuzz and the MPs came. Their lights flashed at the windows. Then their vehicles stopped and they got out and held a consultation on the sidewalk. Jed remembered from his own experiences in World War II that when arresting deserters the usual procedure was for the civilian police to make the arrest, then deliver the prisoner to the military authorities, the reason for this being the bounty which the military pays for apprehension of a wanted man. The civilian precinct captain gets the money, which he splits with the arresting officer. The catch, Jed recalled, was that before the cops could serve the warrant, the deserter or deserters had to be identified, a job usually best performed by the MPs.

The purpose of the sidewalk conference was to decide which team should go in. In the end two MPs came up the walk and opened the doors of the meeting house. But instead of entering they stood there, immobilized by the firm hand of the Silence, the odd sight of so many men and women sitting side by side and saying nothing, doing nothing, just being. The fire of oak logs burned bright and a little rain was falling, the drops hissing in the chimney. The MPs removed their helmets, obeying their instructions to be unobtrusive and if possible unobjectionable in performing their duties. One of them took an arrest slip out of his helmet and leaned down, showing it to the nearest Friend, asking whether the master sergeant, Monash and Gully were present. The Friend could be seen nodding his head yes, for Friends do not ordinarily lie, even to MPs, and above all not during the Silence.

The MP straightened up.

He knew he was in a church, so he hesitated, but he was going to do his duty. The men were here and he would take them out. He spoke to the Friend again and the Friend pointed to the deserters, each sitting with a girl and tightly holding her hand. For it was fine to be a courageous over-the-hill master sergeant or a runaway Marine or a CO living on the fat of the land, but it was another thing to be one minute away from the stockade and the ten to twenty years that the General Court might in its mercy see fit to dish out.

The Silence continued. The Silence held an arm across the door. If someone had tried to run or yelled "Off the pigs" the two MPs would have been inside, shooting if necessary. Fortunately the only person who spoke was the big Quaker who was chairman of the Committee for Guidance and Counseling of the Lemon Grove Avenue Pasadena Meeting.

"Come in, my friends," he said in a deep, strong voice, beckoning cordially to the MPs. "Be seated. Come and meditate with us."

The MPs backed out the door. They did not exchange a word or a look. The big Quaker could have opened on them with an eighty-five millimeter anti-tank gun and they could not have disappeared faster.

"It works, you see," Bob told Jed after dinner. "The right of Sanctuary, one of the oldest legal principles in the world. It's based on the theory of the Contagion of Holiness. If you are in a sacred place, some of the goodness rubs off on you. Demosthenes in the temple, you know. In Roman times, the right extended to fifty paces from the church door—*Christian* church. Oh yes, Justinian and Theodosius were quite liberal about that. The fugitives could sleep in the yard. They also needed somewhere to defecate. Penalty for taking a felon from holy grounds—excommunication. I've seen similar incidents all over the country. Dragging a man out of a seat of worship gives the Army a bad image. They try sometimes but most often the arrest patrol talks to the duty officer on the car radio and he tells them to come back to base. Quaker meeting houses have the strongest charisma. Don't know why."

"I hear the FBI is looking for you."

"Christ, you know it. Had to move away from a stake-out tonight. Only reason my phone isn't tapped is that I don't have one."

"Your mother is worried about you."

Jed brought this out so pompously that his tone bounced back to him and he laughed, Bob roaring along with him, both faces tilted toward the ceiling of the little accounting office where the executives of the meeting kept their books. In that moment father and son looked curiously alike in spite of Bob's beard and the craggy lines on Jed's weathered face.

A blank proxy lay on the table between them. Bob picked it up and signed.

"What's happening, Dad?"

"You might say they ripped me off."

"You mean the company? I thought you owned it. Fifty-third largest in the U.S.A. or something like that."

"Fifty-seventh."

"Whatever. Anyway you—a pillar of the super-rich, guaranteed for life. And nothing ever happens to the super-rich. Or so they say."

"The hell it doesn't, son. You're walking on ice cubes up there. One slip and, wham, you're over a cliff."

Bob nodded, his eyes grave. "Maybe you're talking about turning points. Like getting divorced. Or even not marrying that woman you had before Mom. The one you thought so much of." Jed's eyes narrowed, and Bob added hastily, "Oh, Mom went on about her once or twice. A long time ago, but that's why I figured you had, well, thought a lot of her. I was just a kid then, but kids know more than you think."

"You're still a kid. You're twenty years old."

"I grew up when I dropped out of Harvard. All it took was six months in Viet. Want to see my gray hairs?"

He laughed again, but when Jed didn't join him he sobered.

"I still don't get the ripoff. You mean they cheated you on the trade, your company for their stock?"

"On the contrary, they gave me more than my holdings were worth. Five times more. That's the way these deals are set up. The buyer passes the accelerated figure along to the public in the form of a new stock offering, ten, twelve million to, say—fifty? The figure depends on the state of the market. But I wasn't kidding myself. I had three men on the board, myself and two others of my own choosing. Vishniak had four. His group could fire me any time they wanted to. But I thought they couldn't do without my know-how. I didn't figure on the cost accountants, the corporate boys in the silk suits with the very sharp pencils, whittling my bidding estimates down to where if anything went wrong, I was in deep trouble."

"So things went wrong."

"On construction jobs, things always go wrong. You have to have margin. Only a conglomerate doesn't think that way. They took in an admiral."

"I've seen his picture."

"I'll bet you have. Hair spray-painted Destroyer Gray, a profile like the frigate *Constitution.* With a face like that you *have* to be Chairman of the Joint Chiefs—"

"He was, wasn't he?"

"Sure. Before Viet. Well, Admiral Stranahan and the computers told Vishniak that Basco and Western could spend twenty-five million dollars building a drydock for constructing a nuclear carrier and still underbid a shipyard that already had a drydock. B and W is building that carrier now. We'll lose about ten million on it. So subtracting this and that the first quarter this year wasn't good and the third was terrible. Vishniak needed someone to blame. Odds were that he'd shift the attention from himself."

"For that I don't need a computer."

"You'd be right. The individual at fault, it turned out, was Basco. The president. With voting control of a board of directors you can always come up with a new president. Or so Vishniak thinks. I'm fixing to give him a run for it." Jed's face was grave and heavy. For the first time in Bob's memory, his father looked older than his years. "What's at stake," Jed said slowly, "isn't the money. I have to get that company back. Otherwise, I've got nothing to do. Do you know, the prospect frightens me? I've never had an idle day in my life. I've known discarded old sons of bitches like me who jumped out of windows or turned on the gas."

"Come off it, Dad," Bob said, visibly annoyed. "I don't buy that bullshit. Are you trying to imply you'd go that route? I know you better."

"I never said I would. I've just seen men who did."

"They copped out then."

"They copped out. Mike McGettigan, your grandfather."

"But he *drowned!* You don't mean . . ."

"Yes, I mean. After we split up our construction firm Mike bought a data-processing company, paid like some forty million dollars for it. What he knew about data processing you could put in your eye and one day . . . But what the hell. I won't take it. I don't have to. I'm too rich and I'm too smart. My record as president has been . . . well, aside from the phony losses the accountants have manufactured, it's been good. Right now we're running the kind of poll that tells the story—a proxy contest. I thought you and I should . . ."

Jed's voice trailed off. He put his hands over his face in a tired, uncharacteristic gesture. Bob had never seen his father make such a motion.

"What would you say," Bob remarked at length, "if I told you losing B and W wouldn't be all that bad? In fact," he said, leaning forward with youthful intensity, "it could be the biggest break you ever had!"

"Tell me what kind of drugs you're on. I'd like to try some."

"No, I mean it. You say drugs. I don't hold any brief for the drug culture. That's just another kind of copout. It's as stupid as the corporate game. There's change coming, Dad. It's here already."

"What, son, the Beatnik Revolution?" Jed inquired with dour irony.

"Beatniks, hippies, beards looking for a fix, I don't go with any of them. Or with the other cats either, the hard-core revolutionists."

"Running AWOLs and misfits to Mexico and Canada isn't revolutionist?"

"Not like I'm doing it. I want these cats to have some options." Bob Basco carefully rolled a joint of marijuana and lit up. "You know," he said, "when I was messing through those five-thousand-dollars-a-year prep schools you sent me to, the big book was *Catcher in the Rye.* Well, Holden, the dude in the book, his idea was there were a lot of little kids playing some game in this big field of rye. At the edge of the field was a huge cliff, and what Holden wanted to do more than anything was to stand there and catch them. To keep them from going over: The Catcher in the Rye. Only he couldn't do it. That's the difference between him and me. *I can do it.* And I'm doing it!"

"With the money you got out of that capitalistic monster, B and W."

Jed regretted the remark as soon as he'd made it. Bob's quiet face assimilated the rebuff humbly, as if he had been expecting it.

"Yes, Dad, with the bread you gave me. The dividends, anyway. If you hadn't fixed it so I couldn't touch the principal, I'd be using that too. I'm not the only one who has put in money. Others are out raising more every day. The operation costs—I won't snow you on that. But it works. We have an underground network in every major city and some really classified out-of-the-way stations. And a conveyor chain going, certain truck routes with drivers who will help—certain pilots who make pickups at small airports. We're getting so that with one phone call in any area, a man can be on his way to Canada, Mexico, maybe even France or Sweden."

"And en route, they can tell each other what a hustle they suffered in the 'Pig Nation.' Isn't that what they call this land of the free?"

"That—and some other things. You can expect some phrases like that—yes, pigs—when prowl cars stop kids hitchhiking and tie them up and shave their heads—or beat the brains out of peaceful marchers like in Chicago. There are angry people, Dad."

"I saw that kind of anger on a construction job three weeks ago. I saw them outside my headquarters. Some of them were holding up little red books and yelling, 'Mao! Mao! Mao Tse-tung' or 'Che! Che! Che!' We left them alone, but the ones that had Vietcong flags or carried shit mixed with red pepper in plastic bags, them we threw in the pokey."

"I know about that, Dad."

"And those bums aren't revolutionists?"

"A revolutionist has his own kind of morality."

"If we're quoting Che."

"You were the one mentioned him, not me."

"I'm sorry. I withdraw the comment."

"No need to. But think about this: Do you suppose simultaneous mass meetings at more than twenty campuses, protesting the Chicago scene, were organized by Red agitators? That would take weeks of rehearsing, even in Russia. Anyway, I've told you I'm not revolutionary. I'm against that anger, too. I've taken out citizenship in a different nation, that's all. Ultimately our nation is going to supplant the old."

"Son, what you're talking about isn't two nations. It's two generations. You're yelling at me across the well-known gap and I can't quite hear you."

"I haven't raised my voice above a whisper, Dad. And the gap between you and me is about as wide as a gnat's ass. But call it what you like, your world has rejected you. Maybe you can jam your way back in and recover your company. If that's your wish, I'll do what I can to help you—though I don't approve. But if you lose—or by my terms get a lucky break—you can come with us. You'd be welcome. I've got a place, just a cabin, in southern Utah. Where we put the AWOLs or the stockade escapees that just don't take any chances at all. The real losers. Now don't say it, don't say it." Bob held up his hand. "I'm not expecting you to babysit these cats. I'm aware you don't hold a high opinion of them. That's your privilege, though if you look back you weren't that gung-ho a soldier yourself. You told me one time you spent World War Two shooting craps."

"I did well with the rolling bones. Yes, I came out satisfactorily in that respect. But southern *Utah*, son?"

"That's where it's at. Dad! You said George the trout. Well, they got Georges up there that would make ours look like a minnow. You could fish, you could hunt, you could get things lined up again."

Jed was suddenly deeply touched. He didn't speak for a while. Then he said slowly, "You put out a slick travel folder, son. I appreciate your thought for me."

The red-haired chick who had first welcomed Bob stuck her head into the office; seeing the two men, she moved back hastily. Jed winked at Bob.

"I'll keep that cabin in mind, son. Might be a nice place for a vacation when the shooting is all over. Meanwhile you had better get your ass in there and dance with that gal. I've got to catch a plane tonight, so I'll be going. Thanks for your hospitality. And for signing what you signed."

Driving his rented car to the airport, he thought of what Bob had said about generations. Rejected! A man could be rejected by a woman or an organization, but by a generation? It was a crazy sort of notion. To be lost between generations was another matter. And yet Bob, speaking of his "nation," had said, "You would be welcome."

That statement, strange as it was, had warmed him. If—well, if it were true—if he should lose his fight (not that he could really admit the possibility of losing it) he would need a shelter—even such a shelter as the young and the damned could provide. For damned they surely were in spite of their cocksureness, their defiance, the heat of life in them.

But that hope, the beautiful and hungry lusts of flesh

and spirit, in the end wasn't that all that mattered? Was that what had happened to him? Was that why he found himself in the trouble he was in now? . . . His head jerked up. He had been dozing off, swerving into the right lane; savage freeway horns were blowing at him and a driver's angry face contorted behind shatterproof glass. He corrected his course. Not far to go now to the airport—to the Learjet, the big stretch-out seat and sleep.

No, no, by God! Old he might be, but the heat, the drive were still there, strong in him. He could feel them, and this thrust was what kept him going. That was what the fight to get B & W back was all about. The company didn't matter or the presidential desk or even the money at stake: the real issue—what Felix Rupke with his new, pompous honors couldn't understand, what even Bob had failed to see—was proving that he, Jed, was not some beat-up has-been that you could send to the junk pile—a human being who had run out his string.

He tapped the pocket of his coat where he had put the proxy.

CHAPTER SEVEN

THE Jedson C. Bascos' divorce had not been anticipated, but it had not seriously shocked their friends either. In the circles in which they moved divorces, even Catholic divorces, were common enough. If they had been informed, however, that the cause of the rupture had been an affair on the part of Jed, they might have been surprised. Everyone knew that Dorothy was the flirtatious one. Yet the fact remained that Jed had provided what are generally defined as "the grounds"—though the affair had been broken off before his marriage and resumed only sporadically afterward.

Jed had first met Georgiana Gibbs in 1945, shortly after being discharged from the Army. He had been drafted two years earlier. When he had sweated through a furnace-hot basic at Camp Roberts he applied for OCS and was accepted, trained and commissioned as a second lieutenant. He had spent most of his Army career building shore installations on captured Pacific islands. He had never seen any fighting and regularly supplemented his Army pay with poker winnings, his take sometimes running as high as three or four thousand a month. He had saved more than fifteen thousand dollars when a captain from Connecticut, who had been a professional gambler operating on Atlantic steamers, cleaned him out. The loss had meant as little to Jed as his winnings; he was probably the richest second lieutenant in the 22nd Engineers, 167th Division. He and Mike McGettigan had been partners for three years before Pearl Harbor, and Jed's share of the partnership was worth, at a conservative estimate, half a million dollars.

Jed was already back working with Mike again when Harry Truman, the former haberdasher, announced the Japanese surrender. Jed put on his uniform and went downtown to see what was happening. He felt stupid in the uniform, but to celebrate the end of a war it might be appropriate to show you had participated. Or so he thought. In the Peacock bar at the Mark Hopkins he ran into his commanding officer from Okinawa, Colonel Grey Lusty, a native San Franciscan, who knew everybody in the place and was very active buying drinks and making introductions. Later the group around Lusty went into the Peacock Court, where the colonel had set up a table for twelve people; other friends who had served with him kept coming in and the waiters added a second table and put candles on it.

There had been an electric failure and everyone in the

big, overcrowded room was eating and drinking by candlelight. One of the women, much excited by the victory of the U.S. forces over Hirohito and his dirty yellow bastards, danced with her arms around Jed's neck and rubbed against him enthusiastically with her lower parts. Colonel Lusty had a suite on the upper floors and Jed's partner wanted to go there, but Jed did not accede to the suggestion mainly because he had become interested in another lady at the table.

He could not have said why the term "lady" occurred to him in connection with Georgiana Gibbs, but it did. Not that she gave herself airs. She did not. She was very charming and easy with everyone, turning her head to talk to the man on her left or to the man on her right. She did not dance much but she seemed to be enjoying herself. Jed was not sure which man she had come with—it did not seem to matter. She had rather small, deep-set eyes, in a wonderfully modeled face. Her hair was slicked back with a barrette, not in the current fashion, setting off the beautiful shape of her small, poised head. Her voice made no demands for attention, but he found himself straining to hear it, as if what she had to say was of great moment, and he noticed other people doing the same. She wore a wedding ring and several other pieces of good jewelry. She hardly looked at him, but when she did her glance was open, interested, but uncommitted. He danced with her once. He had never, in the most passionate embraces, felt anything more delicious than the soft detachment of her body.

It was an unusual experience. He could neither reject it nor contain it. Sitting in the room, participating in the celebration, which was historical and also phony, with the candlelight and all, Jed wondered if he had manufactured some concept of this woman which would later disappear. After their dance, he sat beside her at the table, still holding her hand. She asked him about his work and he told her with no brag how he had come out to San Francisco by bus looking for a job and living in a fleabag hotel, and how one day a truck had been parked at the curb with a sign on it, WORKERS WANTED, and how anyone strong enough to climb over the tailgate of the truck had been driven up into the mountains to build a road.

"And you *built* it?" Mrs. Gibbs had said, as if this had been an extraordinary feat. She made Jed realize for the first time what a great thing it had been.

"Mrs. Gibbs," he said, "I had a degree from MIT in engineering. Nearly all the men on that truck had been in some construction trade and several others were university graduates. That was the Depression, you understand —there were good men everywhere with no place to go. There was ability on that truck, Mrs. Gibbs. We could have built the Pyramids, we could have built St. Peter's in Rome, Mrs. Gibbs, with the fellows on that truck."

"And that was your first job?" she'd asked, and he had said, "The first I was in charge of."

He looked past her in the candlelight as if he could see again the stuff they had found piled on the headquarters site, the tools and bedding; there had been a half-built cookshed but no bunkhouse—they'd slept in the truck or under it the first ten days—and behind the cookshed the rolling stock, a secondhand earth-mover and a D6 with a blade on it.

"It had been surveyed. That was about all."

And he remembered how the second week old Mike McGettigan (he hadn't been old then, of course, just the kind of redneck who had been born cantankerous and unpredictable) had started down the mountain to fetch the payroll, yelling casually to Jed in his bullhorn voice, "Take over."

The first command, the one that counted. They'd chewed six blades off that D6, making do for a grader, and at Christmas, in a blizzard, they were still cutting embankments with it, slicing at ground frozen almost rock hard for the first foot or two.

"There was nothing to it, Mrs. Gibbs, once we were started." She had laughed and put her ringed hand on his, holding it as if he were falling to the ground from a twenty-story window, and she had reached out, as a social courtesy, and caught him. "My name is Georgiana," she said, and then took her hand away.

Mrs. Howard Eldridge Gibbs, Colonel Lusty told him later, as the two men walked down California Street to Grant to have breakfast in an all-night Chinese bakery. Howard Gibbs, Georgiana's husband, was an architect. Lusty did not know if they were still living together, but she might be in the telephone book.

Georgiana Gibbs, Mrs. Howard Gibbs, was in the telephone book and she was living with her husband. Jed ascertained both facts later that day. He and Mike McGettigan had contracted to build a series of highway facilities in northern California, but Mike had suggested giving the crew the day off. They would all be hung over from the VJ fiestas anyway. Jed invited her to see *The*

Bad Man with Leo Carillo, in person, at the Geary Theatre and she had declined, for the reason stated. She was living with her husband, although at the moment he was in Los Angeles. Her beautiful voice intimated that although victory celebrations might be an exception, she did not go out with other men. She did not say she would not go out with *him,* Jed; she just said "other men," if that was any palliation, but she did invite him to stop by for a drink, and he accepted.

The house was a small, handsomely renovated Victorian in Pacific Heights. As he stood outside the door he heard a piano inside and someone singing. The singing continued for at least a minute after he had rung the doorbell. Then a girl about six years old came to the door. Her face was a small replica of Georgiana's in every respect except for its sullen expression. She said nothing by way of greeting and left the door open until Jed had closed it for himself.

"Was that your mother singing?" Jed inquired, uncomfortable under her baleful young stare.

"No," the child said. "That was me. Mother can't sing a note." She turned away, adding, "You can sit anywhere you like. She can't read music either."

"Can you?" Jed inquired, half inclined to say something agreeable.

"No," said the child, "but I'm learning."

Jed revised his estimate of her age. She looked like a child of six, but she did not talk like one. She did not talk like a child at all. Her name, he learned later, was Darlene.

Georgiana Gibbs let him stay half an hour. She made him a bourbon and soda and lit a fire in the miniature

Victorian fireplace because the cold August fog had rolled in from the Golden Gate. The firescreen was a brass peacock with a huge, intricately crafted tail. They talked about the people at the victory party, and Georgiana chided him about what she called his flirtation with the civilian's wife who had danced with her arms around his neck. Once, when she went to put a log on the fire, she brushed him with her body, but aside from that she could not have been more remote. He made up his mind, leaving, that he'd had all he wanted of class, but each time he could get to San Francisco in the next few weeks he called her. On one of these occasions he met Howard Gibbs, a bony man with English clothes and an Eastern way of talking. The following day Georgiana met him in Solari's in Maiden Lane and when they walked out she took his arm.

"I want to see you alone," he said.

"I know," she said. "I've thought about you, too."

"Good."

"I don't know if it's good at all. It's very complicated."

"Why is it so complicated?"

"Because I think a cheating wife is the lowest creature that walks, and I won't be one."

"I agree."

"Oh, I'm glad. You've helped me make up my mind about something I've had to do for a long time. After I have, I will be with you, but not before. Will you agree to that?"

"Of course."

"It's asking a great deal. I don't want you to call me. I'll let you know."

"All right."

"That's not a commitment. I don't want a commitment. I don't want promises, from either of us."

"We're not in a position to make promises."

"Oh, you do understand."

"I'm trying."

"That's what I want you to do."

They walked up the alley in the cold summer night and on the corner of Stockton Street he found her a taxi.

"Can I come as far as your house with you?"

"No. He's there."

"But you'll let me know."

"I said no promises, not even that."

"You're making this just as hard as you can."

"I know. But if it isn't going to be something important, then I don't want it."

"Goodbye, then."

"Goodbye."

Jed had his hand on the door of the cab. She moved it away, pushed past him and gave the driver her address.

Georgiana and Howard Gibbs separated two weeks later, and a few days following the separation Georgiana's love affair with Jed Basco began. It lasted, that phase of it, for two years and four months or, to be exact, until four weeks before Jed's marriage to Dorothy McGettigan.

Jed did not give up Georgiana for Dorothy. In a sense, he never gave up Georgiana. No matter where they went or what they were doing, each segment of life they lived together was unique, unexpected, more exciting than any experience could have been if they had not been together.

For Jed, part of this excitement came from a compatibility of judgments and reactions, but part came from a search. He was striving now to possess not only Georgiana's mind but also all that portion of her life that had been frozen behind her elegant marriage to Howard Gibbs, the dutiful, successful and destroyed Howard Gibbs, who now came to the Victorian house only for the purpose of seeing his daughter.

Georgiana was twelve years older than Jed. This fact never seemed important to either of them. It had little physical manifestation. Georgiana had the body and appearance of a woman much younger not only than she was but than *he* was; she also had a sexual hunger, a sexual inventiveness beyond anything he had ever known. She contributed an element that had not been part of the covenant as originally drawn and one that was basically new to him—she gave him love. She was not searching for anything in Jed. She was not concerned with his past. Her interest embraced his future. Because of this element Georgiana developed her own type of possessiveness, making impossible the discussion of certain subjects—conspicuously Dorothy McGettigan. Jed had been making love to Dorothy, on and off, since she was seventeen years old. The meetings took place in Mike McGettigan's house when Mike had invited Jed down for weekends. Dorothy had arranged the occasions with a discretion which indicated careful planning, but she also managed, when she judged the time was appropriate, to become pregnant.

"I think," Georgiana said to him one day, "that I shall go back to Chicago to live. You can still come and see me sometimes there. Will that be all right?"

"For Christ sake, Georgiana," Jed said.

"I thought we were going to have no commitments."

"Moving to Chicago, that's not a commitment?"

"I would say it was a change. Like your marrying the red-haired McGettigan girl. Now do you want to ask me, what McGettigan girl?"

"No," Jed said.

"And if you love me, don't ask how I knew. Maybe it works out best for both of us. Anyway for you. Business has to come first, especially when a big Irishman is holding a shotgun on you with both barrels loaded."

"You're the one that's holding the shotgun. I have no intention of marrying Dorothy McGettigan, now or ever. Unless you make me."

"And how could I do that, pray tell?"

"By leaving me."

"The time has been coming for us just as it did for Howard and me. Before I didn't know how I could stand it. Now I can."

"I wouldn't marry Dorothy if she was the last woman alive. Whether you go to Chicago or not."

"Don't say things you'll have to take back later. Dorothy's a healthy young person. She wants a husband and she set about getting one in the classic way."

"The hell she did. I—well, yes, I laid her. That was before you and I were . . . well before . . ."

"Before *and* after. So far we've been honest. Don't let's stop now."

"Then here's the truth—I don't need the McGettigans. Dorothy *or* Mike. I need you."

"Oh, God Almighty, Jed, what difference does it make?

The McGettigan girl isn't the issue. The issue is that I'm too old for you."

"This happened just one time with Dorothy, just one time since I knew you. I can even spot the date."

"So can the doctor."

"All right, Georgiana. Whether you like it or not you're going to hear it the way it was. You don't have to tell me how you knew. Your ex-husband works for one of the contracting firms we do business with."

"I know all about the housing project."

"So Mike, the stupid son of a bitch, was shooting his big face off there. Dorothy told *him* before she told *me*. We were engaged. Or weren't we? Mike was delighted, of course. One big happy family, big-mouthing it all over. It was just that one time eight weeks ago. Mike and I had contracts to check, and I spent the night. She goes skinny-dipping in the morning early, in their pool, and I sleep in the poolhouse bedroom. So she . . ."

Georgiana Gibbs slapped him in the face.

Jed's arm twitched with the urge to strike her in return. A red blotch appeared on his cheek.

"What was that for?"

"For being a prick. When I wanted to remember you the way you are, the way I love you for being. I know you, Jed—the good in you and the bad."

"The good was that I didn't hit you back."

"Gallantly said. We had something, something real, but you would have grown away from me. You can marry Dorothy or not. Whatever you like, but I think you will because business comes first. With you it always will. For that I pity you."

She left two days later. Jed drove Georgiana and her daughter to the Oakland Mole and put them on the Overland Limited. As the train pulled out, Darlene Gibbs looked out the drawing-room window and made a face at him. Georgiana was nowhere to be seen.

The house on Jackson Street was sold within a month. The new tenants added window boxes and new paint. Jed, driving by, liked it less now. He wrote several times to Georgiana. Twice his letters were returned unopened. Then, unexpectedly, she wrote back. Her letter was a postscript to goodbye, neither embittered nor casual, but filled with a kind of contempt. Georgiana said that she had renewed her acquaintanceship with many of her old Chicago friends. One of them, a banker, was considering her for an administrative post.

"Of course I shall have to take a training course first. Can you imagine me, going to school again?"

Jed, in his answer, enclosed a check for five thousand dollars, which Georgiana never cashed. Perhaps she was getting money from the banker. He wondered whether she had mentioned the banker just to make him jealous. If so, she had succeeded. She had made her choice and by doing so had propelled him into his. This arrangement had best be left as it was, if the sorceries of Father O'Connor were to hold up. Georgiana wrote again for a last time—a brief note, congratulating him on his marriage, and Dorothy opened the letter.

"Who is this Georgiana Gibbs?"

"A woman I used to know."

"A woman you used to screw, you mean. I've heard about her."

"If you heard that, it wasn't true. I never lived with her. I used to take her out sometimes."

"Take her out? I'll bet. She divorced her husband for you. I've heard that too. Well, if she's going to write any more letters, tell her to send them to the office."

"I don't think I'll be hearing from her."

"I hope not." Dorothy looked at the letter, the fine stationery, the dark blue, beautifully formed calligraphy which made Jed think of Georgiana's voice. "I wish I could write like that," she said. "Whether you screwed her or not, her handwriting is elegant. Was she, I mean is she, an elegant person?"

"I suppose you could call her that."

"I can't imagine you with an elegant woman."

"Neither can I," Jed said.

"So you wound up with me."

"That's right."

Dorothy laughed.

"Nothing can make me elegant. Nobody. They tried. The nuns at Santa Catalina. Mother too and her Menlo Country Club. Do I make you happy?"

"Yes, you do."

"All right. But I don't like being second best."

"You're not. You never were."

"Oh, yes I was. And someday I just might get even."

"Not right off, I hope."

"Oh, not right off. Maybe never. But if you screw around, I will. I promise you that."

"Why don't we just drop the subject?"

"All right. Consider it dropped."

"Then come over here."

She came round the breakfast table and sat in his lap. "Oh, God," she said, "why are we such idiots?"

Jed heard nothing concerning Georgiana for nearly four years. Then the information came from a third person, Colonel Lusty. The colonel had retired with the rank of brigadier general and was working for the Rand Corporation. He met Jed in the Rotunda of the Mayflower and they breakfasted together. On his way back to California Jed stopped off in Chicago and went to the address at Eighth and Yakima where Lusty said Georgiana was living: a two-flat house in a desegregated neighborhood.

The deal with the banker had apparently not worked out.

Jed moved her and Darlene to a slightly more expensive apartment near the Ambassador East. He had still by no means given up his resolve to be a good husband, though not necessarily a faithful one.

Georgiana might or might not, for her part, have retained her convictions about wifely fidelity, but if she did, at least her opinion did not hold for husbands. For several years they were together as much as was practical, never in San Francisco and less and less frequently in Chicago, as Jed's operation took him increasingly elsewhere, but in Los Angeles, New York, Miami, as well as the little towns, resembling military posts, near Jed's construction sites where Georgiana's presence, no matter how conspicuous, would not make itself known outside the town borders. What in the end revealed the resumption of the relationship was not the meetings but the checks which, long before the massive gift of Basco Precision stock, Jed sent Georgiana each month. Dorothy was not Mike McGettigan's daughter for nothing. She discovered the payments but did not immediately face Jed with her knowledge. She made no accusations. The checks became what she later called, in one of their quarrels, "My tickets to good times"—a license for gratifying her opportunities for pleasure outside marriage.

CHAPTER EIGHT

FELIX Rupke's hands were sweating and an iron bug kicked whirligigs in his kidneys. He kept leaving his comfortable chair to go to the john. It had all seemed so splendid, so easy, and now . . . God, if they couldn't come up with a simple majority, his future was down the drain.

"Don't you want some lunch, dear?"

His wife Isabelle had stayed home from her own job to help him through this crisis—but her presence had merely become an added annoyance.

"Just coffee," he snapped, fixing his eyes once more on the television set.

In the great brown chamber, the gentleman from Louisiana pushed back his forelock in a well-known gesture.

He had been speaking now for two hours in his deep, baying voice, his glance sweeping mildly over the floor where his colleagues paid him scant attention. Some sat at the little school-like desks, writing or reading or turned in their seats to chat; others moved up and down the aisles, took messages from pages, came and went through the doors at the back. None of this activity was intended, or taken, to be offensive to the speaker. In nearly every respect the proceedings conformed to the normal Senate routine with two salient exceptions. First, a full quorum was on hand; second, the television networks—represented here only on occasions of significant public interest—were covering the scene.

The Senator from Oklahoma, Curtis Eisendradt (R), a clerkly, chubby man, was directing a question to the Vice President.

EISENDRADT: Mr. President, will the Senator yield briefly for a question?

PORTERFIELD: I yield.

EISENDRADT: The Senator refers to the nominee as a distinguished jurist. Did I hear that correctly?

PORTERFIELD: The Senator is correct.

EISENDRADT: Does the expression "jurist" mean that the nominee has had experience in all phases of the law?

PORTERFIELD: Not in all phases. The law is a large field. I know of nobody, including my worthy colleague, who has had experience in *all* its phases.

EISENDRADT: I mean has the nominee ever had experience on the bench? He has been nominated as Justice of the Supreme Court. Has he ever been a judge at any time before?

PORTERFIELD: No.

EISENDRADT: I thank the Senator.

Eisendradt sat down.

"Mr. President!"

A very old Senator with a strong square body and an impish face addressed the rostrum. Although his voice was frail with age, he spoke up firmly. He was Kenneth Goodpastor, senior Senator from Ohio, the Senate's minority whip.

GOODPASTOR: Mr. President, I was distracted. I am not sure that I am following the debate here. What issue did my colleague say was before the Senate?

PORTERFIELD: The nomination of Felix Rupke to the Supreme Court of the United States.

GOODPASTOR: No, sir. I hope, of course, that we can *get* it before the Senate.

PORTERFIELD: We are now discussing it.

GOODPASTOR: No, we are not. We are discussing the question of whether we will be permitted to discuss it.

(*Laughter*)

The telephone with the red tab rang and Felix picked it up. Previously the only direct White House line had been the one in his office, but at the Man's orders one had been installed at the Georgetown house.

"You been listening to that caterwauling?"

"Yes, Mr. President, I have been following the proceedings closely."

"Don't get your guts in an uproar."

"I'm not disturbed at all, Mr. President."

"Quit horseshitting. What do you think?"

"I think if we don't get an aye vote by this afternoon, we're in for trouble."

A snake-oil chuckle oozed through the wire.

"Just what I told Corky McGrath. I told him to get Goodpastor out in the cloakroom and ride his butt ragged. Been after me all week to sign his bill for a Space Medicine Facility in Cleveland. We need that Space Medicine Facility like I need an extra asshole, so if he don't stop crapping around I'll have Corky introduce a new bill, adding onto the Facility at Colorado Springs. That'll bring action. Fast. You wait and see."

"I hope so, Mr. President."

"Hold the left one. I'll talk to you later."

The affirmative vote did not come quite that easily. The tactic relating to the Space Medicine Facility had to be buttressed with another ploy, aimed at Eisendradt, reducing oil-depletion allowances on certain ancient Cherokee leases. But at last it came—Felix's confirmation as the new Supreme Court Justice.

Felix could relax. He had his seat, the Holmes chair, perhaps not the highest paying place in the world but one that would last him to the end of his days, garlanded with honors and beribboned with conspicuity. A lifetime job—or at least, in the words of one authority, "the term is during good behavior, so that it is for life unless a judge shall resign or by impeachment be expelled from office as provided in Section 4, Article 11, of the Constitution."

It seemed strange to Felix that removal procedure should even be mentioned. Only one Justice in history had ever been impeached, some poor rascal back in the early nineteenth century.

Felix slipped so effortlessly into his new routine that one would soon have thought he had known no other. Five days a week a Justice Department limousine waited at his house, the chauffeur decorously opening the door, then driving him downtown where people, noting the official plates, sometimes peered for a glimpse of the wispy figure lounging inside, cigar in mouth, the morning paper scattered around him on the rich upholstery. During the midday recess he lunched, generally in his chambers, on food brought in from the Madison Restaurant, long his favorite; after the session he would spend the evening researching legal points brought up in the calendar cases or dictating notes for the opinion which he later wrote in a tight little script for his secretary to type.

Sundays he liked to play the recorder. He sat when possible in the garden of his Georgetown house or, if the weather was unsuitable, then in his study, a small, neat cubicle with bookshelves built to the ceiling and a large stereo against the wall. He had little manual dexterity. He could not fix anything or make anything. If a drawer stuck or a hinge jammed or a switch needed rewiring he was helpless, yet with the mouthpiece of the old-fashioned instrument held firmly to his lips, his stubby fingers twinkled along the stops like ballerinas performing an intricate drill.

He had picked up the recorder late in life, long after success had come to him and at an age when many men neglect skills which they have long possessed, let alone perfect new ones. Someone had mentioned that the recorder was easy to play and immediately, without knowing why he was thus impelled, he had bought one; within a year he could play and not badly.

His hour or two with music meant much to him, and he permitted no one to interrupt it. The delicate cascades and trills and the proper marching of the notes in the formations conceived in older times by musicians long dead made the world seem orderly, the sort of world that could be regulated by intelligence, negotiation and judicial decision.

Today he was playing in his garden. It was a pleasant morning, warm for a Washington fall. From the yards of the houses nearby, most of them more imposing than his own modest townhouse (but none with a nicer garden!), came the usual Sunday-morning sounds: the buzz of an electric hedge clipper, the plopping noise of racquets against shuttlecocks, the trickle of a hose. Wearing a sport shirt and chinos, Felix sat on a stone bench, Bach's "Fugue in C Minor" in front of him. The sheets rested on an eighteenth-century music stand that had been Isabelle's gift to him on his fifty-ninth birthday. The fugue was difficult, a little beyond his ability as yet; he was not getting it quite right but he was enjoying himself.

"Call for you, dear."

Isabelle's head appeared at an upstairs window. Her hair was in curlers.

"I'm busy. Who is it?"

"Long distance."

What was there about long distance that made you put aside whatever you were doing?

"Mr. Rupke? We are ready with Denver."

"I wasn't calling Denver."

"Denver is calling you. Just a minute."

"I'm on," said Coleman Thorpe. "That you, Felix? Where's Steve?"

"In Texas, last I heard," said Rupke, none too affably.

"No, I'm here. I'm in Chicago," said Vishniak's voice. "Hello, Felix. This is a conference call. Is Herman on?"

"I'm on, Steve," said Pulaski. "Go ahead."

"We need Dan Stranahan," said Thorpe. "Admiral Stranahan is supposed to be on, operator."

"I had Admiral Stranahan for you, sir, but he seems to have . . . just a minute." Then Stranahan's voice came on saying sleepily, "Hello, hello." He sounded as if he'd had a bad night.

"Where are you?" said Vishniak cheerfully.

"I'm at the Sheraton Carlton," said Stranahan. "Right here in Washington. Fact is, I tried to get you last night, to tell you this call was coming through, but you were out, Felix. Don't you have an answering service?"

"Can't afford one," Felix said. "I'm just a government employee, you know."

"How are things down on the ranch, Herman?" asked Vishniak.

"It's raining like hell here."

"It's great here," said Thorpe.

"Oh, it's always great in Denver, the Mile-High City," said Stranahan sarcastically.

"Gentlemen," said Steve Vishniak, "we didn't group up for a weather report. Felix, we've got a little crisis going. We need some action."

"Then you've come to the wrong party," Felix said. "I resigned from the board of B and W, remember?"

"We remember," said Thorpe. "This is strictly off the record. By the way, congratulations. I sent you a wire. Did you get it?"

"I got it," said Felix. "I appreciate your kindness. But as I pointed out—"

"This is just a word between friends, Felix," said Vishniak. "You are the only man who might have the information we need."

"All right, but I won't be involved in any company problems. Now if that's clear, what's the crisis?"

Pulaski and Thorpe started to speak at the same time. Vishniak's raspy tones bulled through both voices.

"Here's how it stacks up, Felix. We've just heard through confidential sources that Allied Investors has bought three hundred thousand shares of B and W. Market price not known but well below the current quote, we can be sure of that. This was a private transaction—our stock transfer agent has no record of it. Now where did Keith Koffend of Allied find that many shares?"

"How would I know?" snapped Felix.

"All right, Felix," said Steve Vishniak smoothly. "Don't get your dander up. When Western acquired Basco Precision, you represented Basco. You were paid one hundred thousand shares in lieu of a cash fee. You wanted it that way, and we went along. You recall that?"

"I do. And that was strictly legitimate."

"Naturally," Vishniak said. "I just want to know if you have sold any of those shares recently?"

"I've sold all of it, Steve," said Felix Rupke. "I have also sold my Standard Oil of California, my IBM, my General Motors, and various other stocks. In view of my appointment, I could not afford any possible future conflict of interest. E. F. Hutton handled the sales for me. The stock was not dumped. There's been quite an improvement in B and W. You haven't been hurting."

"Improvement is right," said Pulaski, "like seven and three-eighths in four days."

"You mentioned a private transaction," Felix said. "I made no such transaction."

"Good God, Felix," said Thorpe, "no one's accusing you of anything."

"We have a damn good notion where Allied Investors got that block," said Thorpe.

"Have we?" said Pulaski. "I've been out here in the boonies. I didn't know that."

"Coleman is right, Herman," said Vishniak. "My hunch is that stock came from Jed Basco. And that it's unregistered—the Class B. Sure, he has registered shares too, but he wouldn't sell those. He wants to vote them. You know the poor hardhat bastard thinks he can get control. He's been soliciting proxies and buying shares, trading in and out but accumulating steadily, the way I hear it."

"Get to the point, Steve," said Thorpe.

"The point," said Vishniak patiently, "is that we think he's been dumping the unregistered stock. The letter stock. We think he sold it to Koffend."

"That's impossible."

"Why is it impossible?" asked Stranahan.

"For one thing, it's illegal."

"You're a lawyer, Felix," said Pulaski evenly. "Haven't you ever heard of anybody doing something illegal?"

"I am not a lawyer now, Herman," said Felix. "I am a judge—a Justice of the Supreme Court. I am not in day-to-day contact with felons. Even if I were, I doubt Jed Basco would be among them. He's too smart."

"Is he?" said Thorpe.

"Maybe he's just smart enough to try it," said Stranahan dryly.

"I would look elsewhere, gentlemen," said Felix.

"There is no elsewhere, Felix," said Pulaski.

Felix said, "Others have unregistered stock. Jed isn't the only one."

"Meaning the seller of this block could have been one of us? Oh, come on, Felix, you know better than that." Thorpe's laugh came over the wire like static.

"Felix," said Vishniak, "what you say is possible but not reasonable. We gave Jed his walking papers, as you know. I'm sure he ran straight to you with his tale of woe."

"He did," said Felix. "I told him to cool it."

"It's clear that he didn't take your advice. A proxy fight costs money, and this must be his way of laying his hands on some. There's another angle—on a smaller scale than the mutual-fund purchase but just as significant—and maybe more dangerous. A Mrs. Oscar Tanheimer, 461 Riverdale Avenue, Bronxville, New York, bought a thousand shares. She made the purchase from someone who called her on the telephone. Mrs. Tanheimer trades in the market. It's her hobby and she looks for bargains but she wants to see what she buys and she ordered the shares delivered to her, which they were. She then sent the certificates to the transfer agent to be reissued in her own name and the agent duly notified her that he had stop-transfer instructions on that class of stock. One assumes that the letter restricting sale or transfer had been pulled off the certificates before Mrs. Tanheimer saw them."

"So?" said Felix, still annoyed that the peace of his Sunday should have been interrupted by this complicated brouhaha.

"So," said Herman heavily, "Mrs. Tanheimer lodged a

complaint with the Securities and Exchange Commission. An attorney named Birnbaum of SEC wrote me a letter, enclosing a copy of the complaint. Wanted us to trace the sale—which doesn't sound so good."

"Not if the SEC is in it," Felix said quickly, all his senses now alert.

"Do you know this Birnbaum, Felix?" asked Stranahan. "If you do, I was thinking—"

"This is not the time for that, Admiral," said Felix. "I'm assuming that the purpose of this call is that you want me to talk to Jed?"

Thorpe's voice sounded shaky. "He'll deny the sales, of course—"

"Not if you trace one to him," said Felix. "Koffend is a pro. Mutual funds are bargain hunters just like Mrs. Tanheimer. Only Koffend knew what he was doing. Mrs. Tanheimer didn't, but a thousand-share breach of regulations can kick up as much grief as three hundred thousand. You are right, you have troubles."

"Will you talk to Jed?" It was Vishniak again, and he was pleading.

"I'd rather stay shed of the whole business."

"As a favor, Felix," put in the admiral. "One call. For auld lang syne."

"All right, then, damn it," Felix said wearily. "Find him for me and I'll make one call for auld lang syne and the memory of my fee. But then I am through."

Vishniak sounded relieved. "And if he's sold the unregistered shares you'll get him to rescind the sale before we're all down the tube?"

"I'll see what I can do, gentlemen," said Felix. "And

now," he added brusquely, "if you will all kindly excuse me, I'll hang up."

Through the window Felix could see the music stand, the stone bench with its cupids and cornucopias. On the seat lay his recorder, but Felix's interest in playing was gone. For auld lang syne, indeed! What kind of plea was that from a former Chairman of the Joint Chiefs? And the others, with their telephones cuddled to their ears, asking his intercession. Oh, it was flattering; he had brought them their biggest acquisition, at a price ultimately satisfactory to all. But part of that price, never mentioned (discretion forbade) in the bargaining, but well understood, had been the move of the conglomerate's legal business to the offices of Cabot, Constable, Page and Rupke. During the next months they had come to rely on him, and faced with this potential *cause célèbre* it was natural they should turn to him.

Christ, you didn't fool around with the SEC! Even a Mrs. Tanheimer—he envisaged her as one of those old ladies sitting all day in a brokerage office, a thermos of martinis in her handbag—even she, with the SEC behind her, could rock a multibillion-dollar corporation to its foundations.

Damn all Mrs. Tanheimers. Damn all former Chairmen of the Joint Chiefs and all junkmen's sons who made it big. Piss on auld lang syne. He was not their bellboy now. He was a Justice of the Supreme Court. He should have told them all to leave him alone. What had possessed him to agree to help? One telephone call. It had not sounded like much. Perfectly ethical: a former client possibly in trouble, and the wish on his, Felix's, part to mend it before it got worse. The SEC as well would be indebted if he . . . well, if restitution was made to the complaining party. But—damn it all! A messy business. He should stay miles away from it. That one call, and then . . . But hell, he wouldn't even have gone along with that request if it had not been for . . . some memory, the sudden nerve-squeeze, almost like a cardiac pain (or what he imagined a cardiac pain would be like; thank God he had never had one). He had no ties with the B & W board, but he had one, slight though it was, with his former client. That was the real reason why he had been so damned accommodating.

A connection. That was it. He had to force his mind to bring it clearly before him. In ordinary circumstances . . . but there was no fooling himself; these weren't ordinary circumstances. So little involved, a poorboy's groat; but political outrage had been touched off by less than that.

Oh, it was hard to give it up. It was so properly legitimate. So useful, too, when in the service of your country you had to cut your honorarium down from more than two hundred thousand yearly, which still, what with taxes and all, left you with car payments to make, to like sixty thousand judicial, black-robed Holmes-chair dollars. Nevertheless, with the press sniffing around (as it already might be!) best to be wary, even when all you were doing extracurricularly was to help out a friend.

And with this thought in mind, an expression of composed fortitude on his face, Felix Rupke walked into his study with his queer, hitching step, turned on his dictating equipment and composed a letter:

Mr. Jedson C. Basco
President, Basco Foundation
1000 East End Avenue
New York, New York

Dear Jed:

As you will recall, in December of 1955 I accepted the post of general counsel for the Basco Foundation, offering my time on a yearly fee to assist you in the charitable and public service operations of the Foundation.

Much as I would like to continue with this work, which still seems to be so eminently worthwhile, I feel it best, in view of my appointment, to submit my resignation, effective as of this date.

I trust you will understand my high personal regard for you and my respect for the activities of the Foundation. I wish you all good fortune and I trust that you will soon find some other person properly qualified to carry on in my place.

Sincerely,
Felix Linus Rupke

Felix snapped off the switch. Though it was still, in the spin of his orderly routine, too early for a drink—a good six hours too early—he mixed himself one anyway, and a stiff one at that; he knocked it back, and then sat down to plan what he would say to Jed about the other matter, when and if he got him on the telephone.

CHAPTER NINE

THE condominium elevator opened into a tiny foyer containing a gold bench and an artificial lemon tree. As Jed touched the bell a heavy dog hurtled against the other side of the door, clawing at the painted steel panels. Someone spoke and the dog fell back, still raging. A small man with dirty blond hair hanging below his shoulders stood in the doorway, smiling shyly at Jed. He looked about nineteen. He was pimply, and he had on round steel rims with very thick lenses. He was wearing a Confederate general's uniform with the slogan "Make Love Not War" embroidered over the left breast pocket. The dog crouched behind him, its belly flattened to the asphalt tile, the lust to kill still rumbling in its nail-collared throat.

"Mr. Basco?" said the boy in a high, sweet baby voice. "Please come in, sir. We have been expecting you. By we I mean myself and John, to whom you spoke on the telephone. I'm Ted and this is Roger." A flutter of his fingers indicated the dog. "*Basta,* Roger," he said. "Mr. Basco is a *friend,* silly."

The police dog stopped growling. He jumped up and gamboled around licking Ted's fingers, the nails of which were enameled shocking pink.

"I must caution you," Ted said as they started upstairs. "Do not touch Mrs. Gibbs in Roger's presence. I mean, like no kiss or handshake. Roger has been programmed to protect her. I mean don't even touch her in conversation. In all other ways, of course, Roger is a dear. Aren't you, Roger baby?"

The huge dog yelped happily.

"I get the message," Jed said. "How is Mrs. Gibbs?"

"Marvelous, Mr. Basco," Ted said. "She's better today than I've seen her in a long time. Just the notion you were coming seemed to perk her up. She plans to entertain you. Which would you prefer, tea or a cocktail? She instructed me to ask."

"Tea will be fine," Jed said.

A telephone rang somewhere. Jed could hear a man's voice answering.

"You must not think, dear, that because I am old and frail that I am not a lucky person. I am very, very lucky and all because of Ted and John. They are so good to me and so good to my pets, aren't you, boys?"

Georgiana smiled across the tea table at the general, then at the man who had followed her in—a cheerful type with the eye cuts and knobless knuckles of a former boxer.

He wore a brown sport shirt and stay-press gray pants and sat beside the door leading to the rear of the apartment, evidently in order to hear the telephone; he had gone back twice to take calls, closing the door carefully behind him each time. Now he was rolling a joint, shaking grass out of a Prince Albert can.

"We like pets," he said.

"You haven't drunk your tea, dear," Georgiana said gently.

"I'll get to it," John said, winking at Jed.

"Do you have many of them—pets, I mean?" asked Jed.

He wondered what they had Georgiana on. She was tranqued—liberally so. To say that she was old and frail was an understatement, but the bone structure of her face had beauty like a flower pressed in an album. The dog lay at her feet, never taking its eyes off Jed.

"Oh, my yes," said Georgiana. "We have Roger, of course. And Twinkie, my parrot. You must have a chat with Twinkie before you go. He adores interesting people. Then there are the Cunards, my cats, named after Lady Cunard, who was a friend of mine at one time. She was older, but she was marvelous to me. So many people are marvelous to me."

"Of course we are, darling," said Ted happily. The front doorbell rang. John nodded to Ted, who skittered off to talk on the intercom.

"I'm very glad," Jed said. Jesus Christ, he thought, what have they done to her, what are they using her for?

"You made it all possible, dear. I knew you'd come to see me someday. I've spoken to the boys about it, haven't I, John?"

"You sure have," said John. He took a long hit off his

joint and pointed the end of it at Jed inquiringly. Jed shook his head.

"Mr. Basco is a mighty big man around these parts," John said. Ted came back and whispered to him, showing him a check. After scrutinizing it carefully, John took a gold pen out of his shirt pocket and endorsed it and Ted went out. John folded the check and put it into the pocket with the pen.

"I planned to introduce you to the Cunards," Georgiana said, "but unfortunately I am not allowed to see them now. I have developed an allergy. I become asthmatic in their presence. This is a dreadful hardship, but I manage to communicate with them by means of ESP. All the Cunards have that gift. It is very common among the Thais, or Siamese, as they used to be called—cats and people alike. They live downstairs now. You shall meet them later."

As if the mention of her allergy brought on an attack, she broke into a fit of sneezing. The telephone rang. Passing Jed on his way to answer it, John leaned over and whispered, "Those filthy cats went to the pound two years ago."

It was the first time John and Ted had been out of the room simultaneously. Jed had a feeling the place was audio-monitored, but he had to take a chance.

"Georgie," he said, "do you still own most of your B and W stock? Our records show that you've kept it."

"Of course I've kept it, darling," Georgiana said. "Why would I sell it? The dividends! They have made possible all this." Her gesture took in the richly decorated room, the crouching dog and the wind-riven lake below the windows. "I would no more have sold it than I would have sold any other gift of love." She looked down at her still elegant hands, on which there were neither rings nor bracelets now. "I gave a few shares to Darlene. I've forgotten just how many. But why do you ask?"

"I'm in a contest for control," Jed said. "I should like the right to vote your shares—if you'll give it to me. Would you be kind enough to sign this?"

"I'm sorry," Georgiana said. "Did the boys explain about Roger? If you will just lay it on the tea tray . . . Have you a pen?"

She was signing the proxy as Ted swished back into the room.

"Bad girl!" he said furiously.

"Why am I so bad?" said Georgiana.

"You know you're not supposed to sign things."

He snatched the proxy out of her hand.

"That's rude," said Georgiana firmly. "I will not tolerate rudeness, even from you."

Ted giggled.

"Oh, yes you will. You will when it's necessary."

"Rudeness is never necessary," Georgiana said. Her voice was papery thin but resolute. The tranquilizer must be wearing off, Jed thought.

"Please give that paper to Mr. Basco," she said.

"She signed something," Ted squeaked as John came back into the room. "She signed that paper."

"So what?"

He took a last hit off his joint and dropped the roach into a teacup.

"She's not supposed to sign anything. You said."

"*Sometimes* she's not supposed to sign anything. Right now she can sign any goddam thing she likes."

Ted giggled. He put his little hand with the enameled nails inside the noble uniform and scratched himself.

"She wants me to give it to him."

He held up the proxy.

"Then give it to him."

Ted walked around the tea table and handed the proxy to Jed.

"Sometimes you get me all mixed up, you big stupid jock."

"You see," said Georgiana with satisfaction. "Rudeness is not necessary. Ted becomes carried away. In my house I will . . . I will not tolerate . . ."

Her small, almost totally white head on its tiny cornstalk neck, the neck carefully wrapped in a scarf pinned at the side with a diamond bar pin, nodded forward, then back against the chair and she was asleep.

"She can't take it," Ted said happily.

John kneaded his bashed-in knuckles.

"Got gism, though," he said, giving credit where it was due.

Jed looked down at him with disgust. "Well, gentlemen," he said, "if it's all right with you, I'll be going now. Do you mind if I glance at something first?"

He crossed to a bookcase on which were arranged a number of photographs in silver frames. The largest, one he had given Georgiana more than twenty years earlier, was of himself, leaning against a back-hoe. Next to it was a studio portrait showing Georgiana in an early-Twenties shirtwaist and long skirt, a shawl over her lovely head: the young Georgiana he had never known. He had been studying the picture since he had first come into the room and wanted to fix an impression of it, as of a beautiful and unknown woman, missed somehow, seen once somewhere and never forgotten—a person who had only a remote connection with the Georgiana who had later said with such shattering effect, "I'm too old for you."

The doorbell rang. John took a small, heavily taped package out of his pocket and handed it to Ted, who trotted off. Jed was still examining the photograph.

"Great-looking chick," said John over Jed's shoulder, his breath ropey with the burned-hemp smell of marijuana. Again Jed had to fight back the impulse to swing at him.

"She certainly was," he said.

"Is," said John. His glance traveled to the sleeping old lady and back to the brilliant-eyed girl in the photograph. "Oh, I get it. You figured that is Mrs. Gibbs? By no means. That's Darlene, her daughter. She found the clothes in a trunk and uses them in her act. You never knew Darlene?"

Jed had picked up the photograph to study it more closely. He set it down where it had been.

"Are you serious?"

"Mr. Basco . . ." John seemed genuinely puzzled. "Look again. You never heard of Darlene Johns, the folk singer?"

"I'm afraid not."

"You don't dig the scene then. Darlene made it in Folk, not all that big, but big. She writes to her ma sometimes. Singing right now in D.C. She and the old lady, they don't get on too good. But I guess at one time they could've been lookalikes. Now would you kindly give back the proxy?"

Ted had come back into the room and was standing behind Jed. The dog lay at Georgiana's feet. He switched his tail, looking at John. Jed judged that while he was programmed to defend Georgiana automatically, he would act in behalf of John only on signal. Best then to get out of his immediate range, also away from Teddy-boy, who might have a weapon. He walked into the hall, John following and Ted maneuvering fast to cut off the stairs.

"I don't understand your request."

"A proxy has been bought and paid for."

"You mean Mrs. Gibbs signed a prior proxy form?"

"Right on. Mr. Vishniak sent a friend up here. He laid three slices on us and she signed."

"She could have mentioned it to me."

"Her memory isn't so good."

"So now she's signed two. How about five thousand from me if the last quotation was three?"

"That would be fine. Except the last proxy signed is the one that counts, the way I heard it."

Jed was almost to the stairs. Even if he could get down before the dog, there was still the front door and elevator. And the elevator was on the ground floor. Whoever had come for his package five minutes earlier would have taken it down and left it there.

"Your information is correct."

"You vote Mrs. Gibbs's shares, we're in trouble with Mr. Vishniak."

For an ex-pug turned pusher, John had done his homework.

Jed was several feet closer to the stairs now with Ted squarely in front of them—and Ted could not weigh more than a hundred and ten pounds, soaking wet.

"I'm wondering how you came to be connected with Mrs. Gibbs. And in what capacity."

"She advertised for a handyman. And I'm pretty handy."

John raised his left shoulder a half inch before throwing the right hand—a telegraph-puncher; you knew why he'd never made it in the ring. Jed ducked the swing and kicked him in the balls. Half turned, Jed dove for Ted and caught him in the belly with his head; they rolled downstairs together. Ted seemed cold-cocked at the bottom, but he must have had the dog whistle on a string around his neck. The big hound never laid foot on the stairs—he was in the air all the way down and he got Jed once in the armpit and once in the shoulder before Jed could unlatch the deadlock and open the front door. The hound, lunging for the kill, slammed it shut himself.

Jed still had Georgiana's signed proxy in his pocket.

"We've given you anti-tetanus, but not the rabies antitoxin. The first procedure is to quarantine the dog. If he isn't rabid you're in no danger."

"It won't be possible to quarantine the dog. The owners would not agree."

"You could compel them."

"I'd prefer not to."

The young doctor, earnest and well scrubbed, sat by, clipboard in hand, while Lebinson, chief of staff, asked the questions. Dr. Lebinson had not been on call that afternoon but had volunteered to come in when told who the patient was. He took the emergency report out of the young doctor's hand and studied it.

"For an ordinary house pet to mount such an attack, unprovoked, is inconceivable unless the animal was diseased."

"This dog was trained to attack."

"To kill? Because he could have killed you."

"Yes."

Dr. Lebinson handed the clipboard back to the young doctor. Experience had taught him when to leave well enough alone.

"You will have some pain during the night. We have prescribed Darvon for that and Seconal for sleep. You should stay in the hospital for at least three days."

"I'm sorry, Doctor. I have to leave tomorrow."

"As you wish, Mr. Basco. But you won't be very comfortable."

"I'll have to take my chances."

Dr. Lebinson smiled as if Jed had said something very intelligent. Then the doctors went out and a middle-aged nurse came in and took his temperature.

"They've done that twice," Jed said.

"I know," said the nurse, "but I need it for my records. Dr. Lebinson said no visitors."

"I don't expect any."

"There's one out there now. A reporter."

"Send him in."

"I'm sorry, Mr. Basco. I can't disobey the doctor's orders."

"Then keep him out."

"Very well. I'm going to supper now. Will you be all right?"

"I'll be just fine," Jed said. "Only I'd like a drink."

"You're full of Darvon, Mr. Basco. Drinking is contraindicated."

"What would it do to me?"

"It might cause vomiting," said the nurse.

"I never vomited in my life."

"Of course," said the nurse, her eyes snapping in her worn face, "vomiting does not occur in all instances."

She was the kind of person who grew on you.

"Can you get me a bottle down in the pharmacy? Jack Daniels. Put it on my account."

"I'll see what I can do," the nurse said.

She went out and Jed closed his eyes. The nurse might be right about the liquor. He was not feeling well. He opened his eyes to find a man standing over him, holding a card.

"Peter Baggot, Mr. Basco, *Wall Street Letter*."

"All right, Mr. Baggot," Jed said. "What do you want?"

He looked again, this time more carefully, at Baggot—a man in his late thirties, overweight and balding.

"I'd like ten minutes of your time, sir."

"All right."

Mr. Baggot seemed surprised by Jed's answer. He laid the card carefully on the bedside table.

"I was waiting at your hotel, sir, when I heard on the radio that you'd been in an accident. Was your car badly damaged?"

"It wasn't a car accident. I was bitten by a dog. Any other questions?"

"Yes, sir. Is it true that you have been charged with irregularities in your efforts to obtain control of Basco and Western?"

"Charged by whom?"

"By the Securities and Exchange Commission, Mr. Basco."

"I notified the Securities and Exchange Commission of

my intention to conduct a proxy contest. The Commission acknowledged that notification. I also filed a copy of my letter to shareholders stating why present management should be replaced. There could not have been any charge of irregularities, because there have been no irregularities."

"Is that the only statement that you care to make at this time?"

"I'll be glad to make another if you can suggest what I ought to say."

"All right, Mr. Basco. Thank you very much."

Baggot had taken a pad of paper and a ballpoint pen out of his pocket. He fiddled with these, as if contemplating one more try at an interview, but gave up when the nurse entered, carrying a package.

"Would you like a drink, young man?" Jed asked Baggot.

"A drink would be fine."

"This is bourbon whiskey."

"Jack Daniels," said Baggot. "That's my drink, too."

"Nurse, could you let us have three glasses and some ice?" asked Jed.

"Two glasses," said the nurse, "I don't drink when I'm on duty. I haven't eaten yet. The commissary was crowded, so I decided to bring this up first."

"That was kind."

"I wouldn't let the doctor see the bottle if I were you."

She went out. Jed was pouring, using his left hand.

"Cheers," he said. "I've seen your paper, Mr. Baggot. Your offices are in New York. Did you come all the way to Chicago for this interview?"

"Sometimes I go a long way for a story," said Baggot.

"That's my trade, Mr. Basco. It's not as good a line of work as yours." He smiled as if to erase the sarcasm.

"I'm sorry I could not have been more helpful."

"Oh, there'll be another day," said Baggot.

"I'll drink to that," said Jed.

Baggot also raised his glass. "To another day," he said. "By the way, Mr. Basco—this dog. Why did he attack you?"

"Maybe he didn't like the way I smelled."

"To be frank with you, Mr. Basco," said Baggot, "I don't either."

"All right," Jed said. "To each his own. Now do you mind getting out of here?"

"Delighted, Mr. Basco," said Baggot. "Goodbye, sir."

"Goodbye, Baggot," said Jed.

Baggot strode out, almost colliding in the doorway with the doctor on floor duty.

"I would not drink whiskey if I were you, Mr. Basco," the resident said, looking at the glass in Jed's hand. "Combined with Darvon, that can cause vomiting."

"I believe you, Doctor," Jed said. "I feel quite nauseated."

He was joking, but a few hours later he made the same statement in all seriousness. Dr. Lebinson had left a referral for morphine, one-quarter grain for pain if necessary, and Jed was grateful for it. He stayed in the hospital three days. He had a telephone installed in his suite the second day and hired a girl from a public secretarial service to keep him in touch with his outside activities. He also chatted with the head of a private detective service, ordering a round-the-clock surveillance of the Gibbs condominium on Lakeshore Drive.

CHAPTER TEN

RICE said everything was going fine, just fine, but how could you tell? Rice said you could judge by the percentage of returns from the mailouts. The percentage was good, and Rice was knowledgeable, but with a corporation having close to a million stockholders, the percentile that stood for control was highly variable: up a couple of points, you had it, down a couple, you lost. You could tell what percentile you had but not what the other side controlled. All you knew was that there was mass buying, including the general public who were just in for a free ride. And one hell of a ride it was going to be. Because now not even the bad third quarter or the rumors of trouble with the SEC could hold down the price: the Big Board, which had B & W at 51⅛ when Jed was fired, quoted 64¾, then 70, then 76, escalating faster than a GTO on a two-lane drag strip. Jed, back in New

York, liked to be in Rice's office when the mailman arrived to dump the big sacks on the floor. He enjoyed the excitement of putting the envelopes through the slicer and spreading the signed proxies on the long tables to count. Afterward he would go over to Donovan & Klein's Broad Street office and watch the board.

He had the feeling now that no matter what happened he could not lose; he had always won, and he would bring this off. Let Vishniak's Four chunk in their money, hock their houses, sell their wives' jewelry—in accumulated wealth they could best him three to one, but if the stockholders were with him, and they seemed to be, he would still come out on top.

Even Felix Rupke's warnings failed to upset him. Felix called numerous times—almost daily, it seemed—carrying on about the damned Securities and Exchange Commission's investigation into Mrs. Tanheimer's unregistered stock. Jed insisted that Felix was acting as if the SEC were some sort of Abominable Snowman that could swallow you whole at the least annoyance.

No doubt the SEC could torment you, but that was not its primary purpose. As Jed understood it, the Commission was one of those regulatory bodies set up during the New Deal to see that the public was not bilked. Well, Jed had every intention of treating the public fairly, particularly B & W shareholders. Even Mrs. Tanheimer.

It had been his experience that the technicalities of government bureaus could always be dealt with somehow, and he did not imagine the SEC was an exception to this rule.

Felix Rupke talked about Mrs. Tanheimer almost as much as he did about the SEC.

"You have to take care of her," he said.

"I'm quite willing to," Jed said. "What does she want?"

"That is something you have to work out," Felix said testily. "As I've pointed out to you, old friend, I am not involved in your problem. Not in any way."

"Then what are we talking about?" Jed asked.

"I've explained that too," Felix said. "It's a delicate situation."

"It's a little too goddam delicate for me," Jed said.

"Look, Jed," said Felix, "I can't give you advice. My position is simply that of *amicus curiae*."

"Whatever that is," said Jed.

"Look it up," said Felix. "Because of our long friendship I have been asked by your former associates to inform you of certain developments. I have a feeling—mind you, this is only a guess—that if you gave back Mrs. Tanheimer her money plus a reasonable profit, she would withdraw her complaint."

"Fine," said Jed. "Why didn't you say so in the first place? I thought she was out for blood."

"That is for you to find out," said Felix.

"I'll give it a pitch."

"Good luck, old man," said Felix, and Jed realized his friend now felt the affair was closed.

In due course Rice's lawyers and Donovan & Klein's lawyers met with Mrs. Tanheimer's lawyers and approved the deal which Felix had—well, not outlined but suggested. When they arrived at a figure Jed made out a check which he sent to Bronxville by motorcycle courier, and Mrs. Tanheimer withdrew the complaint. That should have done it. But be damned if Felix didn't ring up again two days later.

"Jed," said the Supreme Court Justice, "I have bad news for you. The stuff has hit the fan."

"What stuff?" said Jed.

"Your unregistered stock," Felix said. "You'll never get away with this."

"I haven't got away with much so far."

"The hell you haven't," said Felix Rupke. "How much of it have you sold?"

"All I had," Jed said.

"That's what I thought," said Felix. "You could pull a felony conviction, you know."

"The SEC puts people in jail? I never heard that before."

"The SEC doesn't put people in jail," Felix said. "But they can forward a criminal reference report to the Justice Department asking the United States Attorney for the district in question to submit the evidence to a grand jury. If the grand jury indicts, the Attorney General's office issues a warrant and the individual served is brought to trial. If found guilty, he can go to jail. It could happen to you, Jed. Birnbaum has the case and he'll take it all the way."

"Who is Birnbaum?"

"Milton Birnbaum. Chief Counsel for the SEC's Eastern Federal District."

"Do you know him?"

"I've met him on a few occasions."

"Then why don't you go and see him? Get him to call off the hounds?"

There was total silence at Felix's end of the line—shock or the effort to suppress some indefinable fury.

"I can't do that," he said at length.

"Felix," said Jed Basco, "you are an eminent man, I know that very well. Everyone knows it. And you're only involved as an *amicus curiae*. No, I didn't look it up, but I asked somebody and I know what it means now. What I don't understand is why Vishniak is upset that the SEC is after me. I should think they'd be feasting."

"No, Jed, they're in trouble too."

"Why?"

"Because, in an illegal stock transaction, everyone is responsible before the law, clear back to the board of directors of the company that issued the stock in the first place."

"Aha!"

"I wouldn't sound so pleased."

"You're giving me some new ideas."

"The only one I'd consider is what to say to the Chief District Counsel. Because you're the one who will be talking to him, not I."

"Suppose," Jed said at length, "suppose they go ahead and prosecute. How long would it take?"

"It could take weeks. Or it could slam through much faster. It depends how they look at it."

"If they slowed down a little, the annual meeting would be over before anything happens. Then I'd have my company back. I could settle on any terms he wanted."

"That's a chance I wouldn't take. Even with a new board B and W might not approve your settlement. You could buy yourself a minority stockholders' suit."

"Is this the *amicus curiae* speaking? Or my old friend Felix?"

"I recommend you rescind every deal you've made for the letter stock. Negotiate with the holders and pay them off the way you did Mrs. Tanheimer."

Jed jotted some figures on a scratch pad.

"At current prices, that would cost me more than I can afford."

"Get it."

"And where would you suggest I find the money?"

"Out of your current profits in B and W stock."

"I've put those profits back, and more, to buy additional stock. I'm margined up to the neck."

"Then sell some of your holdings."

"Those holdings are my bid for control. I won't sell a single share. That's final."

There was a perceptible pause before Felix said, almost apologetically, "In that case, there's just one other way."

"I can't think of any."

"You've too much on your mind, friend. You don't recall the other time when you needed cash in a hurry and didn't care how much you paid for it?"

It was stuffy in the paneled telephone booth. Jed pushed the door open. "Mormon Creek Cutoff," he said at last.

"As the young people put it," Felix said, "right on."

Jed grunted. He understood now why Felix had functioned effectively as a counselor to the great.

"I remember the deal now. I'm just trying to think of the guy's name."

"Say no more," Felix said. "I trust that it will come to mind. Goodbye."

Jed cradled the telephone. In the crowded room beyond

the booth, the stockbrokers' customers were banked like spectators at a prizefight. Jed stared down at his pad. Without conscious direction he had printed the words HUDSON RIVER FEDERATED INVESTORS.

He printed because that was the first way he had seen the name—inscribed in Victorian gold and satin black across the façade of a red brick building that had once been a spaghetti factory but had been remodeled into small offices, boutiques, bookshops, bars and restaurants.

He looked up the number and the operator dialed it for him.

"Jed C. Basco," he said to the secretary who answered, "calling Mr. Rafael Angiacomo."

The receptionist beckoned to him as he left the booth.

"There's a young lady to see you. I put her in the small conference room."

"Who is she?"

"She wouldn't give a name. But I recognized her."

"You mean you know her personally?"

"I *recognized* her, Mr. Basco. Darlene Johns, the singer. I've seen her on TV."

"Well, would you apologize to her for me and tell her that—"

"I won't take much of your time, Mr. Basco."

Jed turned. The girl must have been watching; the door of the conference room, to the right of the switchboard, was open.

"I'm Darlene Johns," she said. "Could we please talk, if only for five minutes? It really is important."

She was thinner than she had appeared in the photograph and she had on very different clothes, but the resemblance to Georgiana was there—the younger Georgiana he had never known. Often—during their love affair—he had imagined what she had been like in those years. It was a wild concept, romantic—a young man's dream, and he was young no more and had never, as he saw himself, been romantic. Yet now face to face with this dream Georgiana, he had an impulse to say something ridiculous like "But of course, what is it? I'll do anything you want. . . ."

The pressure of the day's affairs and the fact that the receptionist and the girl, Darlene Johns herself, were both staring at him made him check this impulse and he said only, "I'd be glad to see you, but I have an appointment. Could we set it up for some other time?"

"Later this afternoon, then. Or perhaps this evening?"

"I'm sorry. I'm going out this afternoon."

He turned away, but she stopped him.

"Mr. Basco, I know that in your way you've been kind to my mother. You went to see her recently, so you're familiar with the situation."

"Yes, I know."

"Is a little of your time too much to ask?"

The girl kept her tone low, but the receptionist was watching her with the devious sympathy that women reserve for each other when some male is behaving badly.

"Perhaps tomorrow, Miss Johns."

"Very well, I'll call you tomorrow."

The girl said something more, but Jed did not hear the last sentence. He was already out of the door, charging toward his limousine.

"Tell me, Mr. Basco," said Angiacomo, "is it still standing—the bridge we built? You know—Mormon, what was it, River?"

"Mormon Creek Cutoff," Jed said. He found he was holding Angiacomo's little damp hand—a curiously small hand for so big a man. Mr. Angiacomo would not let go. His cordiality was impressive. He led Jed around the desk, introducing him to a small, much older person who had risen from a chair in front of the window.

"It din fall down yet?" said Mr. Angiacomo. He quickly answered his own question: "No way it could fall down, Mr. Basco—the way we had it financed, that bridge is going to stand forever. You remember Mr. Harry Gardella, my associate."

Gardella and Jed shook hands.

"Rafael is a big joker, Mr. Basco. Someday he finds out—I'm not his associate, I'm his boss. Pleased to meet you."

"Delighted, Mr. Gardella," Jed said.

"That bridge will be there after we're all gone. It's solid. Twelve percent, payable ninety days. You remember, Harry?"

"I forget," said Gardella, winking at Jed. "I only remember when they don't pay. Mr. Basco must have paid."

"On the dot," said Angiacomo. "Twelve percent, that's from the old days. Everthing going up, but our old customers come back. They know where they can get a square deal."

Jed could remember clearly, even if Gardella could not, his previous visit to this office. The Mormon Creek job, contracted with a California utility district, had run out of funds when a flash flood washed out a diversion tunnel. The firm had needed three quarters of a million for emergency construction. Recourse to a Cosa Nostra lending house, even one with Angiacomo's legitimate credentials, was not approved practice in the engineering field: rates were usurious and delinquency was rumored to involve unusual penalties. Jed always felt lucky to come out as well as he had, and the necessity for the loan had much to do with his decision to break with Mike, whose improvidence with company reserves, as much as the flood, had precipitated the crisis.

Jed had never expected to find himself sitting across from Rafael Angiacomo a second time.

"What are you charging these days?" he asked.

Rafael Angiacomo turned his hand palm upward on the table in a compact, momentous gesture signifying We are brothers, who cares? Speaking across Jed to Gardella, he inquired, "An old customer, a *gumba* like Mr. Basco?"

"Whatever he wants," said Gardella. "A famous name. It's a pleasure he walks in. You want a cup of coffee, Mr. Basco?"

"No thanks," Jed said.

"This time of day, I like a little espresso, a *grappa* in it. For my stomach."

"None for me," said Angiacomo.

"You boys settle it," said Gardella.

He walked out. Angiacomo drew a line on a sheet of stationery, then looked inquiringly at Jed.

"I need five million dollars," Jed said.

Angiacomo put the pencil down.

"We're big, Mr. Basco, but we're not that big. How long will you be using this money?"

"Thirty days, Rafael," Jed said. "Twenty-one, to be exact."

"Until the meeting, huh?" said Angiacomo. "Sure, I read the papers. *Wall Street Letter* says you got an even chance. Don't tell me the figures. If they say even, I say two to one, your favor. I know you. They tried to give you the shaft, you ram it right back, all the way up. But three million is the top. Even Harry, he can't give you more than that. The super top, three million five. Twenty percent interest for thirty days."

"Four million."

Angiacomo covered his eyes with his fingertips, looking about ten years older.

"For that, I have to ask someone else. Not Harry. He can't say nothing. I told you the truth, he works for me—he only says boss because he's so old, he's ashamed I give him orders. I could ask this other party, but he don't okay these jumbos. I ask him twice, both times he turned me down. Once for an executive like yourself, a man in high position. You gonna give collateral?"

Jed shook his head. Angiacomo groaned.

"To lay this off, I'd have to phone twenty-six cities, believe me. And twenty-four will say no." He pressed an intercom switch. "Harry, will you kindly come back here a minute? I wouldn't ask unless it . . . No, *gumba,* we got a lunatic sitting here, spreading numbers around. He thinks we're crazy too."

Shortly after the Exchange closed that afternoon, Jed Basco walked into Stanley Donovan's office and laid down a certified check for three million eight hundred thousand dollars for deposit in his trading account. He had decided to ignore Felix's advice about settling his difficulties with the Securities and Exchange Commission. The problem, even magnified to Felix's proportions, could not compete with the fact that Angiacomo's three million eight hundred thousand could change Jed's acquirement of Basco & Western from a likelihood into a certainty. Once he had the company, *his* company, back into possession, he could pay the damn hood shylocks, settle for the sale of the unregistered stock—handle everything as it should be handled, cash on the barrelhead. If nervous minority stockholders complained he would take care of them when the time came. First things first.

He was grateful to Felix, if for nothing else for remembering the Mormon Creek Cutoff.

CHAPTER ELEVEN

JED arrived at Kitty's house in Oyster Bay at half past four. She made a drink for him and tea for herself and they sat on the terrace of the guest house which the Bramsteads, Kitty's in-laws, had given their son as a wedding present. The guest house had four bedrooms, a den, living room, a patio and a boathouse (but no dock) in contrast to the twenty-two bedrooms, three-acre garden, six-car garage and large private dock belonging to the main house.

Kitty had done well when she married Willie Bramstead, financially and personally. Willie was a very nice boy. Correction—man. He was over six feet tall, large of bone and lean of frame. He had an open look and a most cordial way of smiling and moving about in a room as if to see that everyone present was seated comfortably and had whatever food and drink they wanted. All this was very engaging. To make it even more so, Willie was a great doer of favors. He would make an extraordinary number of telephone calls to see that a friend obtained the theater tickets or hotel accommodations he wanted, either in New York or in Europe.

Willie Bramstead had met Kitty when she was on a guided tour of England. Willie, at the time, was visiting friends in Cambridge. Their marriage, as Mrs. Bramstead put it, was one of those things that simply had to be and it had worked out wonderfully despite the fact that Kitty, who had seemed so immature as a bride, soon acquired a settled, almost motherly way about her, while Willie became more gregarious and more boyish. He was not satisfied with working in the Bramstead family business, which was rope. He had no objections to rope. He even used to joke about it, in his easy, charming fashion. "No member of my family was ever hanged." He spent a year in the Peace Corps and another as an unpaid, volunteer social researcher for the Mayor's office. During the summer he sailed. He was a highly skilled skipper of six-meter boats and had taken many cups in the races sponsored by Seawanhaka, Larchmont and the other yacht clubs on the Long Island and Connecticut sides of the Sound.

Jed asked Kitty if Willie had kept his enthusiasm for sailing and she said he had.

"That's really why we stayed here after Labor Day, so he could sail a few more times. He loves to go out even if he's alone and especially when the weather's gusty. I like him to sail, it's so good for him. He's been very uneasy lately."

"What about?" asked Jed.

"About his *choice,*" Kitty said. "You know. The choice of what he really wants to do in life. Most people don't know it, but he's a very serious person. It would be terrible if he wasted his life just accumulating money, which we don't need. I wish I could help more, but we do have these talks and I know that eventually he'll find the right thing."

"I hope so," Jed said.

"Oh, I know it may seem silly to you, Daddy," Kitty said quickly. "You've always worked so hard. But you sort of had to, didn't you?"

"You're damn right I did," Jed said. "I still do."

"Well, in a way I suppose you do, but Willie is different in that respect. Right now he's interested in religion. That may really be his future, right there."

"I never knew he was a religious person," Jed said, genuinely surprised.

"He isn't," Kitty agreed. "He's interested in it as a discipline. Don't say anything about this. I'm not sure he wants me to talk about it, but he's been going up to town three days a week to work at St. John's. He commutes on the Chris-Craft. He's been today. I hope he tells you about it. I know he'd like to have your ideas."

"I doubt that."

"Now, Daddy," Kitty said urgently. "Don't be stuffy. Not that you are as a rule, but you can be disapproving. Try to see this from Willie's point of view. Oh, there he is now."

The blue and white power boat, its big twin inboards lifting it high at the bow, made the turn opposite Lloyd's Neck and headed for the Bramstead boat dock. Willie was sitting under the cockpit awning. He lifted his hand, and Kitty, rising, waved back happily as the boatman, reversing his engines, eased up to the padded float. Willie jumped out and made the stern painter fast himself. He had on a light gabardine suit and a Racquet Club tie and was carrying an alligator briefcase; he looked more like a young stockbroker than a man trying to save the world. He kissed his young wife warmly, then shook hands with Jed.

"Have I time for a swim?" he asked Kitty.

"Of course, darling," Kitty said. "But the water's quite cold."

"How do you know?" said Willie. "Did you go in?"

"No, darling," Kitty said. "I can tell by looking at it. You know I can't stand it when it's cold."

"Just a quick dip," Willie said. "I've been looking forward to it all day. Hot as hell in the damned sacristy."

"Why, I would think it would be cool there," Kitty said.

"In the cathedral, yes. Not in the sacristy . . . I didn't get too much done."

"I'm sorry, dear."

"What the hell," Willie said. "You win a few, you lose a few. Would you care for a swim, sir?"

"Not me, thanks," Jed said. "But you go ahead."

"I won't be long," Willie said.

He had a swim and later they dined on the terrace. Kitty had places set in the dining room, but Willie pointed out there wouldn't be many evenings left when they could still eat outdoors, so Kitty personally moved the settings outside and then lighted the electric brazier for warmth. Willie had read in the *Letter* about the proxy fight but made only a passing reference to it.

After they ate Kitty asked Willie if they might not have coffee in the house. It was chilly. Zoltan, the butler, brought in Sèvres demitasses and a bottle of brandy for fortification. Only then did Jed bring up the matter of the proxy, asking whether Kitty had received it in the mail.

As if this were the cue they had been waiting for, Kitty looked at Willie, passing further responsibility for the conversation to him.

"Yes, sir, we did receive it. We've had quite a few talks about it. It's—well, it's not exactly a simple proposition."

"What Willie means, Dad," Kitty interpreted hastily, "is—we're for you. We want to help. It's just that—Willie doesn't believe in corporations. In running them, I mean."

"No, honey, not in running them. In *corporations*. You said it right the first time," Willie declared manfully. "I do not believe in the idiot corporate brain."

"Not *you*, Daddy," Kitty said anxiously. "Willie has the greatest respect for your brain."

"I'm not making myself clear," Willie said.

"No, you're not, dear," said Kitty. "You were very clear when you explained it all to me. You must be the same way with Daddy."

"Well, sir," said Willie, swirling the brandy in his sniffer glass. "The idiot brain I mean is the corporation cost accounting sheet. What's being earned, what's being spent. Figures on a piece of paper. That is the factor that determines human life today. Yet it's essentially inhuman.

It holds people in bondage."

"You don't act as if you lived in bondage, Willie," Jed said.

"No, sir," said Willie politely. "But I don't actually work for a corporation. Oh, I know I profit from one—from several corporations. But I don't participate in management."

"You don't attend shareholders' meetings?"

"No, sir."

"It's a principle of his, Daddy," Kitty interjected. "He's never been to a shareholders' meeting in his life."

"In other words," said Jed, "you differentiate between drawing income from the idiot brain and directing its activities. I must say I don't quite follow that."

"Tell him about the plan, dear," Kitty said. "This is the part that makes it consistent, Daddy," she went on. "I was confused too till I knew what Willie was going to do."

"I'm going to give my money away, sir," Willie said. "Our money. Kitty is with me all the way."

"Oh, I am, Daddy," Kitty said, "I really am. It's a wonderful plan. And it's so simple."

"Not in a lump," said Willie seriously. "I realize that the trusts, both of them, are set up so that we can't touch the principal. But we have the income. We know how lucky we are in that respect. We can use it as we see fit."

"I'm sure," Jed said. "I'm assuming that you mean—in the form of betterment, is that it?"

Willie hesitated.

"It's more than that, Daddy," Kitty said almost reproachfully. "Betterment is such a stuffy word. What we have in mind is to . . ." Her voice trailed off.

"Well, I suppose this will sound stuffy too, but what we propose is—work for humanity. The problem is to find the most effective way." He waited for some response from Jed. When none came he said almost aggressively, "If you don't approve, sir, I'm afraid there's nothing I can do about it."

"He may even go back into the Peace Corps, Daddy," Kitty said.

"That's odd," Jed said. "Bob, your brother, is working for peace too. That's what he's using *his* income for—running deserters and COs out of the country."

"Bob's a revolutionist, Mr. Basco," Willie said.

"He says he's not."

"He thinks the social structure as we know it will collapse. We don't," Willie said.

"We just want to eliminate the bad parts of it," Kitty said. "The Peace Corps might be one answer. St. John's might be another. They're very much interested in Willie at St. John's."

"I would imagine," Jed said gently.

A silence followed, broken when Willie rose to put his brandy glass back on the tray.

"I hope you get back your company, Mr. Basco," he said. "For your own sake, that is. I'm only sorry that we can't help more actively. But Kitty knows my views on that. And she agrees, don't you, dear?"

Kitty favored him with a brilliant smile.

"Of course, darling," she said.

"Well," Jed said, "I think I understand. Anyway, it's been a fine evening. And now it's time I was getting back to the city."

MacNeice, who had driven Jed out, was waiting in the driveway; Jed had one foot in the limousine when Kitty ran out for a last kiss.

"Oh, Daddy," she said, "thank you for coming." She turned, so that her left hand was hidden from Willie, and stuffed something into his pocket. As the car moved out of the Bramstead compound onto the blacktop road, Jed switched on the tonneau light to check what she had given him. It was a signed proxy.

CHAPTER TWELVE

DARLENE Johns had made it pretty big in Folk. Not all that big, but she wasn't playing basket houses either, the little clips where they hand around a can for contributions after each set. Before she was eleven she was gigging with black combos in the busted neighborhoods where her mother took apartments when she was on the shorts. Then Jed's money came, and Darlene could have gone to Radcliffe or Sarah Lawrence but those slick rich chicks dug Folk about the way they dug sex, in her opinion. She picked Cherry Hill, Maine, where her original compositions turned on the dorm mother, a Folk fan, who advised her to split after her sophomore year, what was she wasting her life for?

She owned guitar by that time, not *a* guitar—*guitar.*

She could tune one thirty-two different ways, which gave her sound some difference, to say the least. She spent Christmas holidays that year with her mother, then thumbed to San Francisco because she might have a chance, she thought, in the small experimental clubs where they would try out anyone with an instrument and a song. In those days acid was legal; if the people dug you they could be generous to young singers. After San Francisco there was Gerdes Folk City in New York. She gigged in the Bitter End and Fred Weintraub's Gaslight and cut an album for Vanguard and dropped her boyfriend, Johnny Matzen, the lame bass player, for Hood Olson, VP of another record company. Johnny OD'd soon after the split, and the fellows in his group, the Lease Breakers, blamed it on her, as if you could ever blame a junkie's finish on another person.

Had you put him on it? Then take the blame if you wanted to put yourself down. She didn't. She had liked Johnny, not loved him. You didn't have to love a man because you happened to be sleeping with him and he happened to be black.

She had loved—still did love (if you could use that word for a non-sex relationship)—Gunther Troll. He was the man after Hood. "The strangest human being," she said with great intensity, "the strangest and the nicest I've ever known. Physically, he's repulsive. He's a giant and he weighs three hundred pounds, but all of it is talent. He's walled off, separated somehow—living out of his time and place. And you are too, you know," she said to Jed with a flick of her eyes like a feathery touch brushing some deep place in his being.

"I'm afraid I don't know what you mean by that," Jed said.

"Well, I take it back. I don't know why I said it. It could even be wrong. Not walled off, perhaps I said that because I had to put a wall around you. I had such a hangup about you and Mother. After she left you she pretended to you she had a good job or a rich lover or something, whereas the truth was . . . different. Then you found her again and gave her all that money, but I still hated you. And I was jealous of Mother for having loved you enough to give up everything else. I've never loved anyone except Gunther."

"He's your accompanist?"

"No, Mac Oakley is my accompanist. Harry Silverman is my manager. I could get another Mac Oakley, no sweat. I could find a dozen Harry Silvermans, though Harry is all right. I could never, as long as I live, find another Gunther. I get some musical idea, and he turns it into a million-selling record. Don't ask me what he does. He's just all music. Sometimes he writes the words, sometimes I do, but mostly the music is his. Everyone—you wouldn't believe the names—has tried to get him away from me. They can't. Once we had a quarrel. I don't know, some ridiculous argument, and he split. I couldn't sing for two weeks. I don't know why I'm chattering away to you like this. Is the food any good in this place?"

"Not bad at all," Jed said. And he added, "We were talking about your mother. That was what you told me you wanted to discuss."

"I do," said Darlene, "but let's order first. I'm starving."

Jed picked up a menu and without further intimation of

his intentions found Carlo, the maître d'hôtel, standing beside him. The cassoulet for M'sieur, the coq au vin for Madame. The menus were snapped away, and the drinks appeared: a Jack Daniels for Jed, a strawberry Pepsi float for Darlene.

"I want you to call off your goons," she said, "those private eyes you hired to watch her apartment. You're doing more harm than you can imagine."

"I don't think your mother's in a good situation."

"Of course she's not. So why make it worse?"

"If the narcotics division busts the place, they'll take her in as an accessory."

"You don't imagine, in Chicago, an operation like that exists without money being paid for protection?"

"So much the worse for your mother. Of whom I happen to be very fond."

"So am I, believe it or not. I got a look at this a few months ago. At first I was—well, you could say horrified. A square expression. The kind you would use, Mr. Basco."

"Jed."

"I'll stick to Mr. Basco. As I was saying—then I got another look at it and I decided it was not so bad."

"Maybe your mother's dog didn't take a piece out of you. Or the fags try to beat your brains in."

"So what explains the goons' desire to get even for your lumps or your interest in Mother?"

"Let's put it this way—those operatives are there for the express purpose of protecting her. Also, since the narcotics division does not seem concerned, to gather evidence that would clear her in the event of—"

"A bust? You're dreaming. Nothing would clear her in

the event of a bust. It's her house. John and Teddy are her guests. Nobody would be able to prove that she wasn't part of the operation. In fact, though she's sometimes tranqued to the ears, I'd say she knows. Maybe not all about it, but more than she lets on. They're using her. I'll admit that. But she's also using them. She gets a lot out of the arrangement."

"Like what?"

"She's lonely. And she's old. Take it from there."

"You take it, Miss Johns. Without some change in her environment, and fast, she may not get much older."

"I've told you why I think she will. But suppose she doesn't, here's what she has now: two homos that cheat her and live off her but also give her all sorts of little attentions—the kind their kind always gives old ladies, in memory of the witch, I guess, who made them what they are. She loves those attentions. She loves that little family of queers, she loves her dog. What I mean, she's living. All the money you gave wouldn't have made that possible for her. And didn't. For a long time."

"How did she get mixed up with them in the first place? Or is that a square question?"

"From anybody else it would not be. From you it is. You are or you have been president of a big company and you've built things out of concrete, so I suppose you must be reasonably smart. Are you going to tell me you can't figure out how she came to contact a couple of pushers?"

"I knew she was taking something. I didn't know it was main-line drugs."

"It wasn't at first. You and she made the big break, and you married. That was in the late Forties. After which

Mother and I enjoyed the rainbow years of mean landlords and rats and walk-up cold-water flats until you rubbed your magic checkbook."

"You seem to remember a great deal."

"My memory is excellent, Mr. Basco. I recall among other things that you took her on trips with you. You would leave her alone for weeks at a time. You'd wave bye-bye and go home to your Irish wife with all the money and your two dear children that you thought so much of. Then a call would come through and Mother would pack a suitcase and meet you in some Christ-forsaken place you couldn't even find on a map, and I suppose she behaved as if everything was just dandy. In between she got hooked on tranquilizers, and from there to the big H. She met Ted and John because they sold to her. In the end, after you'd dropped the B and W stock on her—which incidentally she didn't realize at first was a goodbye gift—"

"It was not a goodbye gift," Jed interrupted with some heat. "I most certainly never intended it that way. I was—as it happened, I was busy as hell, and I had some trouble with my—"

"Yes, with dear Dorothy. She'd found some checks and wrote to Mother about them. I suspect you never knew about that, did you?"

"Your mother was . . . not quite . . . like herself about that time. I may have been remiss. I didn't keep in touch as much as I—"

"One might just say that you acted like a prick. All the stock you paid her never quite compensated. Here's one angle that might interest you. Ted and John didn't put her on the stuff; they got her off it. How's that for a twist?"

"I find it difficult to believe."

"Really? Run it through the computer again, Mr. Basco. Here was a woman with a big income from a trust, which those boys could not get their grubby hands on. That was bad news—but they still had the place on Lakeshore Drive, which was the most respectable front two pushers could ever want. Only small-time pushers are junkies themselves. They wanted Mother cured, and fast, because if anything happened to her they would lose their beautiful set-up. They got wise to your flatfeet right away—they have their own security procedures—and they've been blowing their minds. So I ask you again, won't you please lay off?"

"All right," he said.

She stared at him. "Do you mean it?"

"Of course."

"Why, you're human after all."

"How did you think I'd be?" Jed asked, and as her thin face softened, she looked exactly as Georgiana must have at twenty-one (when he, Jed, had been nine years old).

"A real son of a bitch," she said.

"I'm glad you've changed your mind."

"I didn't say I'd changed my mind. I just modified an opinion." She looked at her watch. "Oh my God! I have an interview with *The Village Voice* at two-thirty and then I have to go to the Limelight and . . . goodbye, Mr. Basco. You *will* keep your promise, won't you?"

"I will," Jed said. "When can we have dinner?"

She waved her hand. "Call me, call me . . ."

Some kids had crowded into the foyer, waiting for her, and she paused, scribbling her name on any scrap of paper pushed toward her. She had on sandals, peace beads, a heavy Pucci silk blouse and funky levis with an American flag stitched on the back pocket. Jed stayed at the table only long enough to pay the check.

Now he found himself sitting at a smaller and much less elegant table in a very different type of establishment, wondering why further encounters with this girl were either desirable or necessary (it had suddenly appeared that they were both).

He could not have told why he wanted her—whether to regain that segment of the past which, had he had access to it, would have made him whole, or to force a place for himself in the generation working so hard to destroy him. For whatever this generation was, whatever the fierce, angry nature of its rebel drives, Darlene was one of its idols. Having her would be forgiveness, obliteration of mistakes, reinstatement of a kind he needed urgently, immediately; and having her, he had been realizing these last days, was something he intended, that he powerfully sought, cost what it would and ridiculous as it might seem!

OPENING TOMORROW NIGHT
MISS DARLENE JOHNS IN PERSON
FOR ONE WEEK ONLY

The "E" would not turn on, so her name came out Darlen. Electricians had been called to fix it and they didn't have much time, less than three hours till the first set. One workman, on a crane elevated from a truck in the street, fiddled with the neon wiring, yelling instructions through the window to a helper inside. The room would seat between four and five hundred, with space for fifty standees to the right of the bar; an overflow was expected at the opening because one of Darlene's records, "They Can't Cut the Clouds Down," had just made the top forty, lyrics by Richard Kraemer, music by Gayle Wyllie.

They can cut all the trees in the forest
Till there's not one left to stand
They can shoot every deer in the mountains
Till there's not one left to die

Backed by an electric five-piece combo, Darlene rehearsed as waiters began setting tables with an annoying clink of silver. She stopped in the middle of the first reprise.

"Shall we all play clash the spoons?" Her sweet voice was right on pitch.

A captain, a small Greek with a hairpiece, capable of very emphatic gestures, sent the waiters away and the rehearsal continued.

But they can't cut the clouds down
They can't kill the sky.

A blonde in a silver maxi with a sulky, going-to-work pout on her soft, sad mouth touched Jed's shoulder.

"What yawl doin' by your lonesome?"

"Waiting for somebody."

"Want to buy me a drink while you're waitin'?"

"You name it."

"I'm a champagne drinker, honey."

"Give the lady some champagne."

"And a glass of water, Clemence," said the blonde.

"Coming up," said Clemence.

The water glass had nothing in it but ice.

Jet lit his pipe, watching his companion take her first sip of champagne. When she took her second, the pout become fuller and she sipped some ice water. Jed signaled for the waiter.

"Clemence, take away the spit glass."

The waiter looked uncertainly from Jed to the blonde.

"What do you mean, spit glass?" said the blonde.

"For a champagne drinker, you don't drink much champagne. You use your mouth as a conveyor to pass it into the other glass. I don't mind paying for the wine, but I want to see you drink it."

The blonde laughed. "Why, honey, that acid is bad for the kidneys. My doctor told me that, and I trust my doctor."

Jed pointed at the glass with the ice in it, and the waiter took it away.

The blonde was unperturbed. "You sure been around, honey."

"Not all that much."

"*All* that much." She laughed again and took some more champagne in her mouth. This time she swallowed it.

"I like the taste of it. It don't bother me none. But I swear to God it's no good for the kidneys."

Darlene had taken the song from the top for the last time. She walked off; the bandstand went dark. The Greek approached Jed's table.

"Miss Johns say, would you kindly come back to her dressing room? She can see you now."

"Will you excuse me?" Jed said to the blonde.

The latter raised a pudgy hand: a queenly gesture of acquiescence.

"Enjoy," she said.

The dressing room was the size of a Texas casket. Jammed into the small space were a wardrobe trunk, two chairs, a shelf with a mirror lighted by bulbs in wire-screened sockets, and three people: Darlene and two men, one seated, one standing.

"They are the same lights you had last year, doll," the seated man was saying. He was a frail black with a Muslim-type mustache and goatee.

"Last year they weren't in my eyes, Mac."

"I'll dim them if you want, doll," he said, "but they're the same."

"I can't feel anything. I can't feel *them* out there. I have to see something or I can't *feel.*"

"There was nobody out there but the waiters, sweetheart," said the man named Mac. "How can you feel waiters? It's bad enough to hear them."

"I know about waiters," said Darlene. "I was talking about the fucking lights in my eyes. I *want* them the way they were last year."

"I'll dim them," said Mac. He nodded politely to Jed and left the room.

"That was my sideman, Mac Oakley," said Darlene. "He used to be a gaffer."

"Mac's the best side in Folk, bar none," said the standing man. He was stooped and nattily dressed, tall and lightly perspiring. One side of his mouth tilted upward like a comedian timing a laugh.

Jed, who had been standing half in, half out, felt suddenly grateful.

"I'm Harry Silverman, Miss Johns' manager," he said.

Darlene looked from one to the other. "I'm tired, Harry. Do you mind?"

"I can take a hint," said Harry. "Good night, Mr. Basco. It's a pleasure to have met you. Have a good sleep, Darlene. You were right on tonight. Right *on!*"

"Good night," said Darlene.

She got up and closed the door. "Have a good sleep, Darlene. Have a nice day, Darlene. When did that kind of dirt start going around?"

"He's right, though," Jed said. "You were very good."

"Thank you, sir," said Darlene, "and thank you for the wine. There I go, dishing out the same old crap." She mimicked herself, blowing kisses to imaginary admirers. "Thank you all, you darlings!" She resumed her seat, facing the dressing table on which, in addition to the bottle Jed had sent her in its bright foil collar, were various makeup jars, used tissues, hair curlers in several sizes, a small electric coffee pot, a rabbit's foot, some money (bills), more money (change), part of a portable dryer, and a dim scourge of cigarette butts, half-eaten bread crusts, gum wrappers, unidentified pills and partially empty coffee cups.

Darlene carefully removed her false eyelashes and put them in a box, then unzipped the full-length royal-blue brocade satin costume.

"I hate a run-through. I don't feel easy until the people are out there. People who have paid."

She stepped out of the gown. She had on only a bra and

panties. She reached into the trunk, found a makeup-stained fur-collared Japanese kimono; she turned her back to Jed while she put it on.

"We could open the wine," Jed suggested.

"We could if you like warm champagne."

"It's not bad over ice."

"I think I'll just have coffee. Would you care for a cup?"

"All right."

Darlene filled the pot at the sink and plugged it in. She sat down and began to set her hair. She seemed to be making a definite effort to ritualize her role—a star receiving a gentleman caller in her dressing room.

"Perhaps you'd like me to go out. While you dress."

"No. I'm naked as a jaybird half the time with this room full of people. *That* wouldn't give you a bad idea about me. But—*something* gave you a bad idea. I could be wrong, but that's how it seems to me, and I—shit! There I go. Getting it all fucked up."

She jerked painfully at a curler. Jed could not tell whether her last remark applied to her hair or their conversation.

"Last time we met," he said, "you suggested that I call you."

"I did," said Darlene. "And you did, and you were sweet. I want to tell *you* why I didn't return your call. *Or* thank you for the flowers or—anything." She gestured toward the bottle. "I'm afraid you have confused me with my mother, Mr. Basco, but I'm nothing like her. I think you'd better leave me alone." She poured out the coffee. "Cream and sugar?"

"No, thank you. Just black."

"It's only simulated cream anyway." She handed him his cup and sat with downcast eyes. "I'm sorry but that's the way it is."

Jed tasted the coffee. It was vile.

"All right," he said. "I'll accept that."

"I just want you to understand."

"I do."

"No, you don't. I'm a Pisces, and Pisces people can read minds. *You do not understand.*"

"Then tell me."

"You saw that picture in Mother's apartment. You mentioned it in the French restaurant, when we were talking about John and Ted, that you—"

"I remember."

"—had seen it. That happened to be a picture put out in Folk City. I know it made me a dead ringer for Mother. Perhaps I deliberately laid it on, the resemblance. But that's all it is. We couldn't be more different."

"I am not confusing you with your mother," Jed said.

"No? Then why the telephone calls and the hundred-dollar florist deliveries and stuff? Mr. Basco! I said you were human, but . . . you know . . . you have other things on your mind. Right?"

"Right."

"So if you want to get yourself balled, you ball somebody. And if I want to get myself balled, I ball somebody. You don't come on with this square, old-fashioned pitch. Um-ta-ta"—she hummed—"a sen-ti-men-tal jooourney . . . so if you balled me you'd be balling my mother when you first met her."

Jed put down his empty cup. "As a mind reader you're not doing very well. Check out the dates. I never knew your mother when she was your age. She's twelve years older than I am."

"All the better. Then with me you'd be balling your big love, *before* you knew her. The fantastic freakout orgasm of all time."

Jed looked at her. She had taken off the cold-creamed kimono and was putting on street clothes. What she said might have some truth in it, but the very fact that she guessed was what impressed him. Had he really thought of her in these terms? Or was she making him a surrogate from some notion which, reversed, was really her own rather than his?

"I wanted to know you better. That was about all I had in mind."

"And I was such a nice person," she mimicked. "Such a talent. Well, as long as we are laying the cards face up, here are mine. You'll recall another picture right beside mine. A picture of you in a big silver frame. That lovely object went with us on all our travels, from San Francisco to Skid Row Chicago. Mother always had it prominently displayed. Except when my father came to see me. Then she hid it in a drawer. I knew why she did that. I knew exactly what the score was. Now I know *you* and I'm not too happy about that. Unless hate would be a reason for going to bed with you, I'd say you were the last person in the world I would ever sleep with. Thank you for promising to leave Mother alone. Now you'd better promise to do the same for me."

He wasn't sure. She was so smart, so hip on the he-and-she of it and yet the put-down seemed overdone, false. He might have walked away with no hurt. He had neither time nor emotion invested in her, but he never considered walking away. The overstated drama of her farewell convinced him, as nothing else could have, that he had something going.

He missed her opening at the Blue Mood. Rice wanted him back in New York for a day, which stretched into three—after which followed a day and a half of highly pressured conferences with Felix Rupke.

Almost a week passed before he got back to the Washington club, sipping a whiskey while Darlene, a marvel of sparkles in her hair, wearing a yellow cowgirl dress and high red boots, poured the chill of roadside blood into one of Gunther Troll's songs, "Freezeup Junction."

That time of night
In Freezeup Junction
Phone pole a-rammin'
Sweet God a-jammin'
Big stick whammin'
Clean through the cab
Road lights flarin'
Pigs come a-tearin'
Trucker with his legs off
Girlfriend on a slab . . .

Jed had decided the best, maybe the only way to see her again was to give a party. He asked Harry Silverman to set it up in the Blue Mood after Darlene's last set.

Harry would know who to ask. "With free booze and folk music, I could fill the Senate Building in half an hour," he said.

The Rug Cutters, booked nearby at the Cellar Door, brought their fiddles and turned on—stringbean men with decal eyes and twiny vinegreen pants and rhinestone-studded neckerchiefs. They stomped the needlepointed stock boots, beating out the news that Jesus didn't drive no fastback Ford. They battled for the microphone with three walking clumps of hair called The Human Condition while a hundred and fifty freeloading guests made soft, applauding noises never heard before in an elite music parlor like the Mood. Chicks in lacquered beehives, billowy skirts and covered-wagon shirtwaists and their bearded friends in dirty jeans patched with symbols of carefully funky elegance slugged down Jed's whiskey and gave back their own offerings onstage, in front of a huge barn-red curtain.

All kinds of people who had not been asked but had picked up the word on the rock-folk-country music grapevine mingled with the invited guests. Shitkicker Cinderellas coming on with their specialties put out such a blast that by 3:00 A.M. nobody cared that the guest of honor had not made it. Darlene was long gone, out the back way without so much as an apology—just a note to Harry, written in lipstick on a piece of cardboard torn off her tissue box: I'M SPLITTING.

Jed telephoned. She was not taking calls.

"I'm sorry," Harry told Jed. "She's manic. You know that. She gets nocturnal highs that I would need a twelve-hour Dexedrine capsule to jump to and then she'll switch into a manic low and split for a couple of days. Unless she has a paid gig to do."

"Where is she right now? Out on the town?"

"Hell no. She has too much sense for *that.* She'll be in her room, most likely, knocked out. Or she'll hit the bush."

"Bush?"

"Weed, Mr. Basco. Marijuana."

"Do you suppose she has somebody with her?"

"No. When she gets these downs she generally wants to be alone. She'll just stay someplace, won't sleep much, won't talk to you till she's climbed back to daylight."

Jed left his guests. He took a cab to Darlene's hotel. When there was no response to his knocking, he paid a maid with a pass key to let him in. The living room of the suite was littered with splinter-size pieces of a broken guitar. He picked up a string coiled in the seat of a chair like a dead snake. He was winding it foolishly around his fingers when Darlene came out of the bedroom in the old kimono with a look of dazed and sullen anger on her face.

"Why did you break the guitar?" he asked.

"I wanted to."

"Are you going to quit playing?"

"I don't know." She stared at him. "Mother's dead. She died last night."

Jed felt as if he would not be able to speak, but he looked at Georgiana's daughter and forced himself to say slowly, "Would that be a reason to stop your career?"

"It might be."

"I don't think so."

"You and I never think alike. On anything."

She put out her hand and took the string he was holding.

"This could strangle a person. I could twist it around my neck and it would strangle me."

"Oh, come off it, Darlene, for Christ's sake."

She held up the string by one end and studied it, then let it fall.

"It could have strangled Mother. Can you imagine that, my little old tranqued-up Whistler's mother deader than a mackerel! Wouldn't you like to ask me how she died? She could have OD'd like my late but unlamented boyfriend. Or the fairies might have forgotten to feed her or . . . just so many different incidents could have taken place. Only they didn't. *Because I killed her!*"

She walked past him toward the bedroom, then changed her mind and sat down in a chair.

"I plead guilty, Mr. District Attorney," she said. "Would you like to be the District Attorney? It's a juicy role."

"I wouldn't know the lines."

"I'll give you the lines. 'Was the crime premeditated, Miss Johns?' 'Yes, Mr. District Attorney, it sure as hell was.' 'Would you care to mention your motive?' 'The motive, Mr. District Attorney, was that my mother kept interfering with my life. She totaled out her own, or you, Mr. District Attorney, totaled it out for her, and when one has a leftover life to ramble through, nothing helps you along like interfering with someone else. Like, for instance, keeping the person in question away from some man.' "

Jed tried to take hold of her, but she held her body stiffly apart. He could smell pot on her breath.

"I still don't have a clue to what you mean."

"I don't blame you," she said. "I barely understood it myself. But this much I know: I killed her tonight. All of a sudden. I was going on for my first set and Harry came back and handed me a telegram. It was from her, asking me to come home before going to Little Sur. While I was reading it he said to me, 'Is it from your mother?' and I said, 'No, my mother is dead.' Harry was shocked. He said, 'When did she die? Is that what was in the telegram?' and I said, 'No, but she's dead.' And I'm telling you the same. So don't turn on for me because I look like her. I may look like her, but I'm not her. *I'm not her*. Can you grasp that fact?"

"I think so." Oddly enough, knowing Georgiana was still enjoying her spaced-out existence freed Jed more than knowledge of her death.

"I'm not sure," said Darlene. "You loved her. In spite of all you did that was so bad. Or even because of it. I respect that, it has value. Not many men love. Not many men that I know at least. Would you like a drink?"

"Not right now."

"I don't want one either. So just stay like you are and hold me. Just like you are doing, that is perfect. Only not because you are pretending I am Georgiana. I am Darlene, I am Darlene, *I am Darlene*."

"You are Darlene."

"Not good enough. *Not convincing*. Maybe you want to think of me as Georgiana. *Maybe you're still on that kick!* Which is horrible. Could that be?"

"No."

"I wonder."

With a look of infinite, childish tenderness, she touched his lips, traced their shape with her fingers, then pushed her hand down his body.

"Try this," she said. "Try saying, I love you, Georgiana, I want to make love to you, Georgiana. That's how you feel. *So say it!*"

"I want to make love to you, Darlene."

She moaned, turning in his arms. The kimono opened and so did her legs.

"Oh, that's right . . . that's it, Jed. It's not hers any more, it's mine. Put it inside me. *Put it inside of*—who am I?"

"Darlene, Darlene, Darlene, Darlene . . ."

CHAPTER THIRTEEN

PETER Baggot had just finished one of his regular interviews when he saw the little man come in. He would not have noticed him except that he walked with a queer, hitching limp and carried a folded umbrella which he was using as a cane, although the weather would have suggested opening it. Looking neither right nor left, he jostled a pretty girl who had entered at the same time and she gave him a bad look but he never even noticed it. He just limped past her into a jampacked express elevator, slamming his umbrella against the door to keep it from closing on him—a wispy, thrusting little man in dark glasses, used to having things his own way.

The girl walked up to Peter Baggot, and this time she smiled. She herself had no umbrella—her only protection against the rain was a blue scarf with frivolous gold thread running through it.

"I'm sorry to be late, Peter," she said. "Ada went to coffee first, and I had to wait until she . . . Why, what's the matter?"

Peter Baggot, like the man in dark glasses, had sprung forward, manually obstructing the operation of an elevator door to the annoyance of the passengers already inside. He said, "Go on into the coffee shop and order, baby. If I'm not there in five minutes, forget about me."

"Why, Peter," said the pretty girl with no change of expression, "you son of a bitch."

But the door had closed.

Peter Baggot scowled at the floor indicator. He weighed a series of rapid options, all of them related to the basic conjecture: When a Justice of the Supreme Court of the United States entered a building housing a variety of government services, with which lay his concern? Was he on his way to the United States District Attorney for the First Federal District? Or a cup of tea with the Office of State Department Security . . . or the Internal Revenue Service? Poor guesses, all of them.

Peter Baggot had been a knockabout, freelance journalist most of his adult life, with a consuming interest in finance. Finance was money, and money was power and power fascinated him. He held no particular brief for the culture in which he lived. He knew its faults, but he did not feel himself impelled to right them. He was an observer and a good one. Having seen the Justice in dark glasses enter the Federal Plaza complex that stormy afternoon, he knew that something newsworthy was afoot.

He rode the elevator to the offices of the Securities and Exchange Commission. When he stepped out the hall was empty. Turning to the left, he hurried along the glistening corridor which, with its recessed neon and shiny tile, made him feel as if he were in the subway rather than many floors above the ground. Baggot was thoroughly familiar with the hallways of the federal complex; they were odorless, soundless and repellant to joy. The only easing of this climate occurred during the morning and afternoon coffee breaks—an alleviation provided, oddly enough, by the imposition of a new restriction. Due to a general tightening of the government purse, brief though that was expected to be, the Commission had recommended that official personnel should not go down to the coffee shop but have their refreshment at their desks. Instead of proving disheartening, this recommendation had a contrary effect. Visits were exchanged, often between employees who would not, under different conditions, have been interested in each other. Electric coffee pots steamed fragrantly, and milk, bread, jam and cookies popped out of drawers and lockers. If a visitor happened along during such an interlude he was often invited to partake of the cheer.

No such offer was made to Peter Baggot. Madge, Mr. Sonet's secretary, was alone at her desk. With a cup at her elbow, she was reading *The Adventurers.*

"He's been called to a meeting, Mr. Baggot," she said. "Is there anything I can tell him?"

The view through the open door beside her substantiated her statement: Sonet was not at his desk.

"No," said Baggot. "Nothing important. I might look in later."

"Yes, Mr. Baggot," said Madge. She resumed her reading.

So Rupke—if that man was Rupke—was not with Sonet. Then where was he? His next most likely target would be Milton Birnbaum, the SEC's Chief Regional Counsel. Never mind *why* he would be seeing Birnbaum. That could be established after the fact, but anybody with the least knowledge of protocol knew that when a Justice of the Supreme Court wanted to speak with a Commission attorney he simply picked up the phone and told the man to come to Washington. Such at least would be the normal procedure unless the business were—well, *ex officio* . . . and not only *ex officio,* but so sensitive the Justice felt it advisable to appear in person, dark glasses and all, out of the wet of a gusty autumn afternoon.

Birnbaum's secretary was young and freckled, with bare, muscular arms. As she typed—working through her precious coffee break—the muscles in her round freckled arms fluttered aggressively and the short red hair bounced on her capable neck. She looked up as Baggot entered, then looked down again, missing his ingratiating smile.

"Can I help you?"

"Peter Baggot of *Wall Street Letter,*" Baggot said. He laid a card beside her typewriter without bothering to smile again.

"Mr. Birnbaum is in a meeting."

Could this meeting, Baggot wondered, be the same to which Sonet had been called?

"I can wait."

"It may be some time."

Baggot had already settled in a chair. He was feeling in his pocket for the makings of a cigarette. Although he was perfectly happy with store-boughts, when he wished to truly enjoy a smoke, or to annoy other people, he smoked home-mades. He smiled again, but to himself.

"I'll work it in somehow."

The secretary flipped an intercom switch.

"I know you said no calls, Mr. Birnbaum, but Peter Baggot of *Letter* is out here to see you . . . and he wants to *wait*."

Watching her face as Birnbaum answered, Baggot judged that her message had been taken as a danger alert. She switched off the intercom.

"Mr. Birnbaum is sorry. He will be tied up for the rest of the day. He wondered whether you could call him in the morning."

"That will be fine," said Baggot without moving. He sat at ease, pulling on his hand-rolled, making calculations. He had put the secretary out of his mind. She, for her part, gave Baggot a terrified glance and raised her hands. The ballplayer's bunchy muscles fluttered once more as she typed faster and faster, apparently confident that he would go away now because the words she had spoken always made people go away, and if he did not go away, the typing at least would be a comfort.

Baggot was thinking about Rupke. The Justice had come in from the street instead of from the garage. That in itself was peculiar. He had undoubtedly been using a private vehicle, a hired one, probably not carrying Justice Department plates. Nevertheless, he had certainly telephoned ahead for an appointment so that the garage would be aware that he was coming in. No one without certification could use the garage at 26 Federal Plaza. All vehicles, whether entering or leaving, were monitored on closed-circuit TV. As an added precaution, there were horn alarms which mooed electronically and stout steel barriers which flipped up and down on treadles to permit or obstruct passage from floor to floor.

The Justice hadn't come through the garage. He might have felt he would reduce conspicuity by walking directly from the street into the lobby, or he might simply have been late and sought to save time by eliminating the half block and the corner turn into the parking area. In any event, he would have told his driver to wait. And where could the driver wait but in the garage? If Baggot could find it, simply following the Justice to his next destination might provide some answers to the possible news story flagged by Rupke's trip to New York.

Baggot descended to the garage. He took his time rolling another smoke, getting himself oriented. Several vehicles, all but one displaying federal plates, were parked in the area set aside for visitors. The limo with the unofficial license was a Tanner rental—and a driver waited at the wheel. He was wearing the dark suit and visored cap of the typical pro driver.

Baggot could hear his car radio. The three-thirty newscast was winding up. Ten, at the most fifteen, minutes had elapsed since he had seen the man with the limp jam into the elevator, but at last the story, if it was a story, had begun to run.

He took one more hit on his home-made. The driver had spotted him in his rear-view mirror. Baggot could tell that without looking. Pro drivers were not private eyes, but experience made them alert to situations—sometimes more so than their employers, to whom they could, and frequently did, communicate their observations. To stand where he was any longer could be risky. Baggot dropped the half-smoked cigarette on the pavement, ground it out and took the elevator back up to the lobby. From the lobby he walked out to the street and stood at the curb until a Yellow came along. He had to circle the block three times before finding a parking place which afforded a view of the Federal Plaza garage door. There was a chance, of course, that the hired limo might emerge before the Yellow had been properly stationed—but the odds stood in Baggot's favor. The Justice, after all, would not come to New York for a fifteen-minute conversation. The meter might run quite a while. As a matter of fact it was an hour and ten minutes before Baggot saw the Tanner come out, and the cabbie, following previously transmitted instructions, fell in behind.

The limousine moved into the traffic, taking its time. At the first intersection the driver made a north turn. A few blocks farther on he swung east and continued until he reached the East River Drive, at which point he headed out for the Triborough Bridge and (was it a safe assumption?) the airline terminals beyond.

But which terminal? Baggot would soon know.

The cab driver, a young black, enjoyed the chase.

"We don't want to tailgate him, do we, man?"

"Hell, no," said Baggot. "Just don't let him get away."

"He ain't goin' no place we ain't with him, less he can fly. If he's watching, he's got us in his sights."

"Figure he's watching."

"Them kind always watch. He driving some big shot—he don't want no tail. He'll watch out of habit. But if he catch us tailgatin', he tells the man. That ain't so good. So we don't tailgate. Like that Pontiac, now. Shee-it—lookit him hump." He laughed, spinning the wheel. "You want to tailgate, Mr. Pontiac, you tailgate. Barreling home to the wife and kiddies. Give that big black Caddy something to look at besides us."

Home-going traffic was dense on the parkway: no problem hanging behind the limo while allowing other vehicles to maneuver in and out. It was almost half an hour before the Tanner wheeled onto the La Guardia offramp.

"Okay to move in close now, boss? Or do we still lay back?"

"Sit right on his license plate if you want to. This is the payola."

"You named it," said the cabbie.

The Justice, it seemed, had arrived in ample time for his flight. The moment to broach him would be while he was waiting for the boarding gate to open. He would have to issue some statement as to why he was in New York instead of Washington, and Baggot would at least be able to make a definite identification.

Baggot hoped that there would be a blessed ten or fifteen minutes before the plane left. He was operating now, as he had from the first, on a hunch, but his intuition, honed by years of training, advised him that the story could be very big indeed.

"He's in the bag now," he told the driver.

It was Baggot's first mistake. Feeling that his fare wanted him to fall back, the cabbie hesitated. Just then one of the mini-buses shuttling passengers around the airport pushed in between the limousine and the taxi; the limo made a left turn as a traffic light went red, but the shuttle stopped and the taxi stopped accordingly while Baggot sat helplessly watching the Justice's car charge ahead, past the La Guardia departure lanes in the direction of the old Marine Terminal. The cab was gaining as the limo jockeyed in an area of hangars, repair shops, fueling depots, small office shacks and airport maintenance yards.

ALL VEHICLES MUST
CHECK IN WITH OPERATIONS
BEFORE ENTERING
AIRCRAFT AREA

The sign roadblocked the four light beams. The limousine executed a right-left jog around it, the driver now well aware that he had a tail and no doubt getting orders from the back seat to floor the pedal.

"Go on," yelled Baggot.

As the cab sped ahead, he saw the sign:

STAY IN DOUBLE YELLOW LINES
SPEED 5 MPH

The streak of white on the driver's side of the cab was synchronized with the airport cop's siren. He did not stop his machine—just raised his right arm in the air and circled it, pointing back toward La Guardia. Then he waited, one foot lowered, while the cab turned around.

The limousine was gone.

"Park by the sign," Baggot told the hacker. He pushed ten dollars at him.

"You see the meter, man? You owes me thirteen."

"So wait for me."

Baggot was out and running.

BUTLER AVIATION

The big painted letters covered the end of the large building, part office, part hangar. Baggot had been here before, his visits timed to the arrivals or departures of people who traveled in private or company-owned aircraft. Previously, he had approached through the legal entrance. Now he tried a door, found it locked, continued on to one that was open and walked through it into an office corridor which led to a hangar filled with planes. Beyond the hangar was another passage, then the lounge, which resembled the central waiting room of an important corporation. Through the windows at the back Baggot spotted a small jet with harshly set-back wings and a nose like an anteater's. The plane was already in motion, heading for a takeoff area. Baggot ran across the lounge. He pressed his face against the window, trying to read the code identification painted on the high rudder, but in the glare of the lights he could not make it out. A young dispatcher was looking at him questioningly.

"You missed your plane, sir?"

"Yes, I was supposed to be aboard that Learjet, the one just taking off. Is there any way of talking to the pilot, asking him to turn back?"

"I'm afraid not, sir."

"My own fault, I guess. I didn't allow enough time for the rush-hour traffic. I'll have some explaining to do at General Electric."

"That was not a GE Learjet."

"You're positive?"

"GE flies in a Gulfstream Two. Once in a while a Hadley-Page. But no Learjet, sir."

"Well, I don't know much about planes. That certainly looks like the one I . . . Do you have a registration for it? Maybe I'm at the wrong port."

"That I can't say. But the registration—yes. We keep a data card on every aircraft serviced here. That was not a General Electric plane."

"Would a corporation executive sign the card? Or the passenger aboard?"

"The pilot signs it. Fills in what type of service is wanted. Arrival time. Estimated departure. All that."

"And you have a registration for the Learjet?"

The dispatcher hesitated, then pulled the card out of a file and flipped it on the desk. There was nothing in the scanty notation that would prove the plane's passenger had actually been Felix Linus Rupke, but now he had one positive fact in the welter of rumors that had sent him to Chicago, ten days earlier, on the trip that had ended with the confrontation in Jed's hospital room.

Jed Basco had lent his Learjet to somebody, and the person who had used it had paid a call that afternoon on Milton Birnbaum. It might not be much, but it was enough on which to base an educated guess. Baggot found a coin and dropped it into a pay telephone.

Luck was with him. Milton Birnbaum had not yet left for the day.

"Yes, Mr. Baggot," Birnbaum said when his secretary put through the call.

"Hello, Mr. Birnbaum," Baggot said. "Regarding Justice Rupke's visit with you today—was any particular subject discussed?"

Silence. Birnbaum was making up his mind—to confirm or to deny? Birnbaum must know, from his secretary's red alert, that he, Peter Baggot, had been seated in the reception room while the Justice was inside. Easy to deny, if that was all, but where was Baggot when Felix left? For all Birnbaum knew Baggot might even have spoken with his visitor. After a pause he said, "The Justice was here today, yes. He and I are old friends. He was in the neighborhood on business and . . . he dropped in for a chat. That was about the extent of it."

"Then I take it your conversation did not relate to the Commission's investigation into certain irregularities at Basco and Western?"

"Hardly, Mr. Baggot, since at the present time I am not aware of any such irregularities. Nor, I am sure, is Justice Rupke."

Baggot did not miss the phrase "at the present time"—Birnbaum's protection in the event that the irregularities later were established and made public.

"I understand, Mr. Birnbaum. Thank you very much."

"Don't mention it. Thank you for calling."

"One more question . . . if I may."

"Yes?"

"If or when," said Peter Baggot, his tone perceptibly hardening, "there are any, er, future developments between the Commission and Basco and Western, can you inform me in advance of official release?"

Birnbaum chuckled, but he did not sound amused.

"Well, that's pretty hard to guarantee, Baggot," he said. "We have a policy here, as I'm sure you know. Whatever happens in this office is considered confidential, until such time as we feel the public ought to be informed."

"I understand," said Baggot. "I would just like to be informed first. In time to have an exclusive story for my paper. That is, assuming that the Justice's visit with you today is not newsworthy."

Birnbaum did not need an umpire to tell him when to pick up his marbles.

"I'll see what I can do," he said. "Goodbye, Mr. Baggot."

"Goodbye, sir," said Baggot.

He hung up, then dialed the Washington office of his paper collect.

"Edgar, Pete here."

"Jesus, Pete, we're just locking up."

"I know. So don't make me repeat. Pull the morgue envelopes on Felix Rupke and Jed Basco and put everything on the Overnight that would indicate a tie-in."

"Felix was counsel for Basco Precision . . ." began Edgar.

"I know all that. The Senate went into it at some length. What I want to know is every place they might have been in contact. The Department of Commerce. Those dams. The whole bit. It's urgent and *classified.*"

Baggot replaced the speaker and went out to where the Yellow cabbie was still waiting. The meter reading, by the time he got back to the city, was twenty-seven dollars. He had the cab drop him off at Danny's Hideaway, where he consumed three whiskeys, a porterhouse with onion rings and a baked potato. Muhammad Ali, Shirley MacLaine and Paul Newman were dining in the Celebrity Room (not together). Newman said hello to him and Danny let him sign the chit. Afterward he went home to a cranny above the East River which he shared with a cat, some photographs, an excellent hi-fi set and the memories of two failed marriages. He felt he had done a good day's work.

Reaching his office in the morning, he found an overnight teletype from Edgar.

RE RUPKE

NO BASCO HOOKUP. SUBJECT SOLD ALL CORPORATE HOLDINGS INCLUDE B & W IBM US STEEL GEN MOTORS ET AL. RESIGNED FROM LAW FIRM. THE MAN'S SPARE TIME IF ANY BLESSED AND SANCTIFIED ONLY BY GEORGETOWN U (TRUSTEE) TEXAS A & M (TRUSTEE) FELLOW AM. BAR. AM. LAW INSTITUTE. AM. BAR ASS. AM. LAW INSTITUTE INSTITUTE OF POLITICAL SCIENCE SCABBARD AND BLADE PI SIGMA ALPHA PHI BET CAP. EVERGREEN FOUNDATION (TRUSTEE AND GEN COUNSEL) SORRY OLD BUDDY

EDGAR

It did not look hopeful, but one fact caught Baggot's eye—the one legal post Rupke had retained was with the only organization which Peter Baggot could not immediately identify. The Evergreen Foundation. What was that? The index of U.S. non-profit corporations gave it two lines: "Purpose: Student aid for overseas law studies, etc. Chartered Delaware 1965." It was a meager lead, but Baggot bundled himself once more into a cab, then onto a plane and flew down to Dover to see what, in the archives of the State Corporation Commission, he could find out about Evergreen.

CHAPTER FOURTEEN

AN attorney for a government authority as prestigious as the Securities and Exchange Commission is no stranger to the forces of influence. Milton Birnbaum knew how pressure was applied. You would receive, from a prominent broker for instance, a letter asking for an interpretation of an SEC ruling which somehow concealed in its carefully oblique syntax a screeching pitch for your connivance in a fraud. Or a go-between would telephone inviting you to meet a third person for lunch and you would decline because, should you accept, a face taut with panic would stare at you from across the table saying, in effect, "Just this one time, old boy, or I'm done for."

The methods of appeal were as various as the nature of man, but nothing in Birnbaum's career had prepared him for a head-on assault by a Justice of the Supreme Court. Felix had said that he would be in New York the following day and could he drop in? (Could the mountain call on Mohammet?)

"I should be honored, Mr. Justice," Birnbaum had said, and Rupke had thanked him.

"Fine, Milt. Would after lunch, maybe three, three-thirty, be convenient?"

Birnbaum had said that three-thirty would be satisfactory. And where, he wondered, did the Justice get that "Milt"? From the New York Bar Association dinner at which they had talked for some five or ten minutes? It was remarkable how intimacy ripened when the great sought favors.

Justice Rupke had not gone straight to Birnbaum's floor, as Baggot had calculated. Instead, he had employed a maneuver designed to mislead any one of the persons in the elevator who might have recognized him and looked to see where he got out. Felix had selected a floor two stories above Birnbaum's. He hitched along the tubular hall, then charged down by way of the fire stairway. The secretary had announced him less than five minutes before Baggot's arrival. At that time the conversation inside was still exploratory.

Felix Rupke had cut a cigar and placed it in his mouth. Birnbaum had proffered the desk lighter. The Justice turned the cigar in his thin fingers, scrutinizing the moist place his lips had made on the end.

"The truth is, Milton, the boys at B and W are worried. Steve Vishniak, the admiral, they're good people, solid friends. Nevertheless, it's not in their interest that I'm bringing this matter to your attention. . . . It's the investors who would be hurt most if things got ugly."

"I understand," said Birnbaum.

"They're disturbed."

"They have reason," said Birnbaum.

The Justice waved his hand. "They have, they have, of course," he said heartily, "but on the other hand . . ." His lips puckered into their characteristic droop.

"I'm afraid," said Birnbaum, "that the regulation is explicit on the point at issue—Section Five, Paragraph One of the Act of 1935."

"Ah . . ." said Felix Rupke. He gave Milton Birnbaum a look which pierced clear to the core of Milton Birnbaum's being. "I had hoped," he said, "that we would not take positions. I've come to you, off the record, to examine some options; that is the full reach of my intent. Do you mind if we pursue that line before we set up an obstacle course?"

Birnbaum thought: Here comes the ballbreaker. All right, I've been kicked before, and your shoe, Mr. Justice, will not feel so very different from what I used to get from the gangland buttonmen.

"We can explore whatever you've in mind, Mr. Justice."

Felix Rupke, his good humor restored, smiled at Birnbaum across the barren, institutional desk.

"Well, for a start," he said, "Section Four, Subparagraph Two, 'transaction by an issuer not involving any public offering . . .' The language defines the exemption given individuals who are not underwriters to negotiate the sales of unregistered stock."

"You feel that the sales we are discussing come under the scope of that exemption?"

"Well, perhaps not all. But let's take a random instance. One thousand shares to Mrs. Oscar Tanheimer, 461 Riverdale Avenue, Bronxville. Mrs. Tanheimer has been reimbursed in full, and she has withdrawn her complaint."

"She did," said Birnbaum. "Mrs. Tanheimer got shares from Donovan and Klein, and Donovan and Klein sold other shares, big blocks of them, to numerous other clients —Keith Koffend of Allied Investors to name one. Donovan and Klein are underwriters. They bought B and W unregistered stock from somebody. Donovan and Klein are guilty in violation of the act, as is the individual who sold them the stock . . . and from there the chain of responsibility extends right back to B and W and its board. No one is exempt, Mr. Justice, not even, regretfully, your friends. You will observe that I did not refer to them as your clients."

"So what are you going to do?" snapped Rupke.

"I'm tracing back those sales."

"And then?"

"Then," said Birnbaum, "I'm going to submit a criminal reference report for the Justice Department against Donovan and Klein, against the original seller of the stock, against Basco and Western and its board of directors, collectively and individually. After that the matter is out of my hands."

Felix Rupke blew smoke rings. They eddied up toward the ceiling like signals from an Apache war party closing in on a wagon train.

"Milt," he said thoughtfully, "you're putting yourself to a lot of trouble."

"Oh, not all that much, sir," Milton Birnbaum said. "This is all fairly routine."

"You're raising a big stink—over nothing." The Justice

was well aware that this last statement was in direct contradiction to his own warnings to Jed, but situations could often alter judgments.

"No, Mr. Justice. My job is to apply the law as incorporated in the Securities and Exchange Acts. I do not feel, with all respect to you, that our functions overlap."

Birnbaum smiled at Rupke. His pale, aquiline face looked engaging when he smiled. It also looked formidable.

"Mr. Birnbaum," Felix said, "I didn't come here to obtain a lecture on jurisprudence. I came to see if we couldn't resolve a sticky situation which could be needlessly costly to the people concerned. Screw all this horsing around. I'm familiar with your record. You were a knight in shining armor out in the Bronx, with a walk-up private practice over a bail-bond office and a few extra bucks a month as a public defender. When you became an assistant county district attorney, you threw the book at all the shitkickers who had once moved you to such compassion. You have an uncle who is a federal judge. He wedged an opening for you with the SEC and you rose through the ranks. Bully for you. But don't blister me with that gleam on your helmet. I'm not dazzled. The SEC, by precedent, has withheld prosecution in cases where, after some regulatory violation, restitution has been made."

Birnbaum sat studying his knuckles, tightly clasped on his desk. If he was having a struggle to keep his temper, the effort did not show in his voice.

"The precedent you mention, Mr. Justice, is the only portion of your argument which I regard as relevant. Yes, there is such precedent—unofficial, of course, but well established. If recision of all the transactions in the unregistered stock were effected before the end of last week, I suggested that I would not press the criminal reference procedure. No such recision, with the exception of the one you noted, has so far been made."

Felix stubbed out his cigar.

"Milton," he said good-humoredly, "I have something to say on that score. This concerns only one of the participants in the negotiation—Mr. Jedson C. Basco. He, as you know, is the prime mover in the stockholders' protest against current management policies. He is, quite frankly, fighting to get his company back."

Birnbaum nodded. "I thought we would come around to Mr. Basco—sooner or later," he said, not without a certain irony.

"Well, sir," said Felix, "I told him your conditions which had, er, been conveyed to me. I told him what he had to do. He agreed. He even went out someplace—God knows where—and borrowed the money."

"Then why didn't he buy it back—the letter stock? Does he still intend to reimburse the buyers?"

"It may be his intention, Milt," said Rupke, "but it's not within his competency. The damn fool put the proceeds of that loan into his brokerage account. He bought more B and W common. Stupid, I'll admit, but he's frantic to win this proxy fight."

Milton Birnbaum, who had turned from his visitor, as if to rest his eyes, now squared his chair around.

"I must limit my concurrence to one phrase, Mr. Justice. Damn fool."

"Agreed," Felix said. "But couldn't you give him just a little more time? The shareholders' meeting takes place in eleven days. I'll make you this promise: After the meeting, Basco and Western will issue properly registered common Class A to all holders of the Class B letter stock. Won't that satisfy the requirements of the Commission?"

"You mean Basco and Western will issue the stock—provided Jed C. Basco wins his fight."

"That is right. You're not running for re-election, Mr. Birnbaum. You hold your office by appointment. For my part, I hope you hold it for the rest of your life. But not if you use it to draw attention to yourself at the cost of financial loss to the very people your Commission was created to protect."

"You mean, if I refuse to take orders from you, you'll get me fired?"

"I neither said nor implied that."

"I understand that implication."

"Mr. Birnbaum," said Felix, "any attorney worthy of his bar certificate must recognize that the intent of statute is as relevant as its language. In this case—"

"—In this case, Mr. Justice," said Birnbaum, "my opinion is what counts, not yours. I don't do business that way."

Two small white patches had appeared on Felix's cheekbones.

"So that's the way we leave it?"

"Yes, I'd say so. And thanks for reminding me what a punk I used to be with my crummy office and my indigent clients—and then what a bastard I was for prosecuting those same types later. Well, you stand arraigned for your own argument, Mr. Justice. I did my best as a public defender. I did what I was hired to do. Later, I did my best as prosecutor and right now I'm doing my best when I send up a criminal reference for these highly placed friends of yours. I've risen as high in my life as I'm likely to, which isn't very high. You, Mr. Justice, have achieved the grandest place our legal system makes available. You're an eminent man, but I don't like eminent people pulling rank on me—and the higher up they are, the more I resent it. I'm going to press my investigation of the B and W stock as hard as I know how and, if I turn up the evidence I need, I'll move for an indictment as fast as possible. So get me fired if you can. At least I'll be able to live with myself."

The Justice got up slowly. The little circles, like poker chips, on his cheeks had regained their normal color, but his voice grated as if he were having trouble breathing.

"You make me ashamed of being a lawyer, Mr. Birnbaum," he said.

Birnbaum also rose. Erect, he was considerably taller than Felix.

"Mr. Justice, you make me ashamed of being a Jew."

Felix rang Jed Basco on the telephone later that day. "He's playing a role, and he loves every minute of it—cleansing the sepulchre. He's going ahead with the criminal reference report."

"How much time have we got?"

"None, he says. But that's an element that is still negotiable."

"What do you mean, negotiable?"

"I'm going to put some muscle on him."

"I thought *you* were the muscle."

"There's still one or two places I can go. It boils down to this: Can you win at the shareholders' meeting or can't you?"

"I can win and I will win. Unless some United States marshal slaps a warrant on me."

"I can see you're learning some respect for the law."

"Felix," said Jed pleadingly, "I've been sitting in a sweatbox for three days. Tell me how this thing can work, so I won't blow my mind."

"Let's put it this way. In between a criminal reference and an indictment there is a twilight zone where delays can occur. The Justice Department can send the case back for further evidence. Getting the evidence will naturally take more time. Then there's a chance that even the amplified report might not be considered substantive. There have been cases where submissions and requests went back and forth until the statute of limitations ran out. You don't need that much time."

"I need eleven days."

"You'll get them. All I can tell you is, you'd better win."

"I'm going to."

"All right. Keep your pecker up. And bear this in mind. Whatever I do from here on in, I'm not doing for you. Birnbaum called me a bad Jew. I intend to make him eat it."

CHAPTER FIFTEEN

"MR. Basco," Rice said, "the annual meeting is now six days away. We are down to the finish line. You need a majority. If you walk into the meeting room with fifty and one one-thousandth of one percent of the stock of Basco and Western, you are tall in the saddle. If you walk in with forty-nine and nine hundred and ninety-nine and nine one-thousandths of one percent, you're dead. I believe you will have a majority. There is no way to be sure."

"Your belief is heartening," Jed said. "On what do you base it?"

They were talking once more in Rice's house on the tall palisade above the river. Waiting for Rice's answer, Jed looked down at the pewter-colored sweep of the chilly water. A barge was being towed upstream. It would be pleasant, he thought, to be one of the men navigating the tugs.

"In the past six weeks," Rice said, "we have talked by telephone or in person with everyone holding one thousand shares or more of Basco and Western stock. We've mailed solicitations to *all* stockholders, each letter setting forth why the recipients should vote for you, and enclosed a proxy card for them to do it with. So far fifty-seven and eight-tenths percent of the proxies returned have been signed in your favor."

"Is that good or bad?"

"It's damn good, but it's not conclusive."

"It's almost eight percent more than the minimum we need."

"But . . . stockholders are a screwy bunch. They'll sign your proxy, then along comes management's letter and they'll sign management's proxy too. The last dated is the one that counts. Some people sign any goddam thing that makes them feel important. Let's say we have a better than even chance. But there are major factors still to be dealt with."

"Go ahead."

"The mutual funds hold big blocks of B and W and they traditionally vote with management. It's all very well to represent yourself as the down-to-earth dam builder being fleeced by city slickers, but the slickers have been paying the dividends and the old school ties look at the monthly statements and ignore the drama. Banks go with management. Trust funds go with management. That is what we're bucking. All I can say is that we're hanging in there. And we'll see what happens."

The dimensions of the contest made it newsworthy. *Time* gave it half a column on the Business page, with a picture of Jed climbing out of a Skip. *U.S. News & World Report* compared it to proxy fights of the past and gave the story a full page. Most of the stories were slanted toward him. *Newsweek* called him "last of the concrete dinosaurs" in a paragraph that provided an expressive profile of his engineering expertise and corporate naïveté. Only *Wall Street Letter* shaded negatives, but after all, *Letter* was not a major opinion maker.

Jed found further encouragement in two happenings which took place on the same day.

A large box airmailed from Durango, Mexico, arrived at the office. Jed hadn't known that Darlene was in Durango. Neither, apparently, had Harry Silverman; she had disappeared after the Blue Mood engagement, and efforts to locate her in Nashville (where she had been scheduled to cut a record), Los Angeles and Chicago had produced no clues. The big box did. It contained a Mexican-style ten-gallon sombrero with turquoise and silver hatband into which she had tucked a note:

> You will look good wearing this while you brand those critters at the stockholders' meeting.
>
> Love,
> DARLENE

Jed regarded the hat as a luck piece and hung it over his bed. He was equally pleased by his son's unexpected appearance at Donovan & Klein's when the market opened. He had shaved off his beard and mustache. He wore steel-rimmed GI-issue spectacles and ODs with battle ribbons and the gold horse's head, the divisional insignia of the First Armored Cavalry. His hair was cut so short his scalp looked naked, and he had bought himself some false teeth in a joke store which gave him a no-time-for-sergeants, hillbilly look. Jed walked past without recognizing him. Bob had to whistle to bring him back.

"The FBI?" he said when Jed had pulled him into his office. "Sure, they caught up with me. They questioned me four or five times. I came up clean because my organization runs itself. All I have to do is spot-check, like in Pasadena, and pass out the money. Now if they want to bust me for something, they can bust me for wearing this uniform. There's a federal law that says I can only wear my uniform when I'm on active duty with the ready reserve. But the FBI isn't looking for butch-haircut First Lieutenant Basco, the hero of Vietnam. They want the hairy son of a bitch who's been running deserters to Canada. I could stand outside FBI headquarters all day long and no one would speak to me."

"I'd still feel more comfortable underground, if I were you."

"I like to be where the action is, and right now it's with you. Also, I brought you something that may help."

"I could use something."

"Then take a look."

The proxy was signed "Dorothy McGettigan Basco."

"How did you get that?"

"I explained to her that without you, B and W would lose its value."

"Her father told her the same thing would happen without *him*."

"She never believed her father. But tell me, how's it going?"

"We've got it locked up."

Jed pulled out tabulations, showed Bob the proxy count, described his trouble with the SEC, adding that he hoped Felix was bringing this problem under control. Bob nodded, his eyes serious and his manner attentive, only occasionally interrupting to ask his father questions.

"But that Mafia money—isn't that touchy?"

"No risk whatsoever," Jed said with conviction. "They'll get back their principal and interest on time. Right out of the company treasury."

Bob lay back in his chair, his blouse unbuttoned in a most unsoldierly manner.

"I wouldn't want to see you in a crossfire between Bobby Kennedy's federal agents and Angiacomo's torpedoes."

"I'm not worried."

"All right, Dad. I just mentioned that *in case* Felix Rupke doesn't score."

"He will, son." Jed made a tight chopping gesture. "I haven't told you everything about my personal relations with the Justice. He's under certain obligations . . ."

"Is Angiacomo too?"

"No, but I don't have to wear a bulletproof vest. Most of Angiacomo's deals are as legitimate as the Chase Manhattan's."

"Bully for him."

"Then what are you getting at?"

"Just that I like to see you with as many options as possible."

"Do you have one to submit?"

Bob Basco wrote a number on a scrap of paper and

pushed it toward his father. "Put this in your wallet. *Just in case.*"

"What is it?"

"A rescue line."

"I'm not tracking you."

"This is the national service number for our Underground. It's a hot line for deserters, COs who don't have CO official status, guys who have escaped from the stockade."

Jed looked annoyed. "You classifying me with those bums?"

"Just to this extent—they want out, and you might too at some point. If you do, call that number."

"Then what happens?"

"Then you go where we tell you—or if you're stuck someplace we come and get you. We've sprung people from county lockups and even post stockades. We've got the know-how, the vehicles and the connections. A few days after you contact us you can be in Canada or Mexico or Sweden. You might prefer Brazil. No extradition."

Jed was still angry. He folded and refolded the slip of paper until it was the size of a dime.

"It will be a cold day in hell before I cop out."

"I hope you have no reason to."

"I won't have," Jed said, mollified. "But I—you know. I appreciate your thought. I do appreciate that."

He dropped the pellet of paper on the desk.

"Put it in your pocket," Bob said.

Jed did so. "Are you satisfied now?"

"I am," said Bob. "And in any case I intend to stay until the fight's over. Let's go to lunch. My treat."

"No, I'll take you to lunch," Jed said. "Any son willing to freight his dear old dad out of the country with a load of military castoffs deserves the best. Where do you want to eat?"

The day of the meeting, the sun burned a furnace-red hole through the smog above the East River. Bob and Jed breakfasted together. MacNeice took away the breakfast dishes and got out the car. Jed wore a charcoal-gray business suit to emphasize his appearance as an executive, but then topped it with the silver-banded Pancho Villa sombrero Darlene had sent from Mexico.

He was just leaving the condominium to drive to the meeting when he found his way blocked by two husky young workmen carrying in his gun cabinet.

"Where'd this come from?"

"You got the order, Wilbur?" said one of the workmen. Wilbur fished an invoice from his shirt pocket and handed it silently to Jed. "Would you sign, sir?"

Putting the paper on top of the cabinet, Jed read it carefully. The other name written on the line designating *Shipper* was Steve Vishniak. Steve must have asked that the invoice be sent up for Jed's personal signature. It was a challenge to single combat.

Well, we'll see about that, Jed thought. But he didn't like getting the cabinet back. Its return was a point of gamesmanship in Steve's favor. It was not a good omen. Jed tried to concentrate on the more favorable aspects of the contest as MacNeice drove to the Waldorf-Astoria, where the meeting was to be held.

CHAPTER SIXTEEN

AS a builder and a construction man Jed had always taken joy in his work. There was excitment in it, especially on the first day when you arrived at the site with the marking tape on the trees and the stakes in the ground and the heavy equipment rolling up and he, the boss, unlocked his trailer and checked the blueprint thumbtacked to the board. There was joy in the stir of intent, pleasure in the creased morning faces of the men in the hardhats, the workers stretching out the kinks resulting from a bumpy ride in a truck, estimating the ground and the weather and the problems of the work ahead. Dealings in finance on the other hand struck Jed as insubstantial, complicated and menacing. In the last few weeks he had acted only out of necessity, staking himself recklessly, eager for a score, but also impatient to shed this distraction and move back to something more tangible.

Standing in the doorway of the hotel ballroom, he was sorry that his fate could not be decided on a different field. Building held no mysteries for him. He understood its essence, but about the real nature of money he knew far less. Here was an oblong, ornate room, filled with perhaps five hundred people moving around, talking, putting their heads together over papers, coming and going through the doors at the back. These were the money people. Give them a stick of blasting powder and they would have blown their heads off. Give them a thousand tons of prestressed concrete and they would have been able to produce nothing better than a titan-size mud pie. But they weren't dealing with dynamite or concrete; they were dealing with money, and in this room it was Jed who was essentially the novice.

"Who is that character by himself up there?"

Jed jerked his thumb at a man sitting at a small table on the ballroom stage. There was a box in front of him with a slit in the top.

"He's the inspector of elections."

"He counts the votes?"

Donovan, to whom he'd put the question, nodded.

Shareholders climbed onto the stage by means of the steps on the right, crossed to the box, then exited down the steps on the left. Some of them signed proxies, leaning on the table to do so, and dropped these proxies into the slit in the box. Others took samplings from one or both piles of mail-out literature and went off, presumably to read what they had selected.

"Jesus, you would have thought they'd have studied that stuff by this time."

"Some of them have, some haven't. And I guess a good many want a second look. They can change their minds as often as they like, you know."

Rice, standing between Jed and Donovan, chewed an unlit cigar.

"Mind if I snoop around a little?"

He patted Jed on the shoulder and walked off, heading toward some elderly people in a corner of the room. Thorpe was addressing them, punctuating his remarks with copious gestures. Pulaski strolled by. He had on a pepper-and-salt suit that looked as if it had been made by a prison tailor, his big beer belly bulging it out in front. He moved along the rows of shareholders in the banks of wooden chairs handing out Xeroxed material. Admiral Stranahan's gray hair bushed above his small, mean face like a soiled halo. He stood near a window, making notes on a scratch pad.

As Jed's gaze cased the room he was surprised to see Kitty and Willie. They were dressed as if for a cocktail party, insulated in a private climate they had brought with them. Kitty must have persuaded Willie that attendance at the meeting was a family obligation and did not connote involvement in a corporate activity. Willie could be counted on to meet social obligations promptly.

"Dad . . ."

Bob Basco took Jed's arm, pressing him back toward the doorway. Donovan and Rice followed them out. The congestion in the mezzanine consisted in two conflicting movements, the shareholders trying to get in butting against those coming out. Many of the latter carried the Xeroxed sheets.

"I've got a copy of it," Bob said in his father's ear.

Jed tried to see the paper Bob was holding, but Donovan had quietly removed it from Bob's hand.

THE WHEELER DEALER AND THE JUDGE.

Jed read that much as Donovan unfolded the copy.

"An article in *Letter* . . ."

Donovan's Irish face revealed no reaction. He stuck the paper in his pocket.

"Let's go down to the bar," he said.

He spread the sheets on the table as the waiter took their order.

"Sweet Jesus Christ," he said as he finished the first page.

"Is it that bad?"

"It is not good."

He handed the page to Jed, who promptly put it down.

"I don't want to read it. Just tell me what it says."

Rice picked up the page.

"*Letter* has discovered there was a, quote, personal relationship between you and recently appointed Supreme Court Justice Felix Linus Rupke, unquote. . . ."

"We've been friends for years. What has that got to do with–"

"Wait!" Donovan scanned the rest of that page, then another. "Hmmm, *Wall Street Letter* reveals exclusively that the SEC has been preparing a criminal reference report."

"What's that?" asked Bob.

"They're tracing the sale of the unregistered stock. But the sales are only part of this stink. *Letter* is implying that you had some kind of hold over Rupke. That you entered into a conspiracy with him to fix your trouble with the SEC."

"Nobody can prove that. What's more, I'm ready to sue them for—"

Rice read over Donovan's shoulder, passing the pages to Bob Basco.

"They allege and I quote that 'Jed Basco visited Justice Rupke in his law offices the day after the President's appointment. At that time the board of Basco and Western had already removed Basco as president of the big conglomerate . . .' Let's see. Some more like this . . . and then . . ."

"Bullshit."

"Take it easy, Dad," said Bob. He put a calming hand on his father's arm. Let's find out what they've got before we blow our cool."

"Listen," said Donovan. "Here it is. '*Letter* has confirmed that shortly before the date scheduled for the annual meeting of Basco and Western shareholders, Justice Rupke flew from Washington to New York in a private airplane. From La Guardia Airport he drove to the office of Milton Birnbaum, Chief Counsel for the Securities and Exchange Commission, with whom he spent over an hour.

" 'Mr. Birnbaum refused either to confirm or deny that the criminal reference proceedings against Jed Basco were the subject of the conversation. Immediately after the visit, Justice Rupke flew back to Washington, using a Learjet owned by Jed Basco. . . .' "

"Why, this is all about Felix! He's the one they're after—not me."

Donovan looked at Bob, then down at his glass.

"Dad, read the next page."

Jed read: "While a member of the High Court, Rupke continued to receive an annual fee of $15,000 for services performed for the Basco Family Foundation, a tax-free corporation set up two years ago by Jed Basco. The fee would seem unusually large in view of the fact that actual gifts to charity, college fellowship aids and other expenditures of the Foundation during a three-year period totaled $11,756. Possibly Rupke was drawing his compensation to advise the Foundation what not to spend money for, in which case it would appear that he earned it many times over. One cannot rule out the possibility that . . ."

Jed's head came up again. He kept his finger on the offending paragraph, as if pressing the throat of an enemy.

"Are we back to the days of guilt by association? Christ, you don't have to tell me what a smear can do. Sometimes it's worse than proof. All right, if that's what Steve and those bastards are counting on, I'll make them change their tune."

Donovan motioned for quiet. Jed's voice was attracting attention.

"Sure, it's a smear, Jed. It's dirty pool. And I agree, the target would seem to be Rupke rather than you. But you must realize the effect this is going to have on—"

"Realize! What in hell do you think I'm talking about? Maybe Steve even *planted* this crap in *Letter*. Whapped it in there to divert attention from our statement to the shareholders showing that current management has been negligent and in addition—"

Bob Basco interrupted. He faced Donovan, his face as angry as his father's.

"Dad's right. The thrust of this isn't directed against Dad. This writer, Baggot, was after political game. He just happened to hit Dad with a stray bullet."

"The check from the Basco Foundation was no stray bullet," said Donovan.

A lump of ice jumped out of a glass, landing in Bob's lap. Jed had hit the table with his fist.

"Gentlemen, we're still hanging in there. The meeting can blow wide open any minute. I'm going to talk to them. Then we'll see."

The shareholders in the big, drafty room with its pink walls and gilt moldings were quieter now. Most of them had seated themselves in the wooden chairs banked in the center of the floor, while Steve Vishniak whipped through the agenda like a hillbilly auctioneer selling a foreclosed farm. Behind him, at the table Jed had observed before, the inspector of elections listened while the lawyers for both sides argued over the admission of certain proxies and the exclusion of others.

Admiral Stranahan asked that the floor be opened for motions and resolutions. Steve Vishniak said that it was so ordered. He nodded to Pulaski, who straightened his soiled tie and launched into a review of management's slate, amplifying each nomination with a dossier of homely anecdotes to show what a comfortable, down-to-earth and, at the same time, brilliant and elevated fellow the candidate was—and how indispensable to the future of B & W. He was winding up his peroration on the last name when Rice nudged Jed. "Here we go," he whispered.

He held up a hand.

"Point of order, Mr. Chairman. We have heard the eminent qualifications of the incumbent directors. Is there—or am I wrong?—a place on the agenda for the Basco and Western Stockholders' Protective Association to present its nominations?"

"The Chair will be pleased to hear any further nominations."

"Thank you. Mr. Jed Basco will address the meeting in behalf of the Association."

"The Chair recognizes Mr. Jedson C. Basco."

As Vishniak spoke a bellboy took a message up to the lectern. Vishniak made quite a performance of opening it. Jed, meanwhile, was charging toward the platform with Rice, Donovan and Bob trailing after him.

Jed was tired now. It had been a long haul, putting everything together, combing the discards of his life for something: he was not sure what—a secret hoard of strength or mislaid loyalty, a treasure or a terror that would clarify the extent of what had happened, as a man whose house has burned might poke in the ashes, the unmelted kitchenware and the scorched springs of the upstairs beds, now fallen to the cellar, looking for his wife's jewels or the body of a child. He was tired but not so tired he couldn't mount one last attack.

There was a brisk, welcoming spatter of applause as he mounted the steps onto the stage—not an ovation, but enough to prove there were some people out there who remembered. He ducked his head and smiled, acknowledging the greeting. Steve was still holding the bellboy's message, reading it, apparently for a second or third time while Jed stood ill at ease waiting for Steve, if not to introduce him, at least to move away and let him speak; he clasped and unclasped his hands, let his eyes roam over the audience, then upward to the ballroom chandeliers, one of them glinting in a beam of light, and in that moment—though there was no possible connection—he could see, as if projected on the ceiling, some kind of tracing or picture, terribly familiar, yet hard to remember—the design he had drawn with his finger in the earth in front of the campfire on the night Vishniak had taken his job away. The design had been a tower, such a tower as a second-grader might draw, with one window, yes, and with curves and crenellations in the roof of it, playful and gay little curlicues somehow full of doom—because inside, if you looked closely, you could see the foundations slowly crumbling.

Steve Vishniak was holding up his hand. When the stockholders failed to pay attention he rapped on the lectern with his big seal ring. Finally the audience quieted and Vishniak raised the message he had been reading.

"Before we hear Mr. Basco's remarks, I must make an announcement. The Board of Governors of the New York Stock Exchange has suspended trading in the stock of Basco and Western."

The reporters were waiting for Felix when he left his chambers. They stuck beside him in the hallway, some running ahead to turn and take pictures, holding cameras over their heads. Others waited outside, standing between him and the big car with the government plates. They were mostly young men, many with beards and long hair. They shouted at him, none too politely, asking about the Foundation salary, how long had he known Mr. Basco, whether he had promised the contractor immunity. Felix snapped his answers right and left, never breaking his stride, head down, briefcase swinging.

The car door slammed. One reporter lost his balance, flipping backward to keep from being run over, and the long-haired and bearded and none too friendly gentlemen of the press snapped their last candids, aiming through the glass at the little man in the back seat, and the big car laid rubber getting out of there.

CHAPTER SEVENTEEN

RULE 499 of the New York Stock Exchange consists of a single sentence: "Securities admitted to the list may be suspended from trading or removed from the list at any time."

Rice called the sentence to Jed's attention, pointing out that the Exchange could act with or without reason:

> Failure of a company to make timely, adequate and accurate disclosures of information to its shareholders and the investing public . . . or other conduct not in keeping with sound public policy or . . . any other event or conditions that may exist or occur that make further dealings and listing of the securities on the Exchange inadvisable or unwarranted . . . in the opinion of the Exchange . . .

The opinion of the Exchange. Arbitrary, ineluctable. Not that there was anything so horrendous, *per se*, in a suspension of trading. Such action was not uncommon. Trading could be resumed as soon as the technicalities that bothered the List Department had been cleared away. But the timing of Vishniak's strategy had been masterful. Jed had tried talking to the stockholders, explaining how management had failed, but he could tell that they were tuning him out. Suddenly he was a bad guy, stirring up trouble with the SEC—gunfire at O.K. Corral! Did General Motors set the sheriff to strapping on his Colts? Did Du Pont or AT&T start bullets buzzing and horses squealing and the bartenders putting up the shutters? Hell no, and as for a man who could initiate that kind of rumble, maybe Vishniak was right, maybe old Basco, the dam builder, had caused the third-quarter losses, not the sanctimonious junk dealer's son. Before he had even finished, some of the bastards were hoofing down the aisle to get new proxy cards.

It took two days to make a detailed tabulation, but Donovan ran a tally of his own and by the time the last voter left the Waldorf ballroom, the Stockholders' Protective Association knew it was done for. Now the problem was to see what could be salvaged.

Rice, Donovan, Jed and Bob Basco and four accountants from Price, Waterhouse, together with a very punctilious lawyer named Threadnall, representing Donovan & Klein, sat late for several nights in Jed's condominium with the papers spread out on the dining-room table and MacNeice tiptoeing in and out, serving drinks and sandwiches. Then abruptly the work was done and Jed was suddenly alone. For some reason he began to think about the old days when Felix Rupke had been a friend, a man making it the hard way. There had been no challenge

Felix couldn't meet, no problem he couldn't fix. Jed would walk into Felix's office with a problem and Felix would say, "Give me the figures."

Never take a note. He might write it up later, showing how it would all work out, but while Jed spoke he would just tilt his chair back and listen, nodding once in a while, letting a picture form in his mind.

Jed knocked back a little whiskey, and hunger for the past rose out of the misery of his bones. Something clicked in his mind and he realized that, even now, Felix wasn't all that far away. It was after three o'clock in the morning, but he dialed a Washington number and let it buzz half a dozen times before he gave up. He turned on a hot shower and was about to get into it when the doorbell rang—not the intercom the doorman used for announcing visitors but the pushbutton of the penthouse door.

Jed hooked a towel around his waist and waited. MacNeice was up. Jed heard him thumping around in his room and then he too was out in the hall, holding a maroon bathrobe closed with one hand and pointing a short-barreled revolver with the other.

He looked around at Jed and both had the same idea. MacNeice knew as well as his boss that Hudson Federated's loan was already five days overdue. This individual leaning on the doorbell could be Angiacomo's collector.

Jed motioned MacNeice to put away his hog-leg. Then he walked past him to the door and opened it himself and in came Felix Rupke, prim as a rabbi in a black homburg hat and a dark Burberry raincoat, shaking the wet off his umbrella. He smiled at Jed but made no motion to shake hands, as if not quite sure of his reception.

"How are you, old boy?" he said. His manner was agreeable and only slightly wary. He handed his hat, coat and umbrella to MacNeice. "Seems as if it's always raining when I visit your fair metropolis."

"Don't 'old boy' me," Jed said.

A queer thing had happened. Here he had been sitting, wishing he could talk to Felix, but now he was in the room, his only feeling was one of irritation. Nevertheless, he put out his hand and gave Felix's little paw a quick squeeze.

"I happened to be passing," Felix said, "and I saw your lights on."

"Bullshit," Jed said.

He motioned his visitor down the hall, not into the dining room where he had been—it seemed somehow demeaning to reveal that he had been drinking by himself at such an hour, an old man in trouble.

MacNeice had left the TV going in the den. Jed turned it off.

"Yes, it's b.s.," Felix admitted. "I came to see you. Counted on your being here, but couldn't be sure you were awake. Haven't you been sleeping well lately?"

"No, not too well," Jed said, "and I've been busy. How have you been, Mr. Justice?"

"Just fine," Felix said. "No thanks," he added as Jed gestured toward the bar. "But I'd welcome a cup of coffee —maybe even a sandwich."

Jed nodded to MacNeice.

"I took a late flight," Felix said, sitting at the desk. "On purpose. Commercial airliner. I didn't have use of a Learjet."

"Oh, you could have, you could have," Jed said. "I still own one. For the moment."

God damn him and his cocky ways, thought Jed. What does he want anyway, to view the wreckage or . . . what? But all he said was "You would have been welcome to it."

"Not now," said Felix. "Discretion—always recommended. Didn't even want to use my office telephone. I suspect it's bugged. In fact, I know it is, and I professionally reject the loss of dignity involved in dropping coins into pay phones like some member of the Mafia, an organization with which I've heard you've been dealing."

"To a limited extent."

Felix shrugged. "As I said, I have been cautious. Then I thought, what does it matter now? If every one of the twenty other passengers on my flight had recognized me it would have made no difference. The news is out. They have blown the whistle on you, my friend, and on myself."

"I've been thinking about that," Jed said.

"Don't. I try not to. *Letter* traced the Evergreen check. I must tell you that there are people on the Hill who'll pay to enlarge it photostatically to ten feet by twenty so the Senate Judiciary Committee can see it better. I have no recourse. You have. That's why I dropped over—to tell you that."

Jed had suddenly forgotten his irritation and he said with a completely different feeling, "That was friendly."

"No, it wasn't," said Felix. "It wasn't a bit friendly. I'm not doing this for you. I have my own reasons for cutting down Mr. Birnbaum."

"All right."

Felix Rupke pushed aside the empty coffee cup. He screwed up his mouth and said, "Give me the figures."

It was a weird reminder of the past. Silently Jed handed over the accountants' arithmetic. Felix studied them.

He said at length, "A hundred-thousand-dollar fee for Rice? That's absurd, even for a crash solicitation campaign. Three hundred seventy-five thousand, putting it in round figures, for expenses. He can substantiate that, apparently, but if you sued him I'm sure you could get some of it back. My advice is don't sue him."

"When have I ever sued over chickenfeed?"

"All right. It may seem like chickenfeed compared to the amount you spent to buy control, but let's remember that you didn't manage to acquire it. How much of your gross worth, for instance, did you have in your margin account at Donovan and Klein's?"

"Maybe seventy-five, eighty percent."

"That's what I thought. What's the balance in—anything you could borrow against?"

"Land, mostly. Some loans. Not too negotiable."

"No, if I remember your operations—and I think I do—land you bought in the area of the dams you built—"

Jed was sensitive on matters relating to his dams.

"That land isn't without value."

"I never said it was. The dams were so beautiful the land around them had to rise in value—even if it was located in some peckerwood canyon you couldn't get to unless you were lowered in a sling. And the loans—they were extended to laid-off construction bosses who'd run on hard times. Or started little companies that hadn't made it. Or left attractive widows who—"

"Some of those. Not all." Jed spoke with little humility and less patience. But Rupke, with the bookkeeping sheets spread before him, was not to be put off.

"Rice screwed you," he said, "but at least he got out two hundred and fifteen thousand, eight hundred and forty-nine proxy letters, with enclosures. Followed most of them up with telephone pitches. He employed forty-two mail girls and ninety-one phone solicitors. He stuck you with a high fee, but it was nothing compared to the shafting Donovan gave you."

Jed said bitterly, "I never could stand him. If there'd been anybody else—"

"He was my client at one time. We dropped him because we had run out of ways to keep him out of jail. Not that he was stupid. Far from it. He proved that when he made you hold still for a twenty percent commission. Even ten percent would have been usurious. What he did was set up a separate corporation to sell the unregistered stock. This corporation, as you'll note here"—Felix extended a document to Jed—"is in the name of Tulane V. Haselton. That's Donovan's brother-in-law. Haselton was not an underwriting firm, and only underwriters and principals can be held accountable at law for illicit sales of letter stock. The Haselton Corporation bought the stock from you outright, then resold it to the hand-picked bargain hunters suggested by Donovan and Klein. On top of his twenty percent mark-off, Donovan would have had a capital gain when he dissolved Haselton Corporation. He couldn't lose."

"He made a tidy bit on the brokerage fees alone."

"All the way up and all the way down. You started buying at fifty-one, with your Class A common as collateral plus the two million four that Donovan—or Haselton—paid for the letter stock. The top price paid for B and W was sixty-eight and a half. Before the meeting the quick-money boys had been grabbing what profits they could. By the time the Exchange allowed the resumption of trading, there was considerable short-side play. The shorts helped on the whole. They firmed up the price when they covered. What was the closing quote today?"

"Twenty-nine."

"So Donovan gave you margin calls through the scale, thirty-eight and a half points' worth. Haselton, mind you, had already taken its profits, and no doubt reinvested them. We don't have the books, but I'd lay odds that with the discount on the unregistered stock, plus the brokerage, plus the profit he, or he and Haselton, made on your total trading, Donovan has packed off twice as much as Rice. These highly remunerated gentlemen you trusted to save your neck ripped you off worse than the opposition they'd been paid to defeat."

"So it would appear."

Felix fussed with the sheets.

"You don't have final figures on your trading balance. You might have enough left to pay Hudson River Federated. Are you going to meet that note?"

"No, I'm not," Jed said. "I need that money, Felix," he implored, as if his friend, rather than the vague and ominous lenders, held the key to his dilemma. "I need it," he said, "for a fresh start."

Felix looked at him reflectively. "I know."

"Look, Felix, those hoods charged me an illegal rate of interest."

"That's how they make their living. Also why you went

to them in the first place. Quick cash, never mind the rate."

"So I'll pay—eventually. What's wrong with my using the money a little longer?"

"It could be sticky."

"So to hell with it. I've decided to treat Hudson River like any other outfit holding paper of mine. And I expect them to treat me the same way."

"They won't. They're still thinking with nineteen twenty-eight brains. I've seen print-outs on them you'd never believe."

"I'm sure nothing good will happen to some penny-ante numbers player who welched on a loan. I put myself in a slightly different category."

"They do, too. They've got more to lose with you."

"I'm afraid I'll have to make my own decision about Hudson River Federated."

The Justice nodded. "Very well. But if you want to close your balance at Donovan and Klein, I suggest you act before Hudson River levies on it. The Justice Department has already asked for a grand-jury indictment against you on the SEC violations. Has the District Attorney's office sent you a summons yet?"

"It came in the mail two days ago."

"So you need a lawyer."

"Not while I have you."

"You've got me for another hour—which will put us close to sunup. After that, you'd better retain one who can work for you publicly. That Threadnall fellow will serve in place of a better. We'll treat him rather badly, so we might as well avoid high fees."

"That's almost a necessity at this point."

"I might concur. *Do not surrender on the summons.* Bail will be set very high. If you stand trial, the penalties, restitutions and legal expenses will absorb the yet unliquidated assets. That's the *best* you can hope for. The worst is all that, plus a stretch in a federal pokey."

"Will the feds issue a warrant?"

"They will. But first Threadnall will call the Attorney General for the Eastern Division and promise to surrender you—setting a date as far ahead as he can. By the time the marshals come to serve the warrant, you'll be long gone. If you have any sense."

"I have sense."

"Good. Pick any destination you've a mind for as long as it's outside the U.S.A. Negotiation is the key—and distance can be an effective arbitrator."

"Have to make a stopover in California."

"Why, for God's sake?"

"To see a woman."

"Good luck."

"Thank you."

"I suggest you make no stopovers. I suppose you will ignore the suggestion."

"I will."

Felix sighed. "With that, however, I will terminate my advice."

Jed said, "Thank you. From the heart. I didn't mean to appear stubborn. I just have to weigh all the choices."

"Of course."

"You have some to weigh yourself."

"Not," said Felix Rupke with sudden weariness, "as

many as you." He added, as if to himself, "I wish I had. I wish I had. . . . And now," he said more briskly, "I'll have that drink you offered a while back. That is, if it's still available."

"It most certainly is."

As Felix crossed to the bar, Jed pulled back the curtains. The eastern sky was still glazed black, but the pink rim at its base bore out Felix's prophecy—that they had talked until morning. Jed fetched a glass of his own and the two stood peering out into the ebb of the electric night. Although Felix had not offered any easy alternatives, Jed felt curiously better. Screw the red tape of law, the coils of indictment, the writ and palaver that could change you in a few days from a free man to a felon.

Don't let it happen.

Devil take them all. Grab what you can and run! That, in effect, was what Felix was saying. And he was right! As they talked on and the sun rose over the sleeping city, Jed's face lost its harried look. He was not broke. Not yet, by God. He could take the Cosa Nostra's loan, the millions they had fleeced in turn from the supine poor, the numbers players, the drug-hooked whores and ghetto landlords, he could take it straight to the Cosmos Bank of Zurich. At a risk, yes. Felix had been most meticulous in warning him of that, but to hell with the risk! The money would put him back in the game.

It was best for him to go; it was the only way. He would do what Felix advised.

Jed understood. He'd been around this man too long not to know how his mind worked. All that talk about stopping Birnbaum hadn't fooled him for a second. Felix had come here to talk because he also was all alone, because (as he'd said) the whistle had blown for him too! He had come, beyond help himself, to give help where he could. He had come as a friend and, as a friend, Jed put his hand on the little man's shoulder. "Thanks, old buddy," he said, and Felix answered—as if some entirely different statement had been made—"I'm all right."

"I know," Jed said, "but thanks anyway." And he added, almost as if he did not wish Felix to hear the words, "I'm sorry for your trouble."

CHAPTER EIGHTEEN

WHEN Jed left the apartment he told MacNeice to look after Mr. Threadnall, who would be living there for a while, and on this particular afternoon Mr. Threadnall advised MacNeice that some visitors might be expected. MacNeice was to say that Mr. Basco was not at home but that Mr. Threadnall would talk to them.

At three o'clock MacNeice leaned over Mr. Threadnall's chair. "The gentlemen are here," he said.

Mr. Threadnall nodded. He got up immediately and went to the front door.

"I'm Alvin Threadnall," he said.

"Walter Broderick, U.S. Marshal's office," said the older of the two men. He produced a badge in a leather case. "We are carrying a warrant for the arrest of Jedson C. Basco."

"I'm his attorney," said Mr. Threadnall. "I'll accept service for him."

"I'm afraid that's not possible, sir. We are required to serve on Mr. Basco personally."

"Mr. Basco isn't here," said Mr. Threadnall.

"You might be mistaken about that, Mr. Threadnall," said the marshal. "To our best information and belief, he *is* here."

"Look, Mr. Broderick," said Mr. Threadnall, "I got word earlier that the warrant had been ordered. I put in a call at once to the United States Attorney and told him I would surrender my client to the Chief Deputy Marshal tomorrow morning, ten o'clock. Would you like to check?"

"No, sir," said Broderick. "When a warrant has been issued, we do not check further. We serve the warrant and bring in the person named. Do you object?"

Mr. Threadnall hesitated a moment. Then he said, "Yes, Mr. Broderick, I do. However, I shall not try to keep you from entering, though in my opinion your conduct is out of line."

He stood aside and Broderick motioned for MacNeice to do the same.

The U.S. marshals searched the penthouse thoroughly, starting in the small rooms off the entrance hall, then moving back to the den, the living rooms, the bedrooms, the patio, garden and service rooms.

It was just as Mr. Threadnall had said. Jedson C. Basco was not on the premises. By the time they left, the marshals were satisfied on that point.

That night, after MacNeice had served an excellent dinner, three more visitors arrived, this time representing

Hudson Federated Investors: Mr. Angiacomo, Mr. Harry Gardella and a Mr. Nick Silva. Silva was short and heavy and wore long sideburns and mod clothing. His head was totally bald, giving him the look of a medieval executioner.

Angiacomo opened the conversation. He professed disappointment at Jed's absence but seemed to find Mr. Threadnall an acceptable substitute. The Italian then complained mournfully about the stupidity of the B & W stockholders.

"How do these things happen? They hurt themselves, then they go home and cry on the pillow. They wonder what they have done."

He would have continued in this vein, but Gardella cut him short.

"Rafael—this gentleman don't need you and I to talk about dumb stockholders. He can tell you more than you will ever learn, studying nights. Am I right, gentleman? I'm sorry, I dint catch your name."

"Threadnall," said Mr. Threadnall. He then very kindly spelled his name for Mr. Gardella, adding, "I assume you gentlemen came to inquire about Mr. Basco's loan with Hudson Federated."

Gardella laughed. His snapping glance polled his group for support, drawing a smile from Angiacomo. Silva was not paying attention.

"We're not worried about Mr. Basco," Angiacomo said.

Gardella leaned forward. "You think you got trouble, Mr. Threadnall? I hope I'm not talking out of place, but sincerely—you should trade your troubles for what we got. People need money today, but they don't look for no loans, they go on welfare. You know something? I got three kids in school. The loan investment business, it's in the shithouse."

"That's not the main trouble, Harry," said Angiacomo.

"No," said Gardella. "Not the main."

"The main trouble," said Angiacomo, addressing Threadnall in a sympathetic tone, "is collections. What goes out has to come back. Hudson Federated, we always been high on collection. Without that we may as well . . ." He raised both hands, palms up, in a surrendering gesture.

"We may as well close up," Silva elaborated in a hoarse voice.

"Cool it, Nick," said Angiacomo.

"Okay, okay," said Silva.

"It's the same in your line, eh, Mr. Thread?" asked Gardella. "Am I right?"

"Well, in my type of work," said Mr. Threadnall, "we operate a little differently. Our charges are correlated to the number of staff hours applied against a given case . . ."

He broke off, annoyed with himself. There was nothing to say, and here he was chattering with these hoods like a housewife borrowing a cup of sugar.

"Mr. Basco owes you three million, eight hundred thousand dollars, plus interest, gentlemen," he said, "and as of this moment he can't meet that obligation. He will have to ask for an extension."

Angiacomo produced a sheet of figures. Placing a pair of heavy horn rims on his nose, he studied the paper, then laid it on the table.

“Thirty-day note, overdue.” He removed the horn rims before speaking further, as if to improve his image.

“I tell you what, mister. You mentioned extension, I say we go along. What do you have in mind? Four days? A week? No problem. I got the note right here.” He laid Jed’s promissory note on top of the other paper.

“Why not a postdated check, Rafael?” said Gardella.

“Can you button your lip, Harry, long enough that I can conduct this business?” said Angiacomo.

“It was only a suggestion,” said Gardella.

Angiacomo snapped the nail of his forefinger against his upper teeth, a Sicilian gesture of scorn, aimed at Gardella.

“You give us a postdated check for Mr. Basco,” he said, “we forget about the new interest. The four days, the seven days—whatever it may be. This way everybody is happy. You get a break and we get a break. Cash flow, that’s the essence of this operation.”

His expression was that of a philanthropist who has just made a sizable donation to charity.

“Hudson Federated has this reputation, money on the day, on the minute. Well, we’re not all that tough.” He winked at Gardella, who, thus restored to favor, beamed happily.

“Live and let live,” he said.

Threadnall knocked the ash off his cigar.

“I’m afraid that a four-day or a week’s extension will not be enough for Mr. Basco. He will need thirty days more. Possibly sixty.”

Nick, the torpedo, raised his eyes, concentrating on Threadnall.

“That’s the best you can do?” said Angiacomo.

Threadnall nodded. Angiacomo seemed unperturbed. There were people in the world, his manner conveyed, who failed to conform to accepted business practices. Experience had inured him to this phenomenon.

"I'll have to put it up to my company."

He took the note from the table, folded it and placed it back in his pocket. All present rose, and Angiacomo and Gardella shook hands with Threadnall. Nick Silva merely watched.

"Is Mr. Basco in Manhattan?" Angiacomo inquired. "No reason I asked. Only—until we get the word on the extension . . ." Angiacomo broke off. "What I mean—as a favor to Hudson Federated, my company—we'd like if he would stick around. You know what I mean? Just till the note is cleared. You understand what I'm saying? We respect Mr. Basco. He don't cause no problem for us, we don't cause none for him."

Early the following morning, Mr. Threadnall took the subway downtown, arriving at the offices of Donovan & Klein shortly after the doors opened. He had with him a withdrawal slip for the balance of Mr. Basco's trading account, signed by Mr. Basco before he left for California. He had presented the slip once before—on the day, in fact, of Mr. Basco's departure—but had been told that the firm's bookkeepers were still working on the account and advised of a date when the check would be available. Today, however, early as he was, he again met with disappointment. The account had been closed by a sheriff's attachment issued in favor of Hudson River Federated

Investors against Mr. Basco's note of hand for three million, eight hundred thousand dollars plus interest for one month and seven days at 20 percent. The attachment left an unpaid balance of one million, six hundred and seventy-six thousand dollars and forty-eight cents still owing on the note.

CHAPTER NINETEEN

THE police had closed off U.S. Highway 1 to northbound traffic at San Luis Obispo to make two southbound lanes, but two were nowhere enough to accommodate the buses, the VW campers, the Vegas, Land Rovers, Corvettes and classic old-time models, the height of rock chic, decorated with decal peace signs, U.S. flags and *Fuck War* bumper strips. In and out of this parade tooled the motorcycle cats, in singles, pairs and groups, tough chicks hunkered down behind with their rumps against the sissy-bar and their leather or Levi bellbottoms wide.

A Korean girl with an Oriental boy and two blacks held up a peace sign as Jed drove past and he took off his big hat and waved. He was pleased with himself at being part of the festival and surprised by the warm greetings so many of the young were offering. He had no way of knowing that his black Continental convertible, his Harry

Truman-style Hawaiian shirt, his pipe, his leathery face made him look so square he was hip. Crowded on the road with two hundred thousand other dudes going to Little Sur, in this golden Pacific afternoon he was a nostalgic superstar, survivor of the lost innocence everyone was sniffing for; he had that priceless status, *period,* among the many ages represented: covered wagon, jazz-era Fitzgerald, Davy Crockett, Alamo, Beatle, Teddy Roosevelt, Woodrow Wilson, Al Capone and Jefferson Davis. He was the true Forty-niner—*nineteen* Forty-niner—and the young freaks, impressed, waved to him, embracing him as one of themselves, a funky, freaky *king,* and he waved back with a noble Roy Rogers gesture, gracefully sweeping off and holding up, poised as if for the fadeout of a movie, the ten-gallon hat with the silver concha band, and then hit the Continental's horn, wishing that it would play reveille like the horn of the car driven by Dorothy's lover and by Dorothy's lover's wife.

Well, the horn might not be an asset. But he would surely like an asset, some kind of a break after his bad dry run. He would like to luck this one in somehow.

He was familiar with the risks. Threadnall had fully briefed him. "They don't want you to leave town," the lawyer had said.

Jed laughed. "They're a little late with that one."

"Yes," said Threadnall. "They seem to believe you are still in Manhattan. Which is all to the good. I've avoided asking where you've telephoned from. I'm not sure this line is clean."

"Threadnall," said Jed, "I wouldn't worry about it."

"But there was an unpaid balance on the note!" said the lawyer plaintively.

"It will be paid. They will have to wait."

"I realize that," said Threadnall, "but does Hudson River Federated? They have a peculiar way of doing business."

"I'm aware," said Jed, "that they expect their money on the line. They may have to learn a little patience."

"It's not a matter of patience, as I understand it, as of face. Prestige, in the Sicilian sense. That seems very important to these people. Mr. Angiacomo called again last night. He said he hoped you'd come and see him. He wanted me to set up an appointment for today."

"So he can give me a concrete boot?"

"Mr. Basco," said Threadnall, "I wish you'd take this more seriously. I would never have recommended your obtaining money from such sources."

"Well, anyway," Jed said, "I want to thank you for all the trouble you've gone to. Not only with our Italian friends—I refer also to the United States Attorney. I know my disappearance has put you in an awkward situation."

"I've been in awkward situations before," Threadnall said without humor, "although not many involving felony indictments."

"You'll come out all right, Threadnall," Jed said soothingly. "Remember, I'm the only one who's been indicted."

He still had in his wallet the pellet-size piece of paper with the telephone number on it that Bob had given him. He hoped he would not have to use it.

Other equipment needed in traveling, consisting principally of five thousand dollars in small bills, he carried in a money belt around his waist. He had bought the money belt in Abercrombie & Fitch's San Francisco store, trying it on under the supervision of a highly approving clerk.

The clerk said that a belt of this kind was the only way to carry valuables when you were going on safari.

The clerk might have had something. This trip to California was a safari of a sort. He should have been hightailing it out of the country. Well, perhaps if he ever caught up with Darlene she might be willing to go with him. But to find out he had to reach her. This was the problem. Jed hadn't heard from her since she had sent the hat, and his letter to Dallas, thanking her, had been returned. Harry Silverman's Nashville office said she was booked into Maxine's on the Sunset Strip in Los Angeles, but when he called Maxine's he found the booking had been canceled because Miss Johns was suffering from acute exhaustion. *Variety* had the best clue: her name in a list of artists who would participate in the rock-folk festival at Little Sur.

Point Lobos and Garrapata Creek, two big bridges, then the smaller bridge across the Little Sur. Beyond the lighthouse a new road had been dozed into the bald-headed hills. At its entrance three highway patrol cars blocked the U.S. 1, and the fuzz, with guns and riot sticks holstered to their belts, waved the traffic east.

Jed had started early in the big rented car. He had allowed six hours for a drive that should take no more than three, but the estimate still hadn't been enough: the pastures set aside for parking were already full, two or three square miles of paint, chrome, rubber and iron. People more accustomed to wheels than legs pushed, sweating, tormented and celebrant, up the trails leading to the bow-shaped hollow of the amphitheater.

Jed climbed. The sun's westering blaze made a camp oven out of the box canyon.

When Jed finally reached the festival grounds a purple band was playing Bob Dylan's "I Shall Be Released," the sound booming eerily into the hills from the big amplifiers.

He looked down the slope toward the bandstand. You could hardly believe that the dark mat covering the sides of the draw was made up of people, enough to populate a major city. In a scoop of hills inhabited ordinarily only by owls and coyotes, they passed jugs around, defecated in the bushes, balled, quarreled, ate and drank, popped pills and smoked bush, fastened to the hillside by the pull of sexual music wired in from half a mile below and the identity of the performers so small they were hardly recognizable.

"Who's coming on? . . . Hell, man, you blowed your mind. . . . That's . . . Souper Grouper . . ."

The bulbs on the crucifix sign came on too early. Yet little light penetrated the box canyon once the sun dropped behind sheltering hills. Some vehicle snaked down a firebreak trail near the center of the bowl, an orange blinker wheeling on its roof.

"That the pigs?"

"No, ambulance."

Word came back from row to row.

"Knifin'. Some cat got bladed."

The next report refuted this.

"Naaah. Woman had a baby."

"There was three this A.M."

"By the same broad?"

"Naaah, meathead, three different chicks, all snuff queens. One died."

Wooden parallels, as high as telephone poles, with banks of lights on them, tilted into the wild lavender twilight. These lights had not yet been turned on, but the bandstand, far below, glowed with the hot brilliance of a sparkler core. People near him were laughing at a youth who had put mustard on his draft card and was letting his girlfriend eat it.

"What does it taste like?" someone asked.

The girl, chewing, could not speak, but the youth answered for her. "Says it's a cross between Spam and chittlins."

Jed worked down the ridge. Progress so far was not difficult—the watchers were not packed tight here on the heights as they were farther down; they offered little resistance to a person passing through their ranks. Many paid no attention to anything happening immediately around them but sat waiting with an idle yet enthralled attention for some tremendous event which, when it took place, would justify their presence here even though its nature was as yet unclear. A pregnant woman came out to sing, her swollen belly outlined in the sparkler-core of lights that was the stage. Clearly she was a great celebrity, for at the sight of her the applause surfed back along the sides and bottom of the bowl until the outcasts on the ridge stood up and clapped or cupped their hands to show some kind of welcome.

Jed wondered if Darlene had received his telegram asking her to go away with him. Harry Silverman might not even have given it to her. That did not matter too much. He thought she would come once he explained the proposition to her. Not necessarily out of love. That word —one of her generation's totems—might have no application to their relationship. A hangup it might be, but a hangup, like love itself, could bind with hoops of steel; Darlene exorcising Georgiana through him, he reidentifying with Georgiana through Darlene. Whatever it was, it worked. If he could save this one thing out of the wreck of his fortunes, he would be out ahead.

On a lower level, a large group of young men, stripped to the waist, were pulling down a beer tent, tearing it in sections which they rearranged on long stakes, each with a hand-lettered sign:

WOUNDS
CHILDREN
VOLUNTEERS
ADMISSION
REST
EMERGENCY
HEAT TABLETS
TELEPHONE
INTENSIVE CARE

A voice on the loudspeaker was calling for doctors to report to the "medical facility."

Blocked for a while here, impatient to get going again (every minute, every second so important now, though he could not have said why), Jed began staring at one of the light towers. A man had climbed onto the first crossbeam of the tower. He was standing there, holding on with one hand, studying the crowd. He had field glasses and he directed his viewing carefully, focusing on the ridge and the slopes leading down from it. Now he was putting the glasses back into their case, suspended from a strap on his neck. He was climbing down from the parallel. As Jed walked toward the bandstand, stepping carefully over prostrate people, tactfully avoiding colloquies with drunks, grass-highs and acid-heads, he judged by the movements of the spectators on the opposite slope that this watcher was keeping pace with him, no longer visible but not to be ignored.

It was nearly seven o'clock now, almost time for the rainbow personalities of the rock and folk universe, the living myths, the million-album sellers, to perform. The crowd had become a nation in itself, freaked out, anarchic and inchoate, subtly developing some kind of hidden madness, no longer amiable and loose, but menacing, slippery and uncertain, burning with that peculiar lust that seizes people when they are jammed into a pattern unfamiliar to them and into a space too small.

At approximately the time that Jed was moving up to the bandstand the Six French Lessons were singing "Sugar Sugar" on stage; a male baby was born to Mrs. Fleetwood, a nineteen-year-old, in the helicopter to which she had been transferred from the ambulance that had brought her out of the canyon. A woman from Cucamonga, California—a Mrs. Meyer Hung Far—died of a heart attack in the arms of her husband, proprietor of the China Cafe in Cucamonga. Hung Far was a well-known collector of rock and folk albums and records. Deputy U.S. Marshals A. M. (Early) Tyson and Dick Haversham were seated in a Chrysler sedan assigned to them by the car-pool dispatcher of the Northern Federal District. They had parked the Chrysler near the trailer shared by Miss Darlene Johns, the folk singer, and another musician, Mac Oakley. In their fact sheet the deputies stated they were aware of some disturbance which occurred later, on the other side of the bandstand, but they did not investigate. The fact sheet did not state (although it implied) that the investigation of local disturbances did not fall within the scope of duty assigned to Tyson and Haversham—namely the arrest of Jedson Basco on a warrant issued in New York.

Jed had paused to drink some of the bourbon he had brought in a silver flask. Pretty square considering what the kids around him were using to turn on. But then some boys offered him wine, welcoming him and making him feel part of the scene. He left them with a warm feeling toward all the kids. Then the mixture of the bourbon and wine began to hit him. He had eaten little all day and he felt lightheaded, floating.

He was not sure when the motorcycles reached the area. It was at some point after he had gulped the bourbon and the time he first saw the Naked Man. He was so full of ambiance now that the motorcycles meant nothing. They came down two firebreaks, splitting off the ridge into the amphitheater—the one on the north and the one on the south. The men riding them had black leather jackets, black leather boots, Levi pants, gloves and goggles. Some let their hair flow back loose. Others wore caps or browbands. Some had girls behind them. Many had names of California towns stenciled in big block letters on their jackets—Ivanhoe, Earp, Inverness, Lodi, San Jose. They jammed in along the front of the bandstand, making the people there move out. There was an imminent, unlimited capacity for violence in them.

Jed was close to the bandstand now. He could hear the music coming over the amplifiers; several performers were singing folk, so he was sure Darlene would soon come on. The liquor had made him tired, blurred his perceptions, but he had no time to waste. Once he lunged against a beautiful blond girl whose curvy hips prevented him from passing, and her big Chicano boyfriend knocked him down. Jed got up quickly, blood oozing from a bruise on his cheekbone. He picked up his hat, which had flown off as a result of the blow, and carefully straightened the crown and brim as if the hat had been injured rather than himself. In another mood he might have tried to kill the Chicano, but now he felt no animosity. He would not have known, moreover, what to swing at, since one version of the Chicano's face hung profiled to him with another version hovering square on, balloonlike, as if filled with gas.

The power inside Jed prevented him from feeling any pain from the blow. He waved off a half salute to the Chicano as he continued on his way.

"Perfectly all right, friend, don't blame you at all," he said.

The Chicano could not hear the words due to the blast from the amplifiers, but he saw Jed's lips moving and swung another punch from back country. Jed neatly ducked. "Better luck next time, old man," he said.

The fracas had started waves of crowd reaction. Eyewitnesses' stories differ, but it must have been about this time that the Naked Man strayed into the area near the rostrum, one pudgy arm raised in the peace sign, walking straight to his death.

The telegram was on the trailer dressing table and Mac Oakley read it.

"A trip—well, ain't that something now?"

He watched her face, waiting for her answer. When she said nothing, he pulled the big bass fiddle to him and touched the E string—*Zhuooongg.*

"He wants you on a trip, why don't he sign his name?"

"He doesn't have to sign it."

Oakley played a soft, deep chord.

"That rich cat you met in Washington. The one that knew your mother."

"Play me something, Mac," said Darlene.

Oakley's fingers wandered into the bridge for a hot blues, "Hate to See You Go."

"You hear that?" he said.

Darlene smiled at him over her naked shoulder. She was sitting in front of the mirror, putting makeup on her breasts. The country dress she would wear for her first set was cut low.

"I heard it loud and clear, Mac, and I appreciate your thought."

"But you thinking about the trip."

"I've had it in mind."

Oakley's fingers, plucking a ditty of farewell, were so long they looked as if they had an extra joint in them.

"Rich man," he said, "poor man. North and South Pole —that's a long trip."

"He wants a long trip."

Oakley strummed without speaking.

"Notion about you and me cutting that album for Vanguard. That just fly away?"

"It didn't fly away. We just never signed it on."

"You ever ask Harry Silverman about it?"

"I don't ask Harry Silverman what I'm going to do. I tell him what I'm going to do."

Oakley beat his foot, keeping time to the deep, slow notes.

"Oh, that's a new gig. Now *you* tell *him*. Wonder if Harry knows that. Does he dig that now?"

"What he digs is no concern of mine," said Darlene.

She pulled the dress up, careful not to soil the bodice with her makeup.

"That what your soul craves now, a rich cat, an airplane ride?"

"It might."

"We could play Vegas. We could play the Lounge at the Sands."

"Now I know who's been talking to Harry."

"Harry has to make a living, same as you and me. We could play the Forty Grand in Sacramento. That place swings. We could play Jones Possum Holler in Nash."

"Come over here and zip me up," Darlene said.

Oakley obeyed. Standing behind her, he moved his hands down to her breasts. Darlene shook her head.

"No, honey," she said firmly. She took hold of his fingers and moved them away.

Oakley sighed. "You like the big-time sign on him, but you're big-time now, all by yourself."

"You and me and Gunther and Harry, we're all big-time, the biggest. We'll play Vegas when I get back."

"When you get back," Oakley said glumly.

A blast of rock from the bandstand shook the trailer. Both fell silent in the manner of people on a train platform when a locomotive is passing.

Darlene said, "Where *is* Gunther? I haven't seen him since early this morning."

"Out front someplace. Stoned out of his mind."

"I worry about him when he's stoned."

"We got other worries now."

He picked up the guitar. "Take it from the top, honey? One more time." Darlene took the guitar and tuned it absently, filling in some country riffs in an easy 4/4 bag. Suddenly there were booted feet running on the packed earth outside the trailer and someone banging on the door.

The critic for *Roll,* a music magazine, seated on stage though out of sight of the audience, worked on his copy out of a portable electric plugged into his car dash. He mentioned favorably Catfish, Country Funk, Far Cry, Elizabeth, Ariel, Flow and Buffalongo, with high marks for his favorite numbers ("I'm an old-fashioned guy," he liked to explain), such as "Raindrops Are Falling," "Hey, Jude" and "Lady Madonna." The folk portion of the program was starting and, with a new joint lighted, the critic pulled himself a deep hit, conscious that spectators were standing, facing away from the bandstand to look at something going on behind them.

CHAPTER TWENTY

THE Naked Man had now progressed some two-thirds of the distance from his ridge-top seat toward the stage. In an evening by no means devoid of ugly sights, he was by all odds the most repulsive.

The Naked Man was a curly-headed, no-neck person with a determined yet inward-turning look like some Botticelli baby grown up and turned crazy. He was the type of individual who should not take off his clothes in a public place. He had a son-of-a-bitching horrible physique. The legs were all right, good sturdy legs, but that was where decency ended. Legs less muscular would have been unable to hold up, much less propel, the meat above them. The Naked Man's entire body consisted of overlapping rolls of blue-veined, sweaty, pale pink flesh.

This architecture did not separate itself into discriminate segments but sort of folded together in a series of creases. Above the groin hung the groin sag, then the belly sag, the inflated tits and so on up to the doomed head and lunatic grin. It was horrible. You knew, in the hysteria of the great crowded pit of earth, reeling with drugs and flayed with threatening sexual music, that such a creature had to die, he had no chance; everyone's impulse was to wipe him out so as (if nothing else) to disown their personal connection with him as a fellow human being.

As yet, no one had touched him. The instinct to obliterate him warred, in his beholders, with the aversion inspired by his repulsiveness. Contact had to be avoided, even the contact necessary to kill. Nobody wanted to strike the first blow. There was that and in addition another fact—the Naked Man, in his pendulous jellylike way, was formidable. The arms, for all their mushiness, were huge; that lard-belly—well, an ordinary blow, even if delivered with force, might make no impression on it. Your fist might just sink out of sight. So the legs continued to propel the whole evil vision forward, and above the legs bobbed the typical fat man's round little scrotum and his penis no bigger than a grown man's thumb joint, just about no penis at all. If it had been an inch shorter he would have had a hole there.

He was getting where he wanted to be. He was getting to trouble. The Angels had seen him. They were motioning him down, and he kept coming on. Annnnh, moaned those around him. He would catch it now, all right. He would get his wish. A sixteen-year-old chick stood up. She opened her mouth wide, her arms pressed tightly to her sides. She clenched her hands and bent forward, shaking as if with some religious fervor.

"Ohmygawdohmigawdohmigawdohsweetjesuslookatthat*thang*," she screamed.

"Set down and shetapp," said a dude behind her.

The folk portion of the festival had now been in progress for some time. Lynn Carter, from the Delta country, had given way to Sinkiller Davis, a solemn singer with a magnificent bass whose specialty was revival hymns and who brought with him a chorus of seven mixed voices. He was dressed in a red velvet cape and matching red velvet cap which hung over to the side of his head. Around his neck he wore a large gold cross. He received a nice reception from the crowd, and the *Roll* critic beat his foot in time to the last hymn as he pecked out:

> . . . Sinkiller Davis and the Seven Deadly Sins came on with a leadweight heaviness that had a beauty all its own. . . .

Sinkiller was not an easy act to follow. Darlene would have preferred almost anyone else. She let as much time pass as she dared before making her entrance with Mac Oakley behind her. She bowed several times and stood looking at the crowd, glad of its warm reception and at the same time frightened by its size. Some trouble was going on, some mess or movement in the area to the right, but she did not (as she said afterward) feel the disturbance involved serious violence. Oakley tuned in, and she lifted her face to the smoky ridges, her shoulders bare in the old-fashioned prom dress of the Twenties.

Love, oh, love, oh careless love
Love, oh, love, oh careless love
Love, oh, love, oh careless love
You see what love has done to me. . . .

The clear, lovely notes reached out into the crowd where anger hung black and the smoke and smell of violence assaulted the senses. A sigh went up and little spins of hope fanned out like a touch of coolness stirring the leaves of some backyard tree in a city street where stifling heat has driven the children and housewives mad all day, the first moment of rebirth on some evening of a ghetto July.

Once I wore my apron low
Couldn't scarcely keep you from my door
Now my apron strings don't pin
You pass my door and you don't come in

The critic took another hit from his joint and fingered out:

> This young woman making her first appearance at this fest captured attention by opening with a folk classic that has come down through the ages. She had the right vibe for the ballad, proving immediately that she was not just another chick singer but a woman of some complexity, even a talent gaining new sound and a bigger audience with each appearance. . . .

Faint as it was, the pecking of the critic's typewriter fretted a distraction under the flow of song. Darlene lifted her eyes to the fringe of faces on the ridge, the ultimate listeners. She looked into the night and the shifting glooms and sorrows of her own life, hoping to shut out the vision of the bikes in front of the bandstand. These were the "hogs," the motorcycles the Angels parked there when they had ousted the early comers from the space between the stand and the first rows of wooden seats. Some of them had waited in line for these preferred positions. Some celebrity rock singer had ordered the Angels in as a personal bodyguard. That rumor was going around. He had needed protection, though no one knew what threatened him. The Angels' pay had been fifty cases of beer and all the reds they wanted. Capsules had spilled over the stage, and the Angels had tossed some into the crowd. They moved in twos like patrolling fuzz, gap-toothed and scar-faced, many with leather jerkins lopped off at the armpit to show their biceps tattooed with serpents, swastikas, spiders, amoebas, weapons, breasts and childhood nicknames.

Now the Angels had left this space and were moving in on the Naked Man. Two or three were very close. They were saying something to him, but because he was freaked out he either didn't hear or didn't understand. His no-neck head wobbled and he pushed one of the Angels with a halfhearted act of insane courage or defiance, poked him on his hairy tattooed chest, visible where the leather jacket fell open. That did it. The weak shove of the Naked Man's huge, weak, babyish arm, glistening with its sowbelly sweat—that was all it took. The Angel back-handed him. His movement was effortless. He just jerked a fist in an expository kind of gesture and the Naked Man evaporated. He was on the ground and the

Angels were beating him. They whacked him with their shortened billiard cues as if they were killing a snake. Their faces showed no anger. They had the propriety of men doing a proper job of work. Three or four crowded in to beat him while the others kept a clear space around to enable the executioners to work freely. This was hardly a difficult task since no one made a move to interfere. The billiard cues, wielded with fearful force, produced a terrible, squashy sound as they mashed the Naked Man's flesh. His features disappeared at once. His thick legs jerked and thrashed, rapidly turning into pulp. For a while his short finlike arms flailed about, then subsided at angles no human arms could ever take. The amazing fact was that he lived so long. He continued wiggling and twitching, as if the blows themselves imparted energy to him. Also he kept uttering stupid noises.

He barked and burbled, ugh, ugh, ow wow, as the blows fell. Then he was silent. The Angels continued to beat him for a while. Then they left.

The moment they had gone, the bystanders became active. Those who had stood by timidly during the killing were now stirred into indignation. They cursed the Angels, saying they should be arrested. One short, middle-aged woman assumed authority.

"I saw the whole thing!" she exclaimed. "It was devilish, the work of Satan. Where were the police? This should be reported. It must be reported at once. This poor fellow is badly hurt."

"Hurt, hell," said a tall black. "He daid, lady." His Adam's apple bobbed up and down in his long skinny throat as he stared at the pulpy mass on the ground.

Oh, Shenandoah, I long to see you,
  Away, you rolling river.
Oh, Shenandoah, I long to see you,
  Away, I'm bound away
'Cross the wide Missouri. . . .

The strong, plaintive tune surged into Jed's nerves. Darlene's voice acted on his bloodstream with a force as potent as the neat bourbon. Her figure on the stage was small, but her voice on the amplifiers was big, unmistakable. She was really here—a fact which in the confusing whirl of the day's events he had begun to doubt: his sudden citizenship, as it were, in a world of off-centered people, few of whom behaved like any people he had previously known, a world which had taken on the edges of a dream, a preposterous fantasy which could not have any roots in truth. That Darlene was part of this, as the *Variety* announcement had stated, altered everything. Now what he was doing here made sense. She was here and he would get to her and once he was with her the bad elements of the fantasy would disappear and proper values be restored.

First, of course, loomed the problem of reaching her. The performers' quarters, or whatever they were using for accommodations, had to be down near the stage—the section where the crowd was packed the tightest and where the kids seemed most freaked out. Though it had taken place not far from him, Jed had not seen the Naked Man's death. Actually, its principal effect had worked to his advantage. There had been considerable movement toward the action on the part of the Angels, whose ranks still partially sealed off the bandstand. Only one mean-looking son of a bitch was still in his field of vision, but as Jed drew nearer to this Angel, he decided that the bastard had to be the biggest, meanest mother of them all. He was six feet four or five inches tall, and his height was stretched another couple of inches by his black helmet. His face was wind-burned a dull red color except for white half-circles under the eyes where his goggles had protected him. The goggles now hung around his bull neck, secured by a chain in back. He had white chapstick on his lips, and above these slanted a sharp vulture-nose. What with the beaky nose and the mean, yellowish eyes encircled in white, he resembled a warrior made up as an owl for a tribal Indian dance. He wore a white scarf at the neck of his jacket, and his black Nazi-style boots had white swastikas on them. He stood at ease, holding his shortened billiard cue, its butt resting on the ground. He was staring out over the crowd, a cigarette hanging from his lips. With no major alteration of his relaxed position or pleasantly stupefied expression, he stuck out one boot absentmindedly, blocking Jed's path.

"Go set down, Pop," he said.

Jed smiled at the Angel. He felt so full of power, so encouraged by the churn of his own blood and the confirmation of Darlene's presence here, that he was quite ready for some great, notable deed; a phony, made-up bastard like the Owl Warrior, big as he was, presented no problem at all.

"Sorry, old buddy," he said. "Got to be down front. Got to see somebody."

"Oh, is that so?" said the Owl Warrior pleasantly.

The Owl Warrior was now joined by another Angel,

smaller and less garish. Instead of the conventional leather jacket he had on a white sweatshirt with the words RED BLUFF stenciled across it.

"What's with this cat?" he demanded.

He looked at Jed, who returned his study with complete good nature. There had been one Angel, now there were two. Still no problem.

"Says he had to move down front. I told him to set down."

"That's right," said Red Bluff, who seemed to rank the Owl Warrior in command authority. "Set down, Dad."

"Look, fellows," Jed said. "Let's talk about this, okay? I've got a friend, a singer, Miss Darlene Johns. Maybe you've heard of her?"

Red Bluff looked at the Owl Warrior, but the latter continued to direct the unblinking stare of his white-circled eyes downward.

"A friend of Miss Johns," he said. "What do you know?"

"He must be some big shot," said Red Bluff. "Are you a big shot, mister?"

"Medium big," said Jed. The bourbon was having its effect on his amiability. He was beginning to feel some impatience. "Let's keep this cool," he said. "Maybe you can help me. What is the best way to get down there?"

"This way," said the Owl Warrior.

He put his hand on Jed's chest and shoved. Jed went flying over Red Bluff, who had moved around behind him and bent down—an ancient schoolboy tactic. Jed fell on his back and shoulders, his head striking the ground heavily. Spectators seated nearby, who up to now had centered their attention on the stage, became aware of what was happening. Some of them laughed, but one large youth jumped to his feet.

"I saw that," he said, addressing the Angels. "It was a stinking trick. What are you cocksuckers here for, to shove people around?" He turned his back on the Angels, leaning down to help Jed to his feet.

"Are you all right, sir?"

Jed tried to say he was all right, but no words came out. His mouth was full of blood. His teeth had snapped on his tongue, cutting it, when he hit the ground. His head ached fearfully, but he was filled with a killing rage. If he had had a weapon at that moment, he would have slaughtered Red Bluff and the Owl Warrior instantly, without hesitation. He put his hand in the pocket of his sport coat, wishing there was a gun in it—as if the wish could bring one—and at the same time clenching his fist and poking one finger forward as if in fact he had a weapon. Just to pretend to have one might have some value. He stood rocking on his feet, glaring at the two Angels.

"Get out of my way," he said.

Red Bluff brought his billiard cue up to a position in front of his chest. Holding it by the middle, as in military bayonet practice, he could strike for the groin, then jab for jaw or stomach with the butt or use the upper portion to bash his victim over the head. Red Bluff had had some training.

Many of those nearby were now watching, waiting for what would happen to a person who had dared defy the Angels. The four now confronted one another across a cleared strip of perhaps three feet of earth on which lay

Jed's big Western hat. The hat had flown off when he was shoved down. Owl Warrior picked it up.

"Nice hat," he said. "Dig that silver band, now. Yeeuuuuuh!"

"Keep it," said Red Bluff, never taking his eyes off Jed.

"No," said Owl Warrior. "You ain't got no helmet. You take it."

So saying, he placed the hat on Red Bluff's head. It fitted moderately well.

"Looks good on you," he said.

"No, it don't," said Jed's befriender. "Give it back to him." He moved forward into the neutral strip separating the opposing pairs. He even raised one hand as if about to seize the hat.

"Give it back," he repeated.

Red Bluff now turned his attention from Jed to the youth. Still holding the billiard cue in ready position, he took the latter's measure. This gave him pause for thought. Red Bluff was small. Owl Warrier, on the other hand, was huge, but big as he was, the youth was bigger: a giant! He wore Levis, moccasins and a leather browband—nothing else. He had the build of a heavyweight boxer or a defensive tackle on a pro football team. Long, wavy, delicately curling hair, light brown in color, hung to his immense, muscular shoulders, but the long silky hair was by all odds the only girlish thing about him. Another sort of hair entirely, a heavy black thatch of it, covered his chest, narrowing to a black streak over his abdomen, where it dove into the pubic regions. He had amazing muscles. Whenever he moved, as in this slight, menacing shift of his arm, bulges and lumps and Himalayas of power shifted under his skin. His mouth was large and his face very handsome. His nose turned up slightly at the end and he had bold, dark flashing eyes, set wide apart under thick brows.

"Give the gentleman his lid," he said firmly.

"What are you," said Owl Warrior, "the property custodian around here?"

"What I am," said the youth, "is sick of seeing you zombies push people around. Give it back to him or I'll kick the shit out of you."

Until these words the Angels, in view of the youth's potentials, had seemed better satisfied with parley than with action. Now their status was in jeopardy. Onlookers were laughing. Owl Warrior lunged with his billiard cue at the youth's groin. The blow was practiced, fast and deadly, but the youth caught it in his hand. He jerked the club away from Owl Warrior and broke it over his knee. He dropped the pieces on the ground.

"Now I'll take yours," he said to Red Bluff.

"Okay, you win," said Red Bluff meekly. He extended the cue, tip forward; as the youth reached for it, Red Bluff smashed him over the head with the butt. The youth pitched forward. He fell on his face in the dirt. For a few seconds his body convulsed and his arms flopped helplessly as if he were having a seizure. Then he lay quiet. There was no sound except Red Bluff's rasping breath and the sweet voice of Darlene, amplified by the speakers.

"You killed him, you son of a bitch," Jed said.

He yelled the words. His voice was out of control and his face contorted. It seemed impossible, unbearable to him that he had no way to deal with these two monsters.

If only he had a gun . . . if only . . . but at least he could still fake it. Still with his right fist in his coat pocket, finger extended, he raised his arm until the pocket was pointing at Red Bluff.

"I'm arresting you," he said. "As a citizen, I . . ."

He did not know what he had been about to say. Something ridiculous like "I take you into custody." For the first time in his life he felt completely powerless and not only powerless but dated, old, absurd. He had no business in this awful canyon, in this night of blood, lust, hate and savage music. Even his quest for Darlene now appeared completely unreal and unrealizable.

"You don't . . . you . . ." he yelled at the two Angels, "do . . . not . . . deserve . . . to live!"

"All right, Dad," Red Bluff said contemptuously.

As he spoke, Owl Warrior, with an equated, indolent scorn, kicked at Jed's genitals. The kick landed on the thigh but close enough to target so that Jed knew he was going to vomit and did. On all sides the crowd, expecting more violence, maybe another death, was falling back, leaving an open space around the combatants. Jed straightened up. Both Red Bluff and Owl Warrior had their heads back, laughing at him—and now Jed, whose vision had improved as if emptying his stomach had removed an impairment, saw that something had happened or was happening to Red Bluff. Red Bluff's body jerked. A look of extreme surprise appeared on his face. He put his fingers against his throat, then took them away, covered with blood. Red Bluff stared at his bloody fingers with disgust, then spun around. The fine ten-gallon, concha hatband sombrero he had appropriated from Jed went flying off, cartwheeling frivolously through the air. With it went the occipital portion of Red Bluff's head, his brains spraying out behind. As he fell, pitching over backward much as Jed had when Owl Warrior pushed him, a terrified, almost wordless kind of yelling broke from the crowd. No one went near the fallen Angel.

"Dead man . . . Jesus, deader than a . . . Watch it . . . .watch out . . . He's . . . look . . . he got . . . a . . ."

"He's got a gun," said a boy of about twelve. Down on all fours, out in front of everybody else, he was staring fixedly at Jed. He had comic-strip eyes, big and round and so close together they seemed to be joined.

"I saw him," he said. "He has a rod in his pocket. He shot the Angel. He said he was going to arrest him," the boy said with utmost clarity, addressing no one in particular, with considerable intent to be believed. "Only he didn't arrest him. He shot him. I saw it."

"Grab him," somebody said. "He's as guilty as the others. Lay up, take hold of him."

No one, however, obeyed the command. Jed looked around calmly. He took out his handkerchief and removed a tiny spot of vomit that had sprayed his coat. He walked away rapidly, pushing through the spectators, many of whom had not paid any attention to the fracas or the shooting, hypnotized by the music and the celebrities they had come to hear. The crowd was still packed thickly here, but he could make headway fairly well. At least no more Angels now opposed his progress toward the bandstand. As he edged his way along, he realized that he had neglected to pick up his hat. The hat—well, he had liked the hat. Something about the hat occurred to him, something that ought to be examined further. But no matter. There were more important issues to consider now.

Darlene was still singing.

> Oh Shenandoah, I long to see you,
>   Away, you rolling river.
> Oh, Shenandoah, I'll not deceive you,
>   Away, we're bound away
> 'Cross the wide Missouri. . . .

CHAPTER TWENTY-ONE

JED had no doubt that the youth had been killed—no one could have withstood that blow to the skull and lived—but the fact that his death had resulted from an impulse to help someone who was being pushed around appalled Jed. He had sensed a goodness in the youth. There was goodness and beauty and strength in many of the people swarming here, the young ones who at times seemed so freaked out and lost.

Jed no longer felt alone. He was a member of a community. He had not belonged here at all; he'd really had no business coming. Yet he had been accepted. If only he could have prevented the tragedy! If only that crazy trick of pretending he had a pistol in his pocket had come to him sooner. But wait—that was silly. Not fake bullets but real ones had killed the Angel. While he had been bluffing with his imaginary gun, someone hidden in the crowd had got off two rounds from a genuine weapon, blasting Mr. Red Bluff in the throat, then in front of the head. He saw again the amazing picture of Red Bluff grabbing his throat, spinning around—and then the second shot, the hat flying off and the bastard's brains with it.

Jed still felt hazy from the heat and the liquor. But there was something about the hat, he was not quite sure what. Suddenly he remembered the man he had seen on the tower, the man who had been studying the crowd through field glasses—God!—a man who had climbed up there to look for *him.* ("We're dealing here," Threadnall had said, "with what is reputed to be a large organization," and so of course it was.) How would they have known where to look? Unless the telephone line at the penthouse had really been tapped, as Threadnall had suspected.

Ridiculous. Only was it? Jed had always counted on his instincts to carry him through any situation, and he'd had the feeling, from the moment that he saw that son of a bitch on the tower, that someone was tracking him. Okay, just a feeling. But take it for an assumption. Take your modern assassination technique of high-powered rifle, telescope-sight shooting. When Red Bluff, with the hat on his head, had stood there alone, the crowd giving him room, he had been a perfect target.

He could have been killed because he had been mistaken for me!

It was a creepy thought, one that he might be a hell of a lot better off forgetting. Nevertheless, Jed could not shake it off. He moved forward cautiously now, taking stock of his surroundings.

Water had been piped into the bandstand area from some agricultural pump, and the plastic pipe leaked at the joints. As a result there was a slushy place between the performers' trailers and the backstage trailer village. Vehicles moving up or down the street were forced to slow down, and the artists on their way to perform picked their way along a narrow path of planks. Jed slogged straight through the mud, his head down like a weary bull.

A few trailers had signs on them, denoting the occupants, but most did not. He knocked on one door, intending to inquire for Darlene, but got no answer. He was turning away when he noticed two little men approaching from the opposite direction. Both were slender and carefully made up. They were dressed identically, in beautifully fitted suits of some light-colored brocade with silver-buckled shoes and tapering, pointed hats. They passed, talking animatedly, ignoring his attempt to attract their attention. As he looked after them a white Cadillac ambulance, coming around a bend in the alley, hit the water, splattering it in all directions. Farther up the alley, a police car was parked, its turret light slowly revolving. Some of the trailer tenants had gathered around it; others were watching from doorways. Someone exited from a trailer and got into the police car. The door slammed and the driver moved up the street. At this the clumps of people started to break up. One very large black lady, wearing an Aunt Jemima kerchief, stood on the step of her trailer, watching the car until it was out of sight.

"Ma'am," Jed said at last, "could you direct me? I am looking for Miss Darlene Johns."

The black lady looked quietly down at Jed, her old face

hung with sorrowful creases. She shook her head, picked up her long skirt and stepped back into the trailer, closing the door.

Jed walked on, more heavily now. The old lady had conveyed a message without words. Jed did not need to inquire further. His pace slowed until it resembled the walk of a very old or sick person. He did not know what to expect. He only knew it was not good.

He went to the trailer where the official car had stood. He had made no mistake. Carefully lettered in black paint, the sign on the door read: MISS DARLENE JOHNS.

Jed understood what the old lady had been telling him. Darlene was not there. No use to knock. He put his hand on the knob and turned it. It was not locked. He stepped inside. All the lights were on, including the frame of bulbs above the makeup table. In the scatter of objects thrown down amidst the pots of rouge and eye shadow lay his telegram.

He closed the trailer door, and for some reason he locked it. He was very uneasy. He crossed to the table and picked up the telegram. The paper was very creased, showing that, whether or not it had been read, it had at least been opened and folded many times. HOW ABOUT A LITTLE TRIP.

He had sent off the message at a moment when, despite losing almost everything he had, he had felt free and strong. YOU NAME THE PLACE AND TAKEOFF TIME.

Now the words he had written with such excitement and anticipation filled him with a sense of desolation. I WILL BE IN TOUCH SOON.

Jed sat down at the chair in front of the mirror. The big

double bed, which could be folded back to form benches, was still open. All sorts of clothes, male and female, were entwined in the crumpled sheets.

The bass string of a bull fiddle pulled Jed's head around. Mac Oakley studied him with red-veined eyes from the other end of the trailer.

"Can I help you, Mr. Basco?"

"I was looking for Darlene."

"Sorry, she's gone," said Oakley. He touched another string. "You see the sheriff's vehicle outside?" Oakley said. "That's how she left."

"You mean she was busted?"

"No, sir. She wanted to go along. After she made the identification."

"What identification, man?" Jed inquired. "What are you talking about? Make yourself clear."

Mac Oakley laid the bull fiddle aside.

"I figured maybe you had heard about it. Most everybody has—it ain't no secret now. You maybe met Mr. Gunther Troll? He was beat to death just now." Oakley motioned toward the unseen crowd. "Out front. He had his clothes off, and they wasted him. They beat on him with these big clubs. The bike riders. Like he had offended them somehow."

Mac Oakley was crying. He got a dish towel from the trailer sink and wiped his face with it.

"Christ," Jed said, shaken. "That's terrible."

"You used the right word, Mr. Basco. It was the worst. That man didn't offend nobody, except he take off his clothes. He had a bad habit doing that, when he was stoned. They brought him here. You could hardly recognize him, but she did. She never made a sound, just nodded her head. It was him all right."

The big ambulance that had splashed filth on him, that must have been . . .

"But why did they bring him to Darlene? I don't get it," he said.

"The people recognize him, Mr. Basco. That's why they bring him. Just hardly nothing left of him. I wanted to go with her but she said, 'No.' I knew what she had in mind. She planned to sit up with him, like family. That's about what it amounts to now."

"Yes, I guess that's right," Jed said. He rubbed his hands over his face.

As if reading his mind, Oakley said, "She ain't taking no trip with you, man. Nor with me neither."

"What's she going to do then?" Jed yelled.

He glared at Oakley as if Oakley were responsible for the cancellation of the trip and all the evil that had happened that night.

"She's goin' to sit with him in some mortuary room. Slumber rooms they calls them. That what she goin' to do. She goin' to have him buried. Then she'll go into one of her black meanies. Way, way down."

Jed nodded. "I saw her once like that."

Oakley pulled the bull fiddle to him and sat holding it but without plucking a string.

"Never, Mr. Basco," he said quietly. "I know what you saw. A *red* meanie. The night she split from your party and you balled her. I know all about that. No offense to you, but she will ball anybody in one of her red meanies. The black meanies is a low. It's different."

"Different how?"

Headlights of a car, making the turn of the street, crossed the trailer windows.

"Nobody can go near her at those times. Not you, not even me. And I'm about all she got left. She'll snap out of it sooner or later."

The car was level with the trailer. Then it passed. Jed exhaled a deep, slow breath. He kept remembering the man on the tower. No doubt it was someone just pissed off at the Angel. That was the only way to figure it if you wanted to be logical, but Jed was past logic; he was at the end of the line.

Darlene was gone. Mac Oakley said so. He would not make a mistake. She was now on a trip of her own, a senseless vigil in a funeral parlor, but the true significance of her departure was that his own trip was canceled—if you could cancel a trip that had never been scheduled, just dreamed. Well, a lot of things were over and a lot of bodies had gone straight from this overcrowded festival into slumber rooms, and even while his head nodded with relief at the passing of the car, even while the last of his strength was flowing from him, he knew that there was a shooter out there; there had been no dream about that, logic or no logic, and he knew that one body he did not want riding in a big squashy-springed ambulance was his own.

His head came up. His eyes finally focused on Oakley, who was still soundless, fingering his bull fiddle. Jed asked a question which he realized at once from the blank look in Mac Oakley's eyes had not been audible, so he said again, more slowly, with considerable effort, "Is a phone around here?"

Oakley nodded. He kept nodding, his head bouncing

softly on his skinny sideman's neck, his hand continuing to rub the strings.

"A telephone you talkin' about? There's one under the bandstand. Maybe two there. They rolled wires in on a spool, seen them do that. I was setting here this mornin' when—"

"Will they let us use that?"

Oakley stopped messing with the fiddle.

"I would say so. No personal calls, but in a case of . . ."

"This is an emergency," Jed said forcefully. He felt in his pocket for a dime, located a miscellaneous handful of change, which he handed to Oakley.

Oakley gently shook the fistful of coins, as if trying to pan gold out of it. He seemed confused by Jed's indicated demand on him.

"You want me to make this call for you?"

"If you'd be so kind," Jed said.

Not for all the money in Fort Knox would he have taken another step into the tiger night. He had not often been completely beat out, but the few times he was he had been smart enough to know it.

Mac Oakley was handing back the change.

"You don't need no money for this phone; it a public service, like. Only if this ain't no emergency . . ."

Jed put the change in his pocket. From another pocket he extracted the pellet of paper his son had given him with the Underground's call number written on it. He unrolled the pellet and looked at the number. It was there, all right. He read it, first to himself, then to Oakley.

"When you call," he said, trying to remember Bob's

instructions clearly, "let it ring awhile. Somebody will answer. You might have to wait, but they'll come on. You got that?"

"I understand, Mr. Basco," Oakley said. "You sure now you don't want to call this number yourself?"

"I'm sure," Jed said, "but I appreciate this. You call the number, and when they answer, here is what you say."

CHAPTER TWENTY-TWO

THE small TV set carried the Senate debate. Felix, entering, was tempted to turn it off. He could have done so. No one besides himself at the moment occupied the reception office outside the White House Oval Room, but a sort of masochistic curiosity compelled him to watch. He set down his briefcase and placed his cane carefully on top of it. When he was seated, his glance returned to the set, where the camera was zooming in on Senator Porterfield.

PORTERFIELD: Will the distinguished Senator from Ohio yield to a question?

GOODPASTOR: I yield.

PORTERFIELD: The Senator made use of the phrase "Potomac Fever." Would he care to define the term?

GOODPASTOR: Gentlemen, it is an ailment which is as ancient as the noble river from which it draws its name. Its symptoms are rapid pulse, egocentricity, cunning, arrogance, and an endless thrust for power. Have I answered the Senator's question?

PORTERFIELD: I should like to add one more. Is there no cure?

GOODPASTOR: In rare instances, the patient becomes his own physician. This is his only chance. He himself discovers, hitherto undiagnosed, some lurking sense of public duty. He may even cough up the phlegm of responsibility. He says to himself, I am a Senator or I am a Cabinet member or the head of a government bureau or even, yes, I am a Justice of a Supreme Court. I have sworn an oath. I have standards to meet. That can happen. Then the fever lessens. A cure may be in sight. But it is rare. Far too often, the afflicted individual puts himself above honor, above the office itself, and even above the law. When he reached this condition, as Felix Linus Rupke obviously did, then even the blindest physician must profess that Potomac Fever has invaded the patient's heart and breast, his political and moral future, and if one pauses by the cursed bedside in pity or dismay, one can hear the unfortunate mutter in his delirium, I am the law, so who is to gainsay me; I am the Constitution, therefore I can do no wrong.

"The President will see you now, Mr. Justice," said a voice close to Felix's ear. The door of the Oval Room stood open and, as he crossed the threshold—was it for the last time?—he could hear the debate initiated by Senator Eisendradt's motion for his, Felix's, impeachment continuing.

The Man had been watching. He had just finished lunch. Ordinarily, he made a ceremony of the meal, but today, as a service tray bore witness, he had eaten at his desk. He had his shoes off and his tie loosened; his big face with its cleft chin and hair-tufted flaring nose was heavy with the countrified guile Felix knew so well. Though no longer a candidate for re-election, the Man had no taste for defeat, any defeat at all, much less the debacle of a significant appointee. Was he even now meditating some pitchman's trick that would block the Senate revolt, quell the spiteful press and the public uproar over that ridiculous Foundation business?

But the Man swiveled his head and looked at Felix with an obsidian gaze, and Felix knew that saving him was not the business of the day.

"Tell you something," the Man said, "if one of your clients—the stupidest, most misbegotten son of a bitch that ever walked into your office—asked if he could take that money, do you know what you'd of done?"

"Mr. President," Felix began, "I still maintain I returned the check, late perhaps, but fundamentally there has been no impro—" in the glare of the Man's eyes the word stuck in Felix's throat so that he sputtered "—priety in what I may, may have—"

"Felix," the Man interrupted, "you would have shut him in a room with no window and no phone and manacled him if need be rather than let him do what you did. For a skunk's collar. A bellboy's tip."

"Mr. President—"

"I want your resignation, Felix," the Man said.

The scaled ends of broken pride stiffened Felix's spine, and his lips pursed into their magisterial droop, for he had been expecting, if worse came to worst, these words and his answer was ready.

"You shall have it whenever you wish, Mr. President."

"I wish it right now," said the Man. "Sign on the bottom."

He took from his desk a typed sheet of White House stationery and handed it to Felix.

Isabelle had finished her drink. Felix's glass was empty too, but, as he made no move to refill either of them, she said tentatively, "Would you like to sit in the garden? It's warm enough."

"Thank you," Felix said, "but I don't know that I'd care to."

"You could slip into your windbreaker in case a breeze comes up. You could play the recorder. That might be nice."

"You go out," Felix said. "Not often we get days like this, this time of year. You like it out there. Sometimes I think you like it better than I do."

"I like it," she said, "but I don't think I'll sit there without you. I'll go back upstairs and work. You can come up when you feel like it." She paused, then added, "Felix—don't forget to return George's call."

"I'll return it in my own sweet time, Isabelle," he snapped.

"All right," she said. "I'll be upstairs in case you want to come up."

The silence set up a secret forum. She was up there, with the door open, waiting, implacable and loving, for the communication that he had withheld.

He walked into the hall and said without lifting his voice, "I resigned, you know."

"I'm glad," she said.

"Are you?" he said coldly. "I'm not."

"You had no choice."

"Perhaps not, but I feel no cause for rejoicing."

"Oh, Felix!" she said.

He sat down in his study. He remembered how before the Man had announced his appointment to the Court, George had buzzed him on the office intercom and told him the appointment would come through.

George had a long ear, and that ear might be working now.

George had left word to call him back.

Felix looked at the telephone. This call, now, could be as critical for his future as his meeting in the Oval Room.

He dialed the office number and the girl put him through.

"Isabelle said you rang up."

"I did, I did, Felix. We have been sitting watching the tube all day—unbelievable. Don't you agree?"

"You mean," said Felix with false jocosity, "you mean you're surprised to find me a *cause célèbre*?"

"Oh, no, Felix," said George Page, "you've always had the makings of *that*."

"You flatter me."

George Page's courtly chuckle rumbled over the line.

"Not entirely, Felix. But it's been sticky. Political football, of course, blown out of all proportion. Never does anything straight out, does he?"

"He was straight out as all get-out with me."

"No options, eh?"

"None."

"Well, I . . . all of us, we've been with you to a man. We were just wondering . . ."

He broke off.

"Go ahead, George."

"Well, if it did happen, Aaron and—the whole firm. We felt we should all sit down and—"

"Counsel together?" Felix suggested sardonically. It was one of the Man's favorite phrases.

"If you want to put it that way."

"That's an excellent idea. But for the time being I'm going to unclinch my guts. Maybe take Isabelle on a trip. Haven't quite made up my mind."

"Felix," said George Page with forensic emphasis, "you couldn't do anything that made more sense. Acapulco. Europe even. You need a breather. It's incredible how you've stood up through it all. Get a tan."

"No partner of the firm has ever acquired a tan, in my memory. But if you insist, I'll try."

The loaded word in this speech had been "partner."

"Ha ha," George said. "Have to tell Aaron that. Well, the partnership, tan or no tan, is still here. We want you to know that. Technically—"

"Technically, George?" Felix Rupke said.

"Well, technically you've resigned here too, you know. Meaning, as I see it, only that at the moment you're not *active*—or—"

"Or that you have a workman busy right now," said Felix heavily, "scraping my name off the door?"

George Page's tone hardened.

"That's not true, and you know it. I was about to remind you that *technically* the name isn't on the door. It can go back there anytime. All I suggested was that we should make some evaluation. That can wait. Have your vacation first . . . and then . . . Felix?"

"I'm listening, George," Felix said.

"That is, unless you're in some tearing rush to get back into harness. And from what you've just said I would gather that you're not."

"I'm not, George. And I appreciate your sympathy. Will you extend my thanks to Aaron and the others? I'll be in touch as soon as I return."

"Good man, Felix," said George Page.

His voice was as easy as a door swinging shut. Felix could almost hear the click of the deadbolt. He knew that the "evaluation" had already been completed and was not reversible—it might be best for all concerned if Felix forever terminated his connections with Cabot, Constable, Page and Rupke. George had been elected to convey the news. He did that sort of thing so well. As a hatchetman, no one could equal your Main Line Establishment stiff. He would whip off that old school tie in the wink of an eye and strangle you with it.

Felix got up and began pacing around the room much as he had in his office (that office where he now could no longer go!) the day after the President's appointment—the day when Jed Basco had come in with his load of grief. He remembered Jed in the sauna, telling his troubles, and recalled his own surprise that Jed, naïve as he was in many ways, had understood so well what had happened to him. One of the expressions that Jed had used came back to him: ". . . distress merchandise. . . ."

Yes, indeed, distress merchandise was what Jed had been and still was—and now Felix, walking back and forth, his limp painfully evident, realized that the definition fitted him better than Jed. For Felix Rupke, former partner in a famous law firm, former Associate Justice of the United States Supreme Court, what lay in store? He had advised a head of state effectively but himself badly; as a result, Jesus Christ could not provide shelter for his soul nor Jehovah, in all his might, forgiveness for his error. Yet what was this irreparable sin? He had accepted a charity-foundation appointment, then resigned the appointment but neglected to return a salary check. Was that so black a deed? And then . . . and then, God damn it all, pressured on one side, threatened on the other, he had traveled to New York and pleaded with a minor official for consideration in behalf of an old friend in trouble. For this he had been cast down from the heights, his honors stripped away as if he had sold nuclear secrets to the enemy.

Not that he didn't understand it, for he did. He understood, as well as if not better than Jed had. You could sign a piece of paper ordering a war that would kill ten million people and future generations might erect statues to you in the public squares. But endorse another slip of stationery like a check and if everything was not in the best of taste, they carted you off to the junk heap and no amount of screeching did a bit of good.

Felix sat down slowly in the desk chair. He and Jed! He was glad that at the end they'd had that time together in the penthouse: the old closeness holding them for a few minutes. He was comforted in that, for better or worse, he had pointed Jed to an escape route. Would there was someone at hand now to do the same for him!

"Get a tan," George Page had said. Old-school-tie George, the hatchetman. A tan, by the standards of TV commercials, cured everything and, if the cure was not complete, at least the tint of your skin provided evidence that your ruin was not total since you could afford surfing and cabanas. Felix wanted no such restorative. What rose in his being as he drummed on the desktop with a paper cutter was a longing for—well, a place where the air was not heady and thin, just common low-grade non-status air, the kind breathed by people without honors or aspirations or the contempt of the carny pitchman with the big tired face and the stony eyes, lounging in the Oval Room, himself defeated, himself also now a reject.

Texas air! Maybe that was it, and on an impulse Felix picked up the telephone, dialed a Texas area code and then a long-remembered number, wondering whether it was still the same, and when a familiar, never-much-liked voice drawled an answer, knowing that it was.

"Hello, Sol. Felix here."

"Why, son," said Sol Bender, casual as if he received such calls daily, "where are you?"

"In Washington," Felix said testily. "Where did you think I'd be?"

"Didn't know, Felix," said Sol Bender. "There's been all this fussing. Even now on the television we heard some yarn that you'd resigned. That ain't so, now, is it, Felix?"

"I'm afraid it's right, Sol," Felix said. "That's exactly what happened."

"Ha just can't believe it."

Felix could envision Sol, in his agitation, pulling his big feet in the Neiman-Marcus loafers out of the desk drawer.

"Something must have gone mighty wrong."

"It makes pretty spicy reading, or so I've been told."

"Son," said Sol slowly, "I don't know if it's spicy. I'll tell you I don't understand it. Just sounds like some cooked-up thing."

"Cooked up. You might call it that. I'll tell you about it when I see you."

"See me?" Excitement percolated into the cracker-barrel voice. "Now, let me fasten on this, son. You comin' back *here?*"

"I've been thinking about it."

That he would actually make such a trip had not occurred to him until that moment, but now that he examined it, he suddenly liked the idea.

There was a moment's pause, then Sol Bender said with the solemnity of a revival preacher at a river baptism, "Then by the holy God my dreams is realized. Always had a feeling they'd come true someday."

"Think you can rustle up some room for Isabelle and me?"

"A room?" said Sol. "Son, all I got is room. I'm living in the little downstairs cubbyhole, the one off the back porch. The big room, that will be yours, the one with the sleigh bed. The commode. The pictures. I permitted no changes since your Ma, since she . . . everything's the same. It's yours, son, as long as you want it."

Such extensive hospitality was a little overwhelming. Was there a decent hotel in town?

"I'll talk to Isabelle about it, Sol. Let you know, okay?"

"Why, okay, son," said the old man hastily. "No rush, no hurry. Take your time. Just one thing."

"Yes, Sol?"

"May I ask you one favor?"

"You can ask anything you like."

"And you'll answer me truly, no matter what it is?"

"I'll answer you truly."

"Will you talk to Rotary?"

"Why, sure, Sol."

"You'll come over and say a few words to the boys? That's a true answer now, son? Because if I tell the boys you're coming and you don't come I might as well quit living in this town. I could have a Dollar Day or a Two-for-One sale every day of my life, and wouldn't nobody come through the door."

"You tell them, if I come to town, I'll talk at Rotary. You have my word."

The purposeful iron drone was audible long before the plane became visible, its running lights feeble in the immense bowl of the night. It circled the field once, then landed easily, plumb in the center of the runway the Underground rep had outlined with road flares. The co-pilot opened the door, and the passengers chinned themselves in, using the roof of the VW as a boarding ramp. Everyone made it easily except for the girl, who had to be hoisted from below and pulled from above. The rep waved, the co-pilot closed the door, and the plane had taken off.

It had all been very simple. Never mind why an Electra

turbojet, remodeled for cargo service and making a regular run between Oakland, California, and Mazatlán, Mexico, could have stopped for engine trouble at an airport where there was no repair shop and then been fixed so fast that it had taken off again within five minutes after landing. That might be a mind boggler, but the details, should the pilot care to insert them in his flight log, would be of interest only to his employers and/or the Air Traffic Control Center at Fremont, California, which might or might not have been tracking him by radar. It was certainly of no concern to the passengers on board.

It was cold in the cargo hold. The passengers had been warned about that. The plane was neither heated nor pressurized except for the cockpit. The passengers might suffer some discomfort, but this would not be serious. To keep them warm, the Underground had issued surplus, heavy-duty Navy parkas and to compensate for the lack of pressurization the flight-plan, they were told, called for altitudes of five thousand feet or less. By the way his ears were popping and his lungs pumping, Jed felt the pilot might not be following the course to the letter. He might have even decided to ignore it. Passenger enjoyment, after all, was not the purpose of the trip. The goal here was to remove five people as fast as possible from the territorial limits of the United States, and this result was being admirably accomplished.

MACHINERY
FRAGILE—FRAGILE

The entire cargo consisted of identical crates, identically marked. The crates were not lashed down. If one became dislodged due to some unscheduled movement of the plane, then there would be a question as to which would prove the more fragile, the crates or the five bodies hunkered in a cleared space in the middle of them. Odds favored the crates, but hopefully there would be no tilting.

Apart from his carelessness about the altitude, the pilot seemed to know his business.

The master sergeant kept talking about his quicksilver mine. He went on about it just the way he had in the Quaker meeting house, answering in detail questions which had not been asked. The constant repetition, like a religious incantation, had induced a new mood in his listeners. In the meeting house they had been skeptical. They had paid attention to him only because the master sergeant's concept was so necessary to him that he somehow compelled their notice. Now they did not have to be compelled. They wanted desperately to know more about it—everything that could be known, the shafts with their ancient timbers, the producing veins of ore, the tunnels firm and earthy and compact with cold, cellary smells. They had accepted the mine. Through endless examination it had become as much of a reality to them as to him and as much of a need. Now as he discussed it in his slow, deep voice, emphasizing some point with lifting, priestly motions of a big hand, they never took their eyes off him—Monash, the stockade escapee, Gully, the conscientious objector, and Gully's girl, whose name turned out to be Vida. Vida was the most earnestly committed of all. She was obviously pregnant. No doubt she had been before, but it had not showed. Now, as is the way with pregnant women, her face had suddenly become peaked and her arms and legs oddly thin. She had left her nice, disappointed rich parents in Pasadena; she had dropped out of college and finally climbed into this icy, lung-squeezing plane, deafened, cramped and aching but believing in the mine, in Gully, in her baby. She pushed her skinny little hand into Gully's parka pocket and held on to his for dear life. She had been shot out of a cannon. She was walking on the moon.

"The reason," the master sergeant was saying, his eyes piercing above his square, clean-shaven jaw, "the *reason* why it laid there so long unworked, a mine like—well, the reason is interesting. I don't know if I explained it. Someone asked about it." He shot an accusing look around—an arraignment of their lack of faith if this audience of his had asked the question, or their lack of acumen if they had failed to. "Anyway, here's how it was. The Spaniards started most of those mines, as you know. That was the whole point of their conquests—gold, Jesus, did they ever want gold. And the Church, the Holy Roman Catholic Church, wanted it most of all. The priests were miners and explorers, along with those frigging monks—every mother-lovin' one of them."

"Right on."

The voice came from the back of the hold, among the great pine-smelling wooden cases, with their cabalistic markings.

The master sergeant turned his heavy-lidded eyes in that direction.

"What did you say?"

"I said 'right on,'" said Monash, unsubdued. He leaned his tough little face forward into the circle of light. "You don't have to inform me about the Church. Let me tell you. I was raised a Catholic. I got wise when I was twelve. The lowest place a man can fall is to his knees."

He looked around, putting himself on record.

"But they were *miners,*" said the master sergeant, almost sleepily—this same interchange in one form or another having been undertaken many times during their days of hiding and planning. "*Miners.* That's the point I'm making, gold, yes, but where there's gold there's baser metals. They didn't neglect quicksilver. Not on your life. Silver—screw off. Too heavy for the galleons, no good at all, but mercury. Ha . . ."

"Fulminate of mercury," said a new voice. It was Gully, his back comfortably settled on a crate.

"You knew that, eh?" said the master sergeant shrewdly.

"I studied geology. I told you that."

"So you did." The master sergeant yielded the point grudgingly. "And the use of fulminate, for igniting gunpowder. They knew that too."

"Naturally," said Gully.

"Not naturally at all," said the master sergeant. "It took study. They were way out ahead there. What were those rocks you mentioned one time, the ones where it's found? My brother was a mining engineer before he bought the motel. He mentioned those rocks, he's had them analyzed, the quartzites, the—serpentines, the—what the hell. You know the ones."

Gully, who had burned his draft card on the steps of Sproule Hall, usually shunned any display of superior knowledge, but with Vida gazing at him with adoration he could not resist a rapid run-through, tactfully understated, of the formations, from the Archean to Quaternary, in which quicksilver is to be found.

"Sandstones," he said.

"Okay, okay."

"Slates, limestones, conglomerates, crystalline schists. Actually, if you want to know, most all eruptive rock from the most active to the most basic. Quaternary—"

"You said that," corrected the master sergeant sharply. It was fine that they had all taken on the mine. Gully with a thousand dollars, cash, from Vida's unpaid, next-term tuition; Monash with the legacy left him by an uncle, the chief undertaker of a seabound Maine village. It was all very well to form a limited partnership, to lay it out and check it night after night with all the shares stipulated, but it was another matter to move on the mine with a proprietary air. He, the master sergeant, was the true proprietor, and his brother, former mining engineer, now rich motel owner, was the one laying on the bread. The master sergeant wanted no mistake on that score. Thus, keeping a tight rein on the whole enterprise, from galleon times through German operation and Mexican expropriation, he described how the German owners had closed the shaft with a dynamite blast so that the Mexicans couldn't get in and how eventually some gringos had come in and built their own shaft, bootlegging the mercury out until . . .

Jed had spread a blanket just beyond the circle of light. He lay almost with the others, but not quite—half included in the talk about the mine, half out of it, no opinion being asked of him, as if the young fugitives had discounted his approval while at the same time remaining fearful of his disdain.

At the hideout they had treated him respectfully, calling him "Mr. Jacks."

The Underground station had been a disused building high in the Sierra foothills, once some sort of vacation hotel. Deer antlers whitened by ancient suns and scoured by forgotten blizzards were nailed in neat rows on the porch. The jeep that had fetched Jed from the festival had driven straight to this place as if pulled by a cable. The driver had been a young attorney who, when not working in the Underground, practiced law in Monterey, specializing, he told Jed, in military defectors.

"Court-martial work," he said. "It's tough, you know. Military justice bears the same relationship to real justice that military music bears to real music."

"That expresses it well, I suppose," Jed said.

"Not original," said the lawyer. "True, though."

Jed had slept in the jeep, slumped like a sack, in imminent danger of being tossed out on the roadside. He had slept most of the time at the hideout, would have slept now if he had not been so cold and his ears had stopped popping; sometimes his head did nod, and once when this happened it seemed to him that he was back in Mike McGettigan's truck riding up into the mountains. He heard a slow voice jawing much the way the master sergeant mused along. That voice from the past hadn't discussed a mine, though. What had the subject been?

". . . know a piece of river bottom you don't have to pump no water to it. Just stick a pipe in the river and you siphon right into the furrows. Once I get me a grubstake I'm going back there and . . ."

Maybe it was the cold that had brought back that memory, that voice. He closed his eyes, trying to hear it once more. He longed now to hear old Mike, God rest his soul, say as he had later said so offhandedly, "Take over."

He had taken over too, goddamn right. He had gone all the way. From that day to this, looking back on it as he had looked back these last weeks, he would have done nothing different. Even losing B & W, once it happened, had not been so bad. He had not chickened at the end. Yet . . . one thing could be different, could be better. This aloneness. So all right. He wasn't in their generation, didn't want to be, from what he'd seen of it. But . . . "Mr. Jacks" and "sir!"? Shit, did that ever date you.

A mine, for Christ sake. They had as much chance with that mine as the farm boy on the truck had had with his apricot orchard. That mine was opium; it was pure pot. If it really existed and it managed to produce one flask of quicksilver he would eat it. But . . .

"Porfirio Díaz," the master sergeant was saying, "the dictator. He had so many medals he took his chest to the service station every day to have it filled with air. He was the one rented the mine to the Germans. Those days a foreigner could get anything he wanted in Mexico. All he had to pay was the government bite. Well, we'll pay if we have to, only what my brother says, he thinks . . ."

The flaps, creaking down for a landing, nudged Jed awake and he sat up, shadows cast by the flashlight wagging over him. Mazatlán. He knew the town. Old Gerard von Seideman, chairman of International Chem, brought a fishing party down there on his yacht. They had all gone ashore, put up at some elegant place way down the beach, ironwork tables and hand-wrought gates and furniture made out of glistening gray driftwood. The Balboa Club. He had taken two marlin, one the trophy catch of the trip.

He rolled up his blanket, his back stiff and sore. If he wired old Gerard and said, "Old buddy, I'm in Mexico, down to my last five thousand clams, partner, how about a little fishing, how about a deal?" Ha! What would Gerard wire back? Congratulations? Old Gerard, with a wen on his face he was afraid to cut, it might be cancer, he would have been reading about B & W, you could bet your boots on that. He might wire back or he might not. Either way it wouldn't matter. Not if you were lost between two generations, one disappointed in you and the other uncertain whether to ignore or devour you.

The plane descended through clear skies to an ample runway. It was two o'clock in the morning. Entrance to the passport deck was divided from the airport proper by a glass window behind which, framed like a department-store exhibit, a big, bald-headed bearded man in a dirty T-shirt made welcoming gestures.

"My brother," said the master sergeant. He waved back at the bald-headed man. Greetings would have been inaudible. All the passengers, it now appeared, had work-permit passports except Jed, who had a tourist card. The passport clerk did not seem happy with the card. He motioned Jed to stand aside while he rubber-stamped the other papers, then wrote his name on them.

"You do not plan to work in Mexico?"

"No, I am here for pleasure."

"Fishing, maybe?"

"Yes, fishing."

"Then where is your equipment?" He looked at Jed with the desolate impertinence of a person who did not mind being teased provided that the joker realized he was not being taken in.

"I can rent equipment in Mazatlán."

"Beautiful equipment," said the clerk. He made no move to stamp the tourist card.

Jed picked up the card. He slipped a twenty-dollar bill under it and laid it down once more, and the clerk, with no change of expression, did what was necessary to provide Mexico with a man who would rent fishing equipment. The twenty-dollar bill had disappeared as if propelled through a hole in the desk.

The name on the card was "Ambrose Jacks."

Jed went to customs inspection downstairs. Monash, Gully and the girl had brought little to be inspected, but the master sergeant's gear was taking time. He had a duffel bag, oilskins, surveying instrument and a footlocker containing smelters, scales, test tubes, boots, a rock hammer and a helmet with a battery-powered flashlight affixed to it.

Jed set on the counter the small PX shaving kit which was his entire luggage—compliments of the Underground.

His suitcase had been left in Little Sur, in the rented Continental: another problem for Threadnall. Or possibly for Avis Car Rental. It did not really matter which.

The inspector did not open the shaving kit. He was looking at Jed's mid-section. His eyes, like the light on the helmet, seemed to be battery-powered; he could see through the parka.

"Kindly open your coat, Mr. Jacks."

Jed raised his right hand to the desk, the tip of another twenty-dollar bill showing between thumb and forefinger.

The inspector sighed. "Put your money away, señor. And *por favor*—open the coat."

Jed unzipped the parka.

"I should like to see the money belt. *Con permiso.*"

"I did not know that clothing was inspected."

"Everything is inspected."

Jed put the belt on the table and the inspector rapidly undid the snap buttons of the four front pockets and the zipper of the large compartment in back, looking at the packets of money inside. He took out one pack of hundred-dollar bills, riffled through it and put it back; in the other compartments he was satisfied to just poke his finger around.

When he handed the belt back he had taken nothing out.

"Enjoy your visit to Mexico, señor," he said.

Jed took his time putting on the money belt again. The customs room, like the passenger lounge, had a glass wall on one side with a door through which those finished with their inspections could pass into the free world. Beyond the door, through the glass, Jed's traveling companions had been watching with interest. Jed had assumed they knew that he was wearing such an article—it was not thin enough to be invisible—but he had been careful not to put it on or take it off in front of them.

They would not, until now, have had an accurate concept of what was in it.

He picked up his shaving kit; though the air in the customs room was warm, he zipped up the parka as if, closed, it afforded some protection. He walked through the door, turning in the direction indicated by a sign pointing the way to the taxis. As he passed the group gathered around the master sergeant he waved off a half salute of farewell. Bunking with this bunch for two or three days did not furnish, in his estimate, sufficient reason for firm parting handclasps. Best thing now would be to get his ass out of the airport and uptown to some hotel.

His leather heels clickety-clacked on the floor of the tiled corridor, not too hurried—careful about that!—but not too slow either. He trod along, shifting the shaving kit from one hand to another, just for something to do, aware of other footsteps catching up. Well, they were young, but if they wanted to mug him for a money belt he would put his back against a wall and do what he could. A little alcove with a drinking tap in it was at hand on his right, and he nudged into it, aware too late that the master sergeant had almost reached his elbow. He and his brother faced Jed, both a little blown.

"Something on your minds, fellows?"

The master sergeant looked crestfallen. It was his brother who spoke.

"Pardon me, Mr. Jacks. That is, aren't you Mr. Jedson C. Basco, the engineer?"

"Does that make some difference to you?"

"No, sir. That is, *El Sol del Pacifico*, that's the newspaper here, had a picture of you. Well, my brother and I . . ."

The master sergeant had his hand out. The silly son of a bitch was trying to shake hands!

"I'm pleased to meet you, Mr. Basco. I was surprised. I

told my brother, Jim, I didn't believe . . ."

"It's an honor, Mr. Basco."

Jim, it seemed, also wanted to shake. Jed obliged them both.

"Thank you, gentlemen. And now if you don't mind . . ."

The master sergeant laid a hand on his arm. A touch, more like. If it had been a grab, then Jed, still spooky, might have swung at him.

"Mr. Basco! We were talking, my brother and I, while you were in customs. This mercury mine . . ."

Jim looked tough as a nut. He could not spend all his time in the office of a motel.

"I've already filed on it—trying now to arrange a grant deed."

"From the government!" the master sergeant put in eagerly. "A deed that would—"

"What it boils down to," said Jim, "we were wondering if you'd take a look at it."

Monash, Gully and the girl had followed and were waiting a little way off, watching the conversation for results rather than trying to listen.

"Perhaps sometime."

Again a hand reached for him—this time Jim's. He was at least eight years older than the master sergeant, and he spoke now with the full weight of these years behind him.

"It's two days' driving, Mr. Basco, into the Cordillera. Four-wheel vehicle. The road ain't much."

"I'm afraid I wouldn't know about a mine. I'm a construction engineer, and right now . . ."

The brother stood square in his path, dirty T-shirt,

beard and all, his hairy legs clumping out of some kind of *lederhosen.*

"Any opinion from you would have value, Mr. Basco. This could be for real. I know it sounds unlikely, but as a businessman I think there can be money, big money in such enterprises. If you won't look at the mine, at least take a look at the car. Best there is, Toyota Land Cruiser. I paid seven thousand clams for it down here, American. Franchise tax, you understand." And now, lightly surrounding, Gully and the other two joining—gently, flatteringly, they herded Jed along. Jed reversed direction, moving not toward the taxis but back toward the tarmac where, it seemed, due to some special permit wrangled by Brother, the Land Cruiser had been left. The group reformed around him, leaning past each other to catch his words. Out on the landing field the big jet was taking off for Guadalajara.

The road tilted and slithered over a stretch of marsh between beach and foothill, then began a slow, tortured climb into the immense and silent night. In the inverted bowls of land and sky the Toyota's headlights, shackled close together like the eyes of an insect, picked their way across shaly slides, stabbed at misplaced rocks (to be crowbarred out of the way) and at times pointed drunkenly into the sheared-off graves of huge abysses. Jim drove till he was tired, then reached back, shaking the master sergeant awake to spell him; the moon lost its battle with the pull of the earth and reeled off to some dim appointment in the west. Talk died out. After a time the sky paled a little, and every now and then they could see the ocean, a patch of lighter blue with a frayed white edge.

Gully, hero of the Sproule Hall card-burning, could not be roused when his turn came. His head hung down as if his neck had been broken by a hangman's rope. Vida, skinnier, paler than ever, more than ever preposterously out of place in this sullen venture of the mine, clasped her little hands around her treasure and her curse, that growing lump in her belly. She slept, curled against her man in the front seat, folded like a fern.

Jed relieved Monash. The Toyota seemed to grow calm, more willing, under the touch of his thick hands. Jed liked the car's performance. All his life he had been susceptible to the attraction of a healthy piece of machinery.

"That's it, honey," he remarked when the left front wheel won a contest with a fallen manzanita log. "You know what you're doing." He gunned the high-voiced little engine experimentally, heading at a rise like a horse to a jump.

The lower quarter of the sky now looked as if someone were squeezing lime juice into it; the mountain night lost some of its harshness. Jed opened the side window of the Cruiser. He put his mouth against the crack. After a while his drowsiness passed and he settled to his job, animated with an intense and steady persistence. He would drive until the sun was up; he would drive all day if necessary. He had not shaved since the morning of the music festival, and the gray-streaked beard had come in thick, giving him a resemblance, persuasive though superficial, to the young men sleeping behind him, all bearded except for the master sergeant.

They didn't fool him. Not for a minute. They had tried to give him the illusion of comradeship, crowding around, flattering him—ha! Oh, he'd take a look. Why not? But he knew the only reason he had turned into a buddy was because they had recognized him as a celebrity. These young men wanted him because he was Jedson C. Basco; he had been up there once, had made it once, and some knowledge or magic from those big-time days, like the major leaguer's golden arm, might still be with him, or enough of it to bring a blessing to the mine.

Oh, he would go along. He would push the tough little car up into these scarred mountains, up this road that other men had used, in times long past, hunting for luck or riches and probably finding neither. He would take a look. If by some wild chance there was anything in this business, he would know what to do. He would come to a phone and call Malm Walter, maybe, president of International Metals, in Winnetka. Get Malm to send assayists, analysts down. Risk a few bucks to find out where they stood. There was a shortage of mercury, that much was true. Seemed like he'd heard the admiral, if he was not mistaken, mention it—and Stranahan knew the procurement problems of the missile age if anybody did.

Always a chance, of course. Plays wilder than this one had come in and paid off at ten thousand to one, not that this changed his frame of reference; in the irremediable rush of time he was still a loner just as he had been before. These military runaways didn't want to work. Sweet Christ, who mentioned work? These little darlings wanted to get rich—right now! They wanted a mountain mine bursting with miraculous wealth.

All right. So they'd see.

He stopped, got a ten-gallon can off its clamps on the side of the car and replenished the gas tank. No one woke, but his passengers breathed differently now; the altitude was higher. A low cloud hung before the Cruiser, dancing with tiny flecks of light like sand in a sunshot wave. The Toyota bucked through and shoved itself snorting out the other side.

"Good girl," he said.

Oh, they weren't fooling him, these pot-smoking Cortezes. They wanted the Seven Cities of Cibola, domed in gold. Well, if there was anything up there, Malm would know the answers pretty quick. Next thing would be to start from scratch and build a road you could put trucks over, provide drainage and a hardtop. Need all sorts of rolling stock: a D-8 Caterpillar with a blade and a ripper; track-mounted air-compressed drills for dynamite preparation. A dynamite crew—Mexicans would do, they were great with explosives. Later on, a Kelleher grader, maybe a backhoe. Culvert pipe. None of this came cheap. Would the motel owner do all the funding? Maybe they were lucky in getting Jedson C. Basco aboard.

The sun was full up now. A mountain lion, sleepy after some pre-dawn feast, warming on a rock, lifted itself and with a superb and leisurely indifference made off up the spine of the hill. Jed laughed. He sat bolt upright, his hands firm and light on the wheel. He felt tireless, unconquerable, as he had felt the night in McGettigan's truck, going to his first job. Let them sleep, the runaway soldiers, the bald-headed bedhouse owner and the girl too young to be a mother. Let them take it easy. They would sweat for it later, they had Jed C. Basco along. He took a hairpin turn faster than he meant to, the offside tire kicking shale over a thousand-foot drop.

"What's ailing you?" he demanded sternly of the Toyota. "Have you blown your brains?"

Joy seeped out of some mysterious source in his soul, into his veins, like a drink of whiskey stronger than any ever distilled by man.

He had never felt better in his life.